Kingston Medland has been writing ~~~~~~~~~~~~~~
hood and completed THE EDGE, his first novel,
at the age of twenty-two. He lives in Northwich
and has just finished his second novel.

The Edge

Kingston Medland

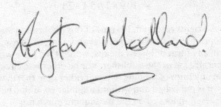

First published in 1994
by HEADLINE BOOK PUBLISHING

First published in paperback in 1995
by HEADLINE BOOK PUBLISHING

A HEADLINE FEATURE paperback

10 9 8 7 6 5 4 3 2 1

ISBN 0 7472 4811 7

Typeset by Keyboard Services, Luton, Beds

Printed and bound in Great Britain by
Cox & Wyman Ltd, Reading, Berks

HEADLINE BOOK PUBLISHING
A division of Hodder Headline PLC
338 Euston Road
London NW1 3BH

For Catherine,
With Love Eternal

Acknowledgements

Thanks to Joan Deitch and Jane Morpeth, and everybody else at Headline. My parents and brother for all their help, suggestions and criticism. Miss Thompson, Mr Hare, Mrs Wye, Mr Stanley, Stephen Gallagher and David Howe, for much advice and encouragement. Thanks to the Writers' Group of Northwich. And you, the reader, for taking the time out and listening to what I have to say.

Prologue
Susan's Death

The Manhattan night was humid.

The rain was torrential, so that you were drenched if you were caught out in it for as little as a few seconds. But while people huddled under store fronts, or cowered under their old, read newspapers as they ran for shelter, one man walked on.

Dressed only in jeans and a white T-shirt, and carrying a gym bag, the rain did not bother him. He did not even notice it; care for it. He might as well have been alone in the world, for as he walked he acknowledged no one. He ignored their laughter, their shouts, telling him to get out of the rain. They could not break through his concentration, and the rain could not touch him. He was immune to everything.

Onward he walked, lost in his own world.

Without cause, without provocation. Without reason or motive, he—

...killed. I watched with glee as the blade from her kitchen, the knife she had used the previous evening for preparing food, now cut across her naked left breast. Instantly there was a fine line of blood which I licked away. A taste for it acquired, I squeezed her breast, bringing more forth; not brutally – gently, as if we were still making love. Her screams of pain, which seconds before had been cries of ecstasy, were beautiful. I gulp the blood, the monster owning me, scooping it in my hands and cupping it to my mouth ... then I place the blade against her throat. Softly tickling her flesh with the sharp edge, I make shallow cuts. This is the moment I savour the most. Their terrified expression when they realise, the daunting horror when they know, with dreaded certainty ... tonight, they will die.

I take a camera from the bag at the side of her bed. Nothing special – just a cheap one. As I listen to her begging and pleading I laugh; not an evil, over-the-top laugh like you hear in the movies, you understand. My laugh. The pleasant laughter of a neighbour who has just told a terrible joke, or of your best buddy as you down a couple of beers together. The gentle laugh of your lover ... I capture her face in the camera lens, and then, after a moment's playful hesitation, push the tip of the blade deep into her throat; silencing her cries for freedom, her cries to end the pain. I am nothing if not obedient.

I sit on top of her naked body, waiting, making small cuts in her chest; across petite breasts, her nipples still hard. Finally, the picture that had rolled out of the camera forms, milky emulsion dissolving and washing away, into a slightly blurred photograph of death. It is not a work of art. Nothing near my best, and certainly not worthy of this private collection. But it is good enough – her eyes bulge as the knife enters her throat, her mouth forms a neat little 'o' of silent surprise as she tries to suck in her final breath. Her eyes are wide, and her eyebrows are raised, as if, even though she knows she is going to die, she is still shocked, even disgusted, by the idea. I stick the photograph above the mahogany headboard, above the dead body, above the blood-soaked sheets. I lean forward and kiss her on the mouth, my tongue slipping easily inside. 'I love you,' I whisper as I push away from the bed, leaving her for the final time, only pausing to clean the apartment of traces to my existence in her life, and to wash myself in her bathroom . . .

—continued on, before entering an all-night diner. Not to get out of the rain, but to eat.

When he had left the apartment building, the moon had been shining in a clear night sky. As easily as he had kissed her lips one last time, the rain had come down. But now, as he sat drinking coffee and eating doughnuts in the early hours, the rain stopped. The moon broke through the clouds and danced with the stars once more.

Danced the night away . . .

PART ONE

Without Motive

Chapter One
Beginnings

The coffee tasted like treacle and the doughnuts were old and stale, but he stayed in the diner until nearly three. At two, sirens had blared through the dead night, and he wondered if his work had been discovered. But it was too early yet. The body would not be found until somebody went into the bedroom, which was very unlikely at this hour. Her cleaning lady in the morning, perhaps? It *was* a weekday when she came, but he was not sure which. So the body would not be discovered for at least five hours. Maybe days ... *weeks* ... when the stench had become so bad you could smell it outside the room, in the corridor and down the stairs of the building – when other patrons would begin to complain about a rotting *dead cat* smell.

Just before three he placed a five-dollar bill on the table, weighted down by the remnants of a doughnut, and left the diner.

It was time to leave this city.

He found a bus depot and walked into the lobby, his clothes still damp, the bag on his shoulder.

'Anywhere out of the city,' he told the woman in the booth when she asked him his destination.

She was old and covered in make-up, a cigarette dangling at the side of her mouth. She looked like Bette Davis.

'Where to, mister?' she repeated, annoyed that somebody had dared to ruin her standard spiel. She did not care about the customers of the bus company, or their needs. All she cared about was the clock on the wall, and how long she had left on her shift. She thought she was going to get by without any crazies, and then in walks this guy, his clothes still wet like he has been sitting in the goddamn rain.

'You choose,' he whispered, a latent air of menace hanging about him.

She thought he was trying to act threatening, and could not comprehend that he did not have to. That she was scared already, without him doing anything. She did not understand that he could kill her without a show of emotion; just for his pleasure ... because he wanted to, and could.

He restrained himself easily.

He remembered the woman's – her name was already forgotten, lost, like so many others – screams, and smiled as he waited for the ticket. It had been a good kill. He was only disappointed that there had been no real struggle, no fight for survival. The monster had missed that.

8

Absolutely looney tunes, she thought, and rang up a ticket for Detroit.

After depositing the gym bag in a locker, he sat in the dirty waiting room, which was nothing more than a large lobby with about fifteen long benches. On several, winos slept through the night, having given up the search for that final drink and deciding to wait and see what the new morning would bring. He watched as one of them coughed and spat phlegm onto the floor, before rolling over, not seeming to wake. There was a telephone booth at the back of the lobby, in front of the rest rooms. Inside the booth, another bum slept. He was huddled in a sitting position, his knees pulled up to his chin, his arms wrapped tightly around his legs.

Except for the occasional snore or grunt that could have come from any one of the drunks, the room was silent. As he closed his eyes to sleep, all he could hear was the rhythmic ticking of the clock inside the woman's booth. Louder and louder in his ears, it kept him awake. His bus would not arrive for another hour, so he continued to try and find sleep. He would dream of his past, he would dream of his childhood ... that short time of innocence and green pastures.

He would ... if only sleep would come.

The clock's incessant count of time was keeping him awake.

At first he had been tired and wanted oblivion but suddenly, he was alert. He felt like a wild animal, a predator, when it has picked up the scent of its prey. There was a challenge here. Somewhere...

He remembered tickling the woman's breasts with the knife, the rush he had felt.

To kill a drunk would be easy. There would be no fun in it; he would be killing for the sake of it – just to pass the time. But to murder one of the winos without there being a witness might be difficult. Especially with old Grouch-bag over there, in her little booth, watching his every move.

Maybe I will kill her, after all ...

He stood slowly and looked about himself, at first unsure of where he was going. Selecting a target, although it did not show on his face, his expression always remaining unfazed. He walked along the side wall, reading the spray-painted messages that covered the scummy white, a mosaic of graffiti.

... hellbent upon destruction ... animal ... Wes and Carrie 91 ...

It went on and on for ever, some nothing more than comical pictures and others that had been done in a more serious frame of mind – pathetic rebellious phrases and insults.

He laughed.

The kids thought they were being tough, doing this – that they had some kind of hardened exterior and could *kick ass*. If he wanted to, he could waste them all, no problem.

And he knew too, even if they did not realise it, that they were actually afraid – spraying the walls to leave a testament of their existence. Something that would always be here ...

10

Wes and Carrie, where are you now?

He went to the bank of lockers and removed the Instamatic from his bag. He let it fall around his chest, hanging from the leather strap he looped around his neck.

When he reached the back wall, he knew that the woman in the ticket booth could no longer see him; nor could she see the telephone booth in front of him, with its sleeping occupant.

He smiled.

It was, after all, a man. A living, breathing human being. The death would not be without purpose as he'd feared. People, somewhere, had to care for him. And these people would hurt – they had to.

This realisation made him step forward and pull the door open. He reached down and put his hand across the man's mouth.

He came around quickly.

'Get outta my house!' the vagrant ordered, his laryngitis-suffering voice muffled and quiet.

He gripped the drunk's throat with his free hand, and saw the horror, the fear, in the old man's eyes.

Don't be afraid. I'm your saviour.

His neck was fragile, and it was going to be easy to break. Just like snapping that of a chicken.

'You'll go into a better life,' he told the wino.

'Hey, man! What the fuck—?'

The voice came from behind. He had been unaware of anybody approaching.

He broke the old man's neck quickly, feeling the

cracking sound in his hand, but not savouring the moment as he would have liked to. Then he pushed back suddenly, catching the teenager, who had placed a hand on his shoulder, off balance. He had to move fast or the ticket lady would hear and come over to see what all the commotion was about. He spun and pushed the kid back into the men's rest room – surprising him with his aggression – where he must have just come from.

'Don't fuck with me!' he hissed, shoving the teenager up against the row of sinks.

In some cases you could be subtle before the kill, no pressure and easy, like making love to a woman before you cut her throat. But the kid had surprised him, so he had to get back on top of the situation real fast.

The teenager pulled a switchblade out and snapped it open.

'You don't want to be pushing me like that, man. It might get you hurt.'

The kid had short black spiky hair, and might have been handsome if he did not look so intense. From the sound of it, he spoke in a language made up of movie clichés. He was trying to be tough and mean, even though he did not seem particularly suited to the role.

The kid should have been at home doing schoolwork or out getting laid, not looking for trouble.

The man who had already killed twice that night was tired, perhaps even exhausted. But now he was looking forward to a third kill. He could feel the kid slowly pulling him into a new high, arousing the monster. He shook his head in dismay, in sympathy. The kid had been in a couple of street scuffles and believed he could look after himself. But underneath that perfect, fierce surface, he could see the sweating fear...

The kid was going to die hard.

Second Grade Detective Jay Austin woke just before the clock radio came on automatically at 7.15. He reached across and pulled the plug from its socket before the radio had a chance to blast loud rock music out at him.

The room about him was bare, and the mattress he slept on was spread on the floor. The bed, along with most of the other stuff from his apartment, was gone.

A few weeks ago he had pulled the night shift of a stakeout, and had come home bleary-eyed in the morning to find his place emptied out. Cyndi had left him, and decided that since they had lived together for a couple of months, that entitled her to all his stuff. Jay had outfitted the Bellevue apartment nearly five years ago when he had first signed a lease on the place, four years before he met Cyndi ... busting her for prostitution with cool detachment before succumbing to her sexy charm.

The radio belonged to her.

She had it set at 7.15, ready to play the rock music of Manhattan's loudest, which she liked at maximum volume. Although he wanted to change it, he found he could not. It was all he had left of her.

Cyndi would be up by now, 7.20, doing aerobics and God only knew what other exercises. Before, Jay would cower deep under the covers, trying to hide from the noise. Now, he rolled over and closed his eyes, doing his best to hide from the memories.

He much preferred to ease into his day. He lay there, slowly drifting into a light slumber, reaching a strange state of semi-consciousness in which, for a moment, he actually believed ... *he could feel Cyndi's steady breathing in his ear* ...

He sat up suddenly, surprised to see that she was not there.

Eight o'clock. Aerobics over, she would be sitting down to a breakfast he would have prepared, her hair still damp from the shower, glistening as she bit into the waffle, cream delightfully covering her top lip as she put back the weight she worked so hard to keep off.

Sunlight flooded into the room – she had even taken the blinds.

He crawled under the pillow, where the sun could no longer pound onto his head. It felt good there, and he drowsed until nearly nine, doing his best to sleep off the bender from the night before.

It was the phone that eventually woke him, dragging him from cloudy dreams and taking him until the seventh ring before he found it under a sheet on the floor. He grabbed the receiver and just before he spoke realised that he had it backwards; the earpiece at his mouth. He corrected it, twisting the cable around his arm as he did so.

'Yeah?' he said, his voice no more than a gruff whisper.

'It's Dooley, Jay. You'd best get down here.'

In his hungover state, the voice seemed to come from miles away, and it took him a second to remember who Mike 'Stoolie' Dooley was. Tall, with a moustache, a beard in mid-growth and a very receding hairline, he was the Desk Sergeant at the 14th Precinct. As that fact came into focus, Jay began to pick up on the beehive of activity which had been in the background of the call all along – phones ringing, people bellowing, a constant low murmur of several other voices and somebody, no doubt in the holding cell, repeatedly shouting 'Fuck!'

'I'm on vacation, Stoolie,' Jay said, and was about to replace the phone when he hesitated. Why was the Precinct calling, anyway?

They all knew he was on vacation, although nobody was aware that he'd spent the past two weeks holed up in his apartment – his *empty* apartment – defeated and hurt and alone, except for the couple of hours when the girl from 'Candy's Call Out' had been around. Then the sex had been pleasurable and that was all. The fact that he was a cop might have made it a little more exciting for her – she had used his handcuffs – but for Jay it had been nothing special, and when she'd left he had felt cheap and dirty. Ashamed.

'I know that, Austin. And considering you're on vacation I hope you don't mind me saying that you sound like shit. Now, like I said, you best get down here.'

Jay could not decide whether Stoolie sounded urgent

or not. There was definitely something in his voice, but the man always had attitude. Jay was sitting in a pool of the brightest sunlight, which wasn't helping his head and he figured the tension he was picking up on might just be his own.

'Why?'

He expected the answer to be something petty about his paperwork, or the Bowloski confession ... *could you believe the guy got his finger stuck in the door, and broke it?* But the reply was enigmatic, strangely evasive.

'I don't want to tell you over the phone. Just get down here, will you? Please.'

'Why?' But Jay was no longer certain that he wanted to know. A quiet fear welled in the pit of his stomach, and his headache faded, his senses becoming more alert as the effects of the drink wore off. *'Why?'*

'It has to do with your sister,' Stoolie conceded.

'What? Has she been robbed or something?' Jay asked. Every time he was at her place he told her about the flimsy, cheeseball locks she had on the door. Drove her crazy about them.

It had been so long since he'd seen her.

Jesus, she'd better be all right.

'Worse. Now get down here.'

In the sleepy town of Haddonfield over 1000 miles away in Illinois, Kirby McCaul rose silently, careful not to wake his parents who were still asleep – and would be for a good few hours yet – in the next room. It was just after 6.00, and he'd woken instinctively at this time as he did every morning. He had once owned a clock radio, but that was a long time ago. One morning it had woken his father, and that was when he had learnt to use it no more.

Now he relied on the alarm clock in his head.

He dressed quickly and moved downstairs, hoping that the creaking floorboards would not wake them, the sleeping beasts, the enemy within.

His father was an irritable drunk – he would spend his nights either at a bar or in front of the television, but everywhere he went there was always a bottle or a can in his hand. When he was drunk, if the slightest thing did not go his way or suit him, then he would beat it ... beat it hard, until it did. And when he was drunk, *everything* went his way. His father was a strong man with large hands; it was a fool who stood up to him or questioned what he did.

His mother was not quite so bad, but in her own inimitable way she frightened Kirby, and he often caught himself wishing they were not his parents. He would always be ashamed of these thoughts, and try to convince himself that he did not mean them ... but he never could. His mother was also an alcoholic, but instead of becoming angry and violent like her husband, she became submissive, giving into his every suggestion and action. Even when she was sober, in his drunken presence she was easily corrupted to his way of thinking.

Kirby believed that his mother was afraid of his

father, living in fear of the man she was supposed to love
... but he would never put that to her in case he was
wrong, and she told him what Kirby had said.

Then some bad shit would come his way.

Often when Kirby rose at this hour to do his paper
round before school, he thought about just leaving the
house and never coming back. But he was only eleven,
and at school he had few friends. It was a crazy idea and
he knew it would have to wait a few years yet. Still, each
morning he considered it, and each morning he found a
reason less for staying.

He reached the door and quietly – forever quiet, his
eternal vigilance – eased it open. He then closed the
door, making sure to lock it. Not that there was
anything in the house worth stealing, but one morning
he'd forgotten to lock the door, and it had been his father
who had found it so and – well, bad shit had come his
way that day.

Bad shit happens often ...

Seated on his bicycle, he looked up at the shabby,
neglected house, at its battered exterior and the room
where his mother and father slept. He wondered why he
always came back.

As he pedalled down the street Kirby could not find an
answer, and did not know if he would return that night.

On the other side of town Dwight Little's wife woke him,
and before his eyelids had even blinked open, she was on
top of him, kissing and holding. Searching for attention
and comfort.

'What did I do to deserve this?' he asked, between long, soft kisses.

She arched her back as she lifted her face away from his. 'Where were you last night?'

She watched his face carefully, looking for anything that would give him away, and tell her that he was lying. Anything in his expression, in his voice. But the answer came smooth and real.

'I got a call from Angie,' Dwight told her. 'I did my best not to wake you. Another of the properties was burned down last night – the Neeley place. They left town three months ago, and since then the property has been for sale.'

Dwight Little worked for a small firm of realtors called Cedar Court Homes, which was part of the much larger Griffin Corporation. Dwight and four others, including Angie Booker, represented most of the ownership deeds and titles in Haddonfield; and they all worked under one man, Richard Griffen.

It was the third building to go up in as many months, and whoever was responsible was keeping the Haddonfield Volunteer Fire Department in business and on their toes. The property, like the other two, had been empty at the time of the blaze and left beyond repair.

Ellen rolled away, and climbed off the bed. Dwight followed and went for a shower while his wife slipped out of her uninspiring nightgown and dressed. She could understand why, even for just a minute, she had suspected her husband of having an affair. She was nearly thirty-five, while he was yet to turn thirty. She was tired, and could feel the pains of age creeping up on her. She wanted to settle down and have a family, before it was too late and time passed her by. She could believe it if Dwight still yearned for freedom and excitement; life's party . . .

Sometimes she felt like she was holding him back, tying him down. She didn't want to lose him, didn't want to see him walk out of her life.

While she listened to the water in the shower, Ellen stared at her reflection in the full-length mirror. There were definite wrinkles in the corners of her eyes, and a permanent line or two across her forehead, half-hidden by her bangs. She was getting old, and couldn't convince herself otherwise any longer.

And while she was showing every sign of the ageing process, Dwight showed none.

The clothes she wore did not help her plight: a straight black skirt that went below the knee, and a soft white blouse with a gold brooch. The clothes of an older person. The kind of clothes she remembered her bookish mother always wearing before she died at the age of thirty-nine, cancer eating her away inside. In the back of her mind, Ellen guessed that was where a part of her fear stemmed from. She had only been a child, and the death of her mother had devastated her.

She changed into one of the tight skirts that had suited her so well a few years ago. Now she just looked silly, like one of those glamour-puss actresses you see on television, trying to look half their age.

Please don't let me be like that . . .

She just wanted to retain a little of the youth she knew she was losing each day. Her husband might not be sleeping with anybody else, but the temptation had to be there. She let the skirt fall to the floor, then hung it neatly back in the closet, stopping to look through the rest of its contents.

In a drawer lay the sexy underwear she had not worn in months – lingerie that had once made her feel good, but which she now hated. These were gifts from Dwight, to make her look more attractive, more wanton. She felt she needed them now.

Ellen unbuttoned her blouse and took it off. She then unclasped her bra and looked, almost with dread, in the mirror. Her breasts were drooping ... *really* drooping.

It would take more than a Jane Fonda work-out to get those suckers pert again.

She laughed, a nervous giggle as she realised how foolish she must look, how pathetic she must sound. The worry was not worth it. All that mattered was their love for each other. As long as that existed, she and Dwight would always be together. Somebody with whom to grow old, somebody to offer you love and comfort, and hold you in your dying years...

She smiled, and her naked reflection smiled back.

She remembered as a child looking into her mother's mirror when the breasts that were her burden now, had first been putting in an appearance. She had marvelled at them, back then. Now she did her best to ignore them.

She hooked the bra behind her back and fastened the

blouse again, this time leaving the top two buttons open and losing the brooch. She pulled the long black skirt on, and found a pair of heels.

Better, she thought.

For a second she actually believed she looked alluring, that she could still walk in a bar and make heads turn. Then she shook her head, bemused, and her reflection, still searching for its own identity, did likewise.

She was being ridiculous.

Dwight loved her...

Soon, she hoped, they would have a child. Four months ago, she had secretly stopped taking her pills. It felt deceitful, but Dwight might argue about her decision. Besides, they had made love rarely since then, and she was afraid they were growing apart. A baby would bring them back together. She was scared and believed their marriage needed that extra incentive if it was going to survive.

Dwight stepped out of the shower, water dripping from his hair, a towel wrapped around his waist. As he dried himself he wondered how much Ellen knew, whether she even suspected. He planned to leave her soon, but – perhaps unfortunately – he liked her, was fond of her, and if it was at all possible, wanted them to stay friends.

They had the potential to be good friends ... but not lovers. He believed that time was gone. Marrying Ellen had been a mistake. In Angie he had found the woman he'd been looking for ten years ago. Back then, the nearest thing to her was Ellen. Now he'd found the prized, cherished passion for which he'd been seeking all those years ago. And by some miracle, she wanted him too.

They could party all night ... unlike the tired, routine lifestyle marriage had brought him. Could still surprise each other. Make new discoveries. It was exciting and thrilling. When he was with Angie, he felt so comfortable. So right ...

These days, when he was around Ellen, he always felt guilty, insecure – forever wondering how much she knew. Like this morning, after she had discovered him missing in the night. She must at least suspect his affair. Dwight hated himself for not having the guts to tell her about Angie, tell her that he wanted a divorce; even though he knew the longer he waited, the worse she would take it, the harder the blow would be.

He could not see how Ellen fitted into his life any longer, but he still cared for her, and did not want to hurt her. He had never wanted to hurt her, and would never see her hurt by somebody else ...

Jay took the time to pull on a pair of jeans and a dirty sweatshirt before dashing out of his apartment and down the two flights of stairs, ignoring the sluggish elevator. When he ran onto the street he felt for his sunglasses and put them on, shielding his eyes from the burning daylight. Dodging the morning traffic, he crossed the road to his beat-up TransAm.

The streets held a dull sheen from the previous

night's rain, and there were fading reflections on the surface. Even though traffic was reasonably light, progress was slow as executives searched for the right place to have breakfast.

Something had happened to Susan.

If it was anything serious there was going to be hell to pay. And if Roger Card was involved, Jay was going to bust his ass big style.

Susan had been fired less than a month ago from TechnoCom, where she had worked under the title of Roger Card's Assistant. She had been proud of the title, which made her feel more than just a secretary – Card often handing many of his menial tasks into her charge.

Responsibility.

That was what he called it. Card promised her that as he progressed through the ranks of the corporation, so would she: she was far too valuable to lose. But Jay had always believed the man was using her – simply lessening the amount of work-time he had to spend in the office.

He had once confronted Card about it – without Susan's knowledge because she would have given him the same old lecture about Big Brother looking after Little Sister, even though she was thirty – and was given some lame bullshit about Susan doing her job *as an assistant*, and doing it well. Card explained that while he gave her extra duties, he also gave her extra benefits.

A couple of months later, Susan was fired, and Jay could only suspect what those 'extra benefits' were. He

24

would never ask Susan about them, but knew that she must have spurned Card's advances, and angered him. Jay also knew that by visiting Card, he himself might have been instrumental in the loss of her job ... and now, he sensed she had lost much more than that.

He brought the car to a screeching halt outside the Precinct building and ran up the steps, a couple of uniforms glancing at him as they left. Inside he spotted Stoolie, now beardless and looking much better for it, who pointed him to Caldwell's office.

Jay made his way through the maze of desks, and a few officers asked him how he was holding up. He nodded and pushed by, knowing that something very bad was coming around the corner, right at him.

When he reached the door, he did not bother knocking.

'You might have shaved. The Commissioner's coming by soon for a press conference,' Caldwell said, and then caught a smell of Jay's breath. It nearly knocked him to the floor. 'And you've been drinking.'

'I was on vacation. What's wrong with Susan?' Jay demanded.

Caldwell ignored the question. Surprisingly, it was easier to break this kind of news to civilians rather than cops. He sighed. It was a bad day when the force lost one of its own, and even worse when a member of an officer's family bought it to the scum on the street. Jay was also a great friend, so he put off the inevitable as long as he could.

'Cyndi left you, didn't she? I know you thought you

loved her, Jay, and it was kind of poetic, you taking her off the streets the way you did. But I told you then, and I'm telling you now – you meant nothing to her. She was a parasite, man. She used you, and you know it. You're doing yourself no good and—'

The words faded away. An empty silence filled the room.

Jay looked at Caldwell's bald head, his world-weary eyes carrying a legion of experience.

'Alan, what's happened to Susan?' he asked softly, looking into those eyes and pleading for the truth.

'Jesus, Jay,' Caldwell sighed heavily. 'You don't make it easy, do you? Jay, your sister, she's . . . she's gone, Jay. Susan's dead.'

Jay felt the strength in his legs suddenly disappear, and he collapsed into the wooden chair behind him. He should have guessed. Everybody had avoided the subject, and as he had come through the Precinct nobody had made eye contact with him. Subconsciously, he had known something like this was coming, but he was still not ready for the shock.

'Oh Jesus,' he managed, and then slowly realised the implications of Caldwell informing him of his sister's death. Alan Caldwell was a good friend, *but he was also a cop*.

'It was murder, wasn't it?' he whispered, stunned.

Caldwell remained silent.

'Talk to me!' Jay demanded angrily.

All the events of the past few weeks suddenly caught up with him. Cyndi's cold rejection, the drink and lack of sleep, and now the loss of the only family he had. Their parents had died when he and Susan were children, and they had been forced to grow up faster than their years dictated.

Now his sister was gone too ... and the real agony began.

In Haddonfield, Sheriff Tom Hasky was the final word in law enforcement.

He was tall at six-two, spritely and athletic. At forty-three his hair was beginning to thin, and he was currently involved in a deep inner struggle as to whether he should shave off his thick moustache, or not. Some people – mainly the doddering old biddies and housewives who liked to keep him informed of all the town gossip, and who could often be found in the kitchen baking cookies for his small department – said the moustache made him look younger. *Just trying to be polite*, he thought. Others, mainly his five deputies, told him the moustache was old-fashioned, pre-dating George Washington himself. But surely this was just friendly banter? Or were they serious, for the first time in their lives?

He tilted back in his chair, lifting one leg up onto his desk, next to the holster and the .45 it held. In all his years at Haddonfield he'd never had to draw the weapon, and never wanted to. He hadn't become Sheriff because he liked the action. If he wanted that he would have joined up at the Academy in one of the cities. He just wanted to help the people of Haddonfield. He could have entered the political arena, but didn't live for it – so he had joined the Sheriff's Department, and years later had found himself running the small building. The gun was beginning to feel uncomfortable on his hip, and he only carried it when he had to.

He would quit soon . . .

'So, what do you think, fellas?' Hasky asked Leigh Nichols – Volunteer Fire Chief and librarian *extraordinaire* – and their visitor, the man from Cedar Court Homes.

Dwight Little, whom Hasky saw as some kind of troubleshooter, was obviously getting angry. But Nichols knew that this was Hasky's way – just being friendly and polite, forming ground upon which he could meet with the unknown and unfamiliar Little. Nichols cut in before Little had the chance to say anything.

'Like I said last night in the bar, Tom – you're getting old, but that moustache, that was old ten years ago! Get rid of it, and see if Alice still recognises you. I'll bet she can't even remember what you look like underneath,' Nichols joked.

'What about you, son?' Hasky asked pleasantly. 'What do you think?'

Dwight was infuriated. Here they were, feeding him some bullshit routine about Hasky's moustache, when he needed facts – something he could take to Mr Griffen. Results and solutions.

'I don't really care about the moustache! I *do* care about the three properties that have been burned down in the past few months. Chief Nichols has put all three down to arson, and I want to know what you are going to do to catch the culprit.'

Hasky was not bothered by Little's outburst. He looked the young man up and down. A fashionable suit, shirt and tie, expensive shoes ... *we're in the middle of a heatwave, buddy, or didn't you notice?* Hasky wore a pair of scuffed jeans and a shirt, while Nichols had on shorts and a T-shirt.

Pretentious and obnoxious. Definitely nothing more, and probably a whole lot less. Hasky looked at Nichols, his best *'Is this guy for real?'* look, and Leigh smiled and shrugged.

Nichols had grown tired of Little hanging around the Fire Department, so he'd suggested they pay Hasky a visit. If Hasky ever found that out, the rest of Leigh's life would not be worth living.

'Coffee?' Nichols asked, trying to break up the battlefield atmosphere that had developed between the other two men.

'No,' Little said, distracted by the question, and Hasky saw his chance to move in.

'Just to keep you informed, Mr Little, there was nothing but a pile of ashes at any of the three sites. Now, if you want to waste my men's time by asking them to dust those ashes for prints, then go ahead, do that. But I'm telling you now, any evidence would have been the first thing to go up in the blazes. At each site, we've been through the damage with a fine-tooth comb – and found nothing. These burnings are professional.' And Hasky smiled, glad to see that Little was, well, *belittled*.

Hasky glanced at the tired Nichols, who just wanted this to be over as soon as possible, so that he could go home and get some sleep. Nichols yawned, hiding a grin which was threatening to explode all over his face. Little was shrinking, like a flower wilting in the sun.

'This isn't just some firebug jerking himself off,' Hasky continued, only pausing long enough to get his breath. 'Not as far as I'm concerned. These places are being left in an irreparable state. Now – why is that? There must be some method to this madness, and I intend to reach the bottom of it. Why are these places always on the market? Why are they always vacant? Now, your average firebug, he's not going to wait until the right property hits the street. He's going to torch whatever building he wants. Either that, or trash cans. It's almost as if these are *selected* targets. If I were you, Mr Little, I'd start looking inside your own corporation. Somebody knows when these places are hitting the open market – after they have been turned down by all of Griffen's friends, and when the insurance value is at its highest. Get it, Mr Little? Somebody, almost definitely on the inside, is making Griffen a lot of money. It could even be you.'

'You sonofabitch!' Dwight suddenly lost his cool and lunged at Hasky.

Nichols intercepted him and forced Little back.

'I think you should leave now,' Nichols advised him calmly, and began to escort him out of the office. 'And think about what Sheriff Hasky said. He may well be right.'

Dwight struggled, but the Fire Chief held him easily, and guided him towards the door. Dwight turned, flustered and angry. He stormed out of the small office with Nichols close behind, past Louise who barely looked up from her nails, and out of the quiet Department building. He slammed the door, making the glass windows shake and vibrate in their large frames.

'You OK?' Nichols asked Louise.

'Sure,' she said, chewing gum and nodding slightly.

Nichols looked at her, discreetly admiring her youthful body and good looks. He wondered what it would be like to be with her, a part of her, deep inside ... *goddamn illegal.* He returned to the office, and found Hasky sitting back in his chair, considering something more than his moustache.

'Give somebody that young a bit of power, and they think they can rule the world,' Nichols said. 'He's jumped up, that's all. No respect. It's that old adage – give 'em an inch, and they'll take a mile. In a day or two he'll simmer down – perhaps even realise that you're right.'

Hasky remained silent, staring into space, wondering how much longer he could find the energy for a job he no longer loved.

'How long have we known each other, Leigh?'

'Oh, I don't know. Has to be getting on for twenty-five years since you first moved into town. You stole my girl in about a week.' Nichols smiled, lost for a second as he remembered Alice Bury, his college sweetheart. Alice, who had run off with Tom Hasky and married him. Who would have believed that that stormy night, when rebellious young Nichols had beat the shit out of the new kid Hasky, would be the birth of a twenty-five-year friendship?

'She just chose the better guy,' Hasky said, likewise losing himself in the memories. 'I'm thinking of giving it up, Leigh. Throwing in the towel and calling it a day. I need more from life than hauling in drunks every Friday night, and busting up domestic squabbles once a week. You really think I should lose the moustache?'

'You never had a moustache back then. Think about it, Tom. I got to get out of here. I don't just fight fires. As you know, I've a library to run.' Leigh smiled, and put on his wire-rim glasses, losing the hard firefighter image in favour of something a little more intellectual. 'We'll talk later.'

'I know you two were close,' Caldwell said, and ordered two beers.

The bar was empty, a dark haven from the bright sunlight of the morning. A waitress busied herself by wiping tables that were already clean.

Caldwell was tall and dressed classy.

Jay could not remember ever seeing him in anything other than a shirt and tie, designer suit and handmade shoes. He had once been visiting Caldwell's home to discuss a case, and found his two kids lazing about in swimsuits, his wife in a pair of baggy shorts, and there was Caldwell, sitting on the patio on one of the hottest days in years – dressed in tailored slacks, a long-sleeved shirt and a paisley tie. As a tiny concession, the sleeves were rolled up, and the man held a glass of ice-cold lemonade in one hand.

Jay remembered that day now.

The case that had concerned them then, the murder of a small boy named Billy Rogers, had long since been relegated to the Unsolved files, despite a perfect description of the killer from the child's mother, who claimed he was her lover. The investigation had driven Jay crazy. The boy's death had been meaningless – without motive. The former lover had just disappeared off the face of the earth, and the boy had been buried deep in a grave of paperwork with other unsolved cases.

Jay hoped Susan would never find a place in that graveyard...

His thoughts were bouncing everywhere, and he did not care so long as they kept away from the taboo subject of Susan's death.

Lorraine, Caldwell's daughter, was seventeen now and studying to work in criminal law. She was developing into quite an attractive young woman. Julian had more of his father's genes. Snazzy dresser for sure, but overweight for his fifteen years and, if the truth be told, damn ugly. But they were good kids, and Jay had gotten to know them quite well since that first visit to Caldwell's home, nearly five years ago.

His wife, Teressa, was a real good woman. A little plump as she got older, but she was caring, and loved Alan more than anything else in the world.

Caldwell was lucky.

Jay was trying to block out and reject what had happened, but all the time his thoughts completed a circle, obsessively returning to the same point on the circumference.

Susan was dead.

'I once saved her life,' Jay said, and was quiet for a sombre second. 'I think now, maybe I should have let her die back then.' He finished the beer and ordered another.

'Slow down,' Caldwell warned.

'I want to go by her place, Alan. Can you fix that?'

He did not care about Caldwell's response, however much he valued him as a friend. He was going to Susan's apartment, and no one could stop him. If he obtained Caldwell's permission and went through the proper channels, so much the better. Hopkins and Deacon would have less time to fuck up the investigation.

'It was messy, Jay. You don't want to see it,' Caldwell told him. 'Besides, I know what you're thinking, and you're wrong. Your judgement is clouded, your opinion influenced by how you feel. Hopkins and Deacon are good men, and you know it. It's pretty crowded over there. Leave it a day or two.'

'And while I wait, the bastard who killed Susan is getting away. I want him, Alan. I want him dead in a fucking body bag!' Jay said, gulping angrily at his second beer.

'Take it easy, Jay. We all want him for what he did, but in your condition, with your emotional attachment, you will probably hinder the investigation more than help it. Maybe you should take a real vacation. Get right out of the city for a while.'

'Yeah,' Jay said with bad attitude as he stood. 'And maybe I should be out looking for that sick sonofabitch!'

He was at the door, silhouetted as light flooded in, when Caldwell called him back. He had just received a call over the radio. Two bodies had been found at the bus depot. Multiple homicide.

'You want to come?' Caldwell asked, knowing that the address was only several blocks from Susan's apartment, knowing that the possibility of a connection was about three million to one ... but that it nevertheless existed. He hoped it would be enough to keep Jay's mind off his sister's death. Enough to keep him from going on some cowboy crusade to find the killer. Something like this might take his mind off vengeance trails and vigilante action ... but then again, it might be enough to push him over the edge ...

Chapter Two
Deceptions and Truths

Surprisingly enough, the chaos at the bus depot was actually a well-organised procedure. To the untrained or inexperienced eye, it might seem a shambles, but there was nobody there who should not be, and everybody was going about their duties with typical haste and efficiency.

White flashes filled the air as photographs were taken – rolls of film accumulating as every detail was recorded from every angle. Bright yellow 'police scene' tape had been used to cordon off various areas of the lobby. Caldwell and Austin ducked under one such strip.

'Hey, Bobby! Who found the bodies?' Caldwell asked a young uniform as he walked by.

Cleanshaven and all-American, that was Officer Bobby Roberts. He had once been a promising college quarter-back with a bright professional future ahead of him until one game, when a line-backer decided to take

37

him out ... for good. His leg had been broken in four places. He now walked with a slight limp.

'The lady in the office, sir,' he replied, pointing to the ticket booth.

Jay was already on his way, and Caldwell knew that his mind was made up. The perpetrator of these crimes had also killed his sister – and if he were to catch up with him, the murderer would be the unluckiest man to ever walk the earth. Jesus, Alan sighed. Maybe it had been a mistake to let him come here.

Caldwell took a step to follow, and then turned back to Bobby. 'Get on the radio and make sure that asshole Brody knows where I am. I'm supposed to be at the Precinct in half an hour for a press conference.'

Caldwell made his way across the lobby to the ticket booth. When he reached it, Jay was already talking to the woman.

'You found one of the bodies, right?' Jay asked succinctly. Time was of the essence. Susan's killer could be on a bus to someplace, and this woman was the only person who could help him.

'I didn't find no body!' she snapped, angry that the assumption had been made. 'I just called the police. The janitor, causing me trouble like always, he found the body. You should go talk to him.'

'We will,' Caldwell assured her. 'But first we'd like to ask you a couple of questions. Do you remember seeing anyone unusual or suspicious last night?'

To Jay, it seemed like she thought about the question for ever. She mulled it over, seemed on the brink of answering, then stopped and thought about it some more. When at last she did answer, her reply was flat and bleak.

'No.'

'There must have been something,' Jay prompted, impatient and frustrated. 'Something that was slightly out of the ordinary. Just take a moment to think about it.'

'What do you think I already did?' she argued. But she paused for a short moment, and the answer that came this time was far more positive than her first response.

'Wait a second,' she said slowly, remembering. 'There *was* a guy. He had me scared for a while, jumping at my own shadow. He came in at ... oh, around three o'clock, maybe a little later. He must have been sitting in the rain because his clothes were still damp. He carried some kind of bag which he left in one of the lockers.'

She stopped for a second to light a cigarette.

Jay looked over to the print crew working the locker area ... *good job, boys. Make it good ...*

'Why do you remember him so well?' Caldwell asked, as she clicked the cheap lighter several times before it worked correctly.

'Damn thing,' she complained bitterly. 'Well, he came to the booth and looked at me with this really dumb expression. Kinda like, the lights are on, but there's nobody home – you know what I'm saying? Anyway, he really gave me the shivers. I asked him where he wanted to go, and he said anywhere. Now, I've been in the bus business for nearly ten years, and I told him straight – that isn't the way it works. He said that I should just give him a ticket, and it didn't matter where to. He had me scared bad, so I punched in a ticket for Detroit as fast as I could and gave it to him. He paid for it, and then he went and sat on the benches over there. I would have given him the—'

'How did he pay?' Jay asked. 'Bills or change?' His mind was racing ahead to Detroit, and he knew he would soon be on his way there. Nothing was going to stop him, or even slow him down. However long it took, however far he had to go – Jay would always be following the man...

But it was all instinct and emotion. He had no evidence.

'It was cash. Bills, I think. But what has—?'

'Bobby!' Jay shouted, holding his hand up to silence the woman.

'Just a minute.'

'*Now*, Bobby!' Jay returned. 'This is important.'

Bobby came over immediately.

'I want you to empty the cash register, and have all the bills checked for prints. See if we can get any matches from around this place. Let's try and narrow down our options here.'

Caldwell watched Jay take charge. He was good, even under the kind of stress he must be feeling, even with that sad motivation. He was one of the best.

Bobby was on his way into the booth when the woman

started to protest. She tried to get a lock on the door, but Bobby had already pushed it open. Jay wondered if Susan had struggled to get a lock on her door, or if the killer had some kind of invitation, if he knew her...

'You can't do this!' the woman protested, pushing at Bobby who firmly pressed on. 'Is this legal? If I lose my job over this, I'm gonna sue all your asses!'

'You will not lose your job,' Jay assured her slowly. 'Bobby will give you a receipt. Leave that in the cash drawer, or the safe ... whatever. In a couple of days we will call you, and you can collect the money. Don't worry about it.'

'Do you remember anything else?' Caldwell asked.

'Just that on his way out, as he was walking by the booth, he turned and looked at me, stared ... through me. Real vacant-like. Death was behind those eyes, I know it,' she said, more dramatically than she needed to.

But on that note, Jay observed that her speech had slowed down a little; as if, for the first time, her disdain for the law was forgotten and she was serious. Previously, she had been speaking so fast you would have believed she was in a race. She did not care about the investigation, or the two dead men. She just wanted to get out of this place and get home. If they had told her the killer was the Man in the Moon she would have agreed, so long as it meant she could leave.

But not for those few seconds...

'Thanks for your time,' Caldwell said, as Jay took off in search of the janitor. 'We'll be in touch.'

As Caldwell was catching up with Jay he noticed an attractive female detective motioning for him at the locker area.

'What is it, Shelby?' Caldwell asked when he reached the woman.

Detective Shelby held up a photograph they had found wedged in a locker door. It was sealed in a clear bag.

'It's clean,' Shelby told him as the forensics crew began to move out of the area. 'But we're sending it to the lab for complete analysis. They found some pictures at the Austin apartment.'

Shelby had transferred to Manhattan three weeks ago. She'd heard that Susan Austin was the sister of a cop, but did not know Jay.

The picture showed a teenager's head pushed deep into a toilet bowl. Blood smeared the white porcelain. A series of bubbles were breaking on the surface of the yellow liquid ... *as the kid kicked and struggled at the end of desperation* ...

'Welcome to Manhattan,' Caldwell sighed quietly. 'You notified the parents yet?'

'It's happening. This is a very bad guy,' Shelby observed.

Caldwell nodded, wondering if the killer had left the city. 'Good work, Shelby.'

Halfway across the lobby Jay stopped next to a man kneeling on the ground. He wore jeans and a shirt with a cheap sports jacket and no tie. His name was Ray Province, and he was the best police artist Jay had ever encountered. He worked fast, and his sketches actually looked like people. Jay had seen some artists whose work was little more than rough caricatures. But not Vinnie. He was responsible for several big arrests over the past few years, and Jay was glad he was here.

'Hi, Vinnie,' Jay said, the greeting spoken blandly, the words at odds with this place of death. 'How are you doing?'

'Not bad, Jay. Hang in there, you hear? We're gonna catch this bad fucker,' Vinnie replied. He had been to Susan's apartment as soon as the call came in, but there was nothing happening. Then the bus depot murders had come through. The possible connection was not lost on him.

Jay was grateful for Vinnie's sympathy but, strangely, did not appreciate it. It only served to remind him of what had happened to Susan. He was going to Detroit, but if he dwelt on his sister's death it would slow him down. Unlike the movies, his grief would not drive him harder and faster. It would probably cause him to break down.

'Listen, Vinnie, I need a big favour. Talk to the woman in the booth, will you, and fix me a picture ready for when I leave. It doesn't have to be anything special – this is just for me. All I want is something that looks like a face.'

'I'm on it,' Vinnie said, and stood.

'And don't let Caldwell know you gave me a preview of who we're looking for. He must suspect that I'm going to Detroit, but that doesn't mean I have to leave footprints in the sand for him to follow.'

'Anything you say,' Vinnie replied.

'Thanks,' Jay said, watching as Vinnie headed for the booth.

At that moment, Bobby was emerging from the booth, having taken several minutes to persuade the woman to sign for the money.

'Pay day, huh?' Vinnie smiled when he saw the wad.

'I wish,' Bobby said, and then motioned Vinnie inside. 'I do not envy you at all.'

Why did I kill the vagrant and the kid?

As the Greyhound rides out of Manhattan, this question haunts me more and more ... like a germ or bacteria contaminating my mind.

Confusion reigns.

The death of the woman – Susan Austin – was nice, but disappointing. I knew her, and she thought I loved her. That was good. That was the best aspect of the whole scenario – her face, her beautiful face, when the knife was on her throat for the first time.

Her voice, frozen with terror. 'What are you doing?'

And then ...

She cried ... she begged. She pleaded, sobbed and wept. 'Please, please.'

Am I beginning to miss the fight? Is it that on

which the monster thrives? It tastes the fear, devours the lifeforce and the soul. It needs the fight, the violent rush as every nerve and cartilage and muscle, every individual cell, tingle and dance in perfect harmony. Sing ...

That is what life and death are really about. The bridge. The carrier ... from one to the next. The struggle, the burning energy, when somebody living must fall over the edge of that deep, dark abyss called Death.

The women rarely resist. They lie back, let me bed them ... let me kill them. Have they never heard of self-defence? Are they all waiting for their knight in shining armour?

It is never enough, anyway.

The kid with the switchblade ... I wish I could go to his home, see his parents grieve. Watch them close their curtains and shut out the world as they mourn. I wish I could see that.

But their deaths were wrong, careless.

Why did I kill the vagrant and the kid? I cannot find an answer, and that scares me. Until now I have always been in control. Check out the past.

Cautious. If I start a relationship, I always keep a mental record of what I touch, so that I can clean it when the monster comes out to play, breaks its chains. I never let anybody take a photograph of me, leaving my picture on an undeveloped roll of film, or lying under a bed, forgotten.

But at the depot ... did I clean the lockers? Are my prints still on the kid's switchblade?

I do not know.

My attitude has never been so cavalier. If they are clever they might relate the prints to the boy I killed last time I was in Manhattan. Get a match ...

The monster of my psyche, the beast that claimed me as a child and made me its master, wants to come out of its cage more and more often. I can hear it rattling the metal bars in brutal torment, can feel it pulling on its leash, see it growling, baring sharp fangs ... demanding the freedom my body can give it.

It is good that I have never been to Detroit before. It has never been a witness to my work. It will be safe.

Detroit will never forget.

He looked up with a start as the passenger in the next seat deliberately gave him a nudge.

The bus was no longer moving. He had not been aware of it stopping.

He looked out of the window, the sun, high in the sky, blinding him. He saw a barren landscape, unmarked by the passage of time for as far as he could see, except for the shifting dunes.

The constantly shifting dunes.

He turned and studied the man next to him. He was heavy and visibly fat; his shirt bulged and his gut protruded, actually flowed over the top of his slacks.

Half a cigar, the type that really smell, stuck out of the side of his mouth, a thick trail of smoke rising from it, scenting the air.

'Engrossing stuff?' the man asked, friendly enough. 'Wouldn't have disturbed you, but this is the only stop on the journey.' And he stood, squeezing his way down the aisle of the bus.

The diner was one of those places that only exist because of the bus trade. Apart from that, the only business it ever saw was the occasional tourists stopping for a break, and the odd trucker who could be bothered to slow down. He went in, found an empty booth and ordered a coffee.

The waitress dumped the cup on the table and the coffee spilled over the brim, caught only by a saucer that was cheap and chipped, like the cup.

The coffee was lukewarm and bad.

Stale doughnuts and bad coffee ... about all he seemed to eat and drink these days.

He laughed quietly, and then began playing games in his mind. 'Simulations', he called them. They gave him a release when one was not physically available, and he enjoyed them. Just to think about death, violent death ... sometimes it was enough to appease the monster.

He smiled at the pleasing fantasies until he finished the coffee.

The smile disappeared fast when the man from the bus suddenly sat opposite him. Fat and ugly, his breathing was heavy and laboured. He spoke between breaths that were like frantic gulps for air.

'What's the coffee like? I have to stop at so many of these places because of business. It all tastes the same after a couple of years,' the man explained. 'Peter Richards. You got a name?'

'Daniel,' he said, and took the hand Richards offered, pumped it heartily. Doing his best to please, to like a man who must be hated by so many just because of his shape and size. 'Daniel Mabe. And yes, the coffee *is* awful.'

Daniel Mabe was not his real name. He had used so many over the years, he could no longer remember the name his mother and father had given him.

'I'll have one anyway,' Richards said, and ordered a cup. 'You married, Danny?'

The man was just trying to be polite, making conversation so that the journey would go by that much quicker. But Daniel could not help thinking that the man was prying, sticking his nose in where it was not wanted.

But what did it matter? Peter Richards was nobody. He could tell his whole life story to good old Pete, and the man would not care or listen because he had enough worries of his own.

'No. Never felt the urge to settle down. Never met the right woman,' Daniel said, and stood. From Pete's expression, Daniel knew the man thought he was leaving. He walked instead to a soda machine, dusty and old, got a Coke and returned. 'What about you? You got a woman?'

The man looked down at his coffee, staring intently

into the black for what seemed like an age before looking up.

'I was married once. She was the best thing that ever happened to me, but ... it just didn't work out. You're too young to understand, Danny. I'll bet you're always falling in love, but I'll bet too that nobody has ever fallen out of love with you. I just came home from the office one day and she was gone. I found a note tacked to the wall, a couple of sentences written on toilet paper.'

The man looked down again, and remembered.

'She made great coffee. It's strange, but I remember that the most. I guess that's why I drink so much of *this* stuff – to rid my mouth of her taste.'

Daniel felt genuine sympathy. A guy like this, in his obese condition, must have to work hard just to get people to like him, never mind love him. He was a loser, and Daniel could relate to that. Only Daniel had fought the system and become a winner. Nothing could touch him now. He controlled everything about him – the man heading for a late lunch, the lady pushing a buggy, the baby in that buggy. All the people on this bus to Detroit ... his presence controlled all their lives.

'What about now? Do you see anybody regularly?' Daniel asked.

'My marriage broke up a few years ago. Since then I have only slept with one woman. We're more friends than lovers. We're always there for each other, no matter what the problem is. We call each other in the middle of the night just to chat. I think it might work out for us,' Richards said, and fumbled for a cigar. 'You mind?'

Daniel nodded silently, an almost menacing look in his eyes, which were cold and deep – staring eternal. The look was enough for Peter Richards.

'Hey, no problem. I can wait until we reach Detroit. Shouldn't be smoking the damn things anyway. Andrea would kill me if she knew. So, what do you do when you're not talking to fat guys in cheap roadstops?'

Andrea would kill me if she knew. You and Andrea are a lot closer than you think. You care for her, and she really cares for you. All the time Daniel was thinking: *A shame for you to die,* even if he did not allow the thought fruition and growth into something far greater and more solid.

Daniel had never worked in his life, not even delivering papers when he was a child. Work was for the poor – something he had never been, and never would be. Money held no value for him. When he killed he did not rob – that was not the motivation – except on occasion a long, long time ago. He had held up several banks in different states, and then killed his partner. He was still getting by on that money.

He could have hitched to Detroit instead of getting the bus. It would have been a lot more fun: a dangerous game of cat and mouse as he killed, waited for another ride, and killed again. But the bus was quicker ... and ever since that Rutger Hauer movie, rides were hard to come by.

He had flown many times, and had once killed a whole family at sea, on board a luxury cruise liner. Killed them, and then thrown their bodies overboard ... *sharp hail cutting my face as the ship cut a course through high waves and strong winds* ... Their disappearance had always remained a mystery. It obviously had to be presumed they were lost at sea – but how? Why had they been up on deck in such bad weather? It was these questions that baffled the authorities.

Murder had been a possibility too incredible to consider.

Daniel smiled.

What did he do in life?

'Me? I kill people, Pete,' he said sardonically.

Richards laughed. 'I don't mind if you won't tell me,' he grinned, his smile hiding a secret truth of his own. 'Hell, maybe we should just talk about movies or something – get away from all this personal crap. So ... where to after Detroit?'

Daniel had not even thought about it until now, because it did not matter. There would always be another town, another city. Another place unfamiliar with his call.

His midnight cry ...

The janitor was a small, rat-like Mexican, unshaven, his skin naturally greasy. He did not seem at all bothered by the fact that he had just found two bodies.

'Oh, come on, man!' he complained, his accent strong. 'Are you fuckin' jokin' me? I got responsibilities, I got work to do. I already spoke to your people, and you're still harassin' me.'

Jay looked up from the dirty, grime-ridden floor.

'This isn't harassment, but it could very easily be,' he threatened, pissed at the janitor's lack of co-operation, and his whole attitude. Two people had been murdered – and all this little rat-bastard cared about was the floor.

Three people . . . Susan – she would have been the first.

He had to get out of here as soon as possible. Before he left for Detroit he needed to call in at Susan's apartment, however painful that might be. Seeing her home for a final time, sealed and isolated. The bloodied sheets . . . the blood, red and – and . . .

Don't think like that.

. . . and dry now, the body gone.

Don't think!

Tears were heavy in his eyes. *Just get the job done and get out of here.*

'You haven't spoken to me yet. So speak.'

The janitor wondered who this sad sonofabitch was, coming in here and ordering people about like he was running the show – ordering *him* about. He had work to do. He decided the quickest way to get all these fucks out of his life was to just tell them what they wanted to hear, as many times as they wanted to hear it.

The janitor had come in with the intention of trying to get the walls cleaned up, but first had to perform his everyday duties; brushing and mopping the floor, wiping the windows, cleaning the toilets.

'I've come in and found kids humping in the shithouse before now. Never found a body, though. This has to be a first. I pulled the kid up out of the head, and all this piss ran off his face. It was disgustin', man. So I let him fall back in.'

Contaminated scene, Jay thought. It was going to make forensics' work more difficult.

'Then I remembered you guys, and fingerprints and all that shit, so I got the fuck out of there. I told Daryl Hannah over in the booth there to call the pi-*cops*, man. Then I went to wake the phone man up, get him out of here before all this shit went down. He's a good guy. I leave him as long as I can most mornings, let him get all the sleep he needs.'

The janitor spat chewed tobacco on the floor, and caught the look of distaste Jay gave him.

'Don't worry about it, man. The floor gets a lot worse than this. Hey, am I going to get anything for this – a reward, or something?' the Mexican asked.

'How about a check on your green card? Now, what happened to the guy in the booth?'

'Chill, man. He's dead, you can see that. Just like the kid. Man, would I like to get my hands on the guy who did this.'

I don't think you would, Jay thought. *He'd eat your fucking heart.* And he turned away, leaving the janitor. The man had been no help.

Caldwell caught Jay up, walking quickly across the lobby.

'What sort of an interview was that?' he stormed,

surprised by Jay's attitude, surprised at himself for letting him be here.

'He didn't know anything. All he did was find the bodies, and you're treating him like a material fucking witness!'

Several cops looked up from their work, but Caldwell's expression was enough to tell them to get on with what they were doing.

'I'm sorry,' Jay said evenly. 'But we have his statement, and that is enough.'

Caldwell looked at his watch. 'I have to get back to the Precinct, get the Vaseline out for that fat fuck Brody.'

Jay did not smile at the old private joke, so Caldwell continued: 'I think it was a mistake letting you be here, Jay. I want to see you in my office this afternoon.'

Caldwell looked at his friend, and placed a hand on his arm. In his eyes he could see all the sadness and sorrow for what had happened, all the hatred for the person who had killed Susan. But mostly Caldwell saw pain, cutting deep into Jay's heart where it would always be felt.

'Jay, let it be,' he appealed. 'Let us handle your sister's death. Your emotions will only get in the way. You're no good to us on this one. Play it by the book and do some traffic duty or something. Take a real vacation – anything to get your mind off her death.'

He gripped Jay's arm tightly.

'You're a good cop,' he told him. 'One of the best. Don't let this ruin your career ... don't let this ruin *you*.'

* * *

Kirby hated Johnny Whittingham.

To Kirby it seemed that Johnny's sole purpose in life, his big reason for living, was to make his life miserable. Not a day went by without Kirby alternating his route to school so that the other boy would not see him. But once inside they shared a lot of the same classes, so to avoid him altogether was impossible.

But sometimes...

Because of his parents, most of the children in the school kept away from him. They were not afraid of him; they just didn't want anything to do with him. He had few real friends, most people believing he was going to follow in his father's footsteps. Even the most stupid and immature children knew that, and knew he was trouble. The teachers too, despite the fact that he was intelligent and shone in every subject, tended to neglect Kirby McCaul because of his parents.

The thinking went something like this: Mr and Mrs McCaul were losers, so why should their son be any different?

He had been in many fights because of his father's reputation. Some of the other kids, Johnny Whittingham for example, felt good when they told tales of how they had beaten up the drunk's shitty son. Probably jerked each other off over it. But Kirby stood his ground. He knew the fights were not his fault, and was not going to get beat up for nothing – so he always did his best to get in a couple of good punches of his own.

He was not built for fighting. He was no weakling, but was more suited to athletics and running than weight-training and football. He was fast on his feet with the few friends he did have, often playing tag; even when they were all chasing him, they could not touch him.

It would be so easy to run ... *run away from Haddonfield, leave it all behind ...*

He was too fast for all the slobs and dorks, and could always outwit them if they tried to use what little brains they did have. But he was no coward, even though running sometimes meant survival. Because of his parents, he feared the way people perceived him. He would not give his peers the chance to even think he was a coward.

And, occasionally, he even won the fights.

Then the Principal came down on him the hardest, because of his father who had spent more than many nights in Sheriff Hasky's drunk tank. The Principal would lecture him for hours, explaining his destiny – 'your inescapable fate', he brainwashed. Told Kirby he would end up in a state penitentiary before he was twenty-five, most likely maximum security.

However much those remarks hurt him, they meant nothing because it was only talk, and the Principal knew nothing about Kirby.

What everybody failed to realise was that Kirby McCaul was one of the good guys. He never went looking for trouble, it just seemed to find him. He attracted it like a magnet, a field of energy, thanks to his parents. Something else everybody failed to realise was that Kirby McCaul was not going to spend his life getting dirty under car engines, or flipping burgers at the local McDonald's. He was going to make something of his life.

Every time they beat him up, they made him stronger, more determined to succeed.

People always seemed to overlook his consistently high grades, and the exceptional work he did using his own initiative – reading up on subjects in his own time at the library. And if it took his fancy, if he wanted to get out of the real world for a short while – a delightful time, however short – if he wanted to escape Haddonfield and all the people he wished he did not know, he would ask Mr Nichols – *hey, Kirby, I told you already, the name is Leigh* – to select him a good piece of fiction. Nothing heavy, just good adventure stories. In his bag today he had *Treasure Island*, which he intended to return after school – *if* he lived that long.

As he chewed the sandwiches he had purchased for lunch, Kirby watched them.

It was incredible, and he wondered if it was the same in all schools. He was wise to it now though, and he watched as the message was passed and read. The reader then circled through the hall and passed it to somebody else. There was a whole network of school bullies. Act independently, and you suffered their wrath.

The message was passed again. That made eight.

Each time the note was read and re-folded the person would throw a casual glance in his direction, and Kirby would smile back as he slowly ate his sandwich.

He was in trouble.

He could feel Johnny Whittingham's cold stare on his back, but refused to turn.

The last recipient of the note went outside.

That was it. The letter could come back inside at any time, but Kirby would not know unless he spotted it by chance. So ... there would be at least eight, probably more than ten. It was going to be a blitz. That had happened once before. He'd fought back then and taken a hell of a beating for his trouble, but that had been nothing compared to what his father had done to him as punishment.

He would not make that mistake this time.

He chewed the sandwich with slow, deliberate contentment, tasting the ham, letting the juices and sauces flow in his mouth before he swallowed.

What was he going to do?

At times like this it was a fool who stayed around for the fight, and a brave man who knew to run. But even that might be difficult. There were going to be too many of them, some of whom he would not even know. A posse, a pursuit team forever snapping at his heels, tiring him, and people watching all the exits. And from far away, Johnny Whittingham, observing studiously and waiting for word of his capture.

It was the last day of school for a couple of months. He

should have expected them to come up with something special.

Kirby finished the sandwich and shook his head with dismay. Nobody would help him on something this big ... but he should not be thinking so bleakly. If they did catch him, what was the worst they could do?

They could not kill him, and on a basic level, that was all that counted.

Survival – making sure they did not put you in the ground with all the old people.

While school was out he would celebrate his birthday. Another year closer to leaving Haddonfield, and the bad family ties which held him there. All he needed was a decent education, and then he could go away to college, some place where nobody knew his name.

Leave here ...

While Dwight was at the office, Ellen went about her usual household chores. She stacked the dishes and wiped over the kitchen. Then she went into the bedroom and made the bed, tucking the soft sheets under the mattress, folding them back tidily, gently running her fingers over the fabric, wondering how long it had been since they had last made love.

Losing herself, she decided to go into the back yard for half an hour or so, but as she passed through the kitchen, suddenly feeling tired, she sat down on one of the chairs and leaned on the table.

All the insecure thoughts of earlier that morning and the middle of the night were coming back at her. She did her best to block them out, but they were like an express train racing to the front of her mind, all-powerful and demanding attention.

The gardening – that was what had thrown her back into the middle of the night. Gardening was something they had always done together, something they found joy in when out there together. Surrounded by beautiful flowers and long grass...

But when was the last time they had been into the garden together?

So long ago, she could not remember.

They used to make love out there, rolling in the long grass, sweltering in the heat of summers past. It was easy to smell the pollen, the drifting scents carried by a cooling breeze, easy to see gorgeous butterflies with their patterned, symmetrical wings, fluttering and dancing in the air ... and two people she no longer recognised, running and playing games with each other...

Her softly falling tears brought her back to the kitchen. She was crying, almost sobbing.

Dwight was having an affair.

She did not need to go into the garden to understand that. She knew what was waiting for her out there now, an ugly troll, ready to jump on her the moment she stepped outside.

She was alone.

The realisation caused a pain greater than anything she could imagine. His love and affection for her had grown cold. Even though Dwight was living with her, she was actually alone. All he cared about was his job and his mistress, whoever she might be. Ellen wondered how long he had been living the lie.

She stood as the well of tears began to dry, and the sobbing eased. She refused to feel defeated.

It was his loss.

She had to believe that.

Richard Griffen sat behind his large desk in the open and spacious office.

In front of him was a thin sheaf of papers.

Dwight Little, one of the people who looked after Cedar Court Homes in Haddonfield, had stumbled upon his insurance claim operation. The lengthy fax represented the sum of Little's findings. It had only arrived a few hours ago, yet it was already Griffen's top priority.

Griffen looked at the photograph of his wife – *ex*-wife, he reminded himself, and wondered why he still yearned for her like a teenager with a crush; why he could not let go.

He was a rich man of self-indulgence, with a malicious streak that ran straight through his heart. He could not understand that it was his weakness for other women – paid-for prostitutes whom he could treat how he liked – that had driven her away.

There was a tear in his eye as he longed for his wife.

It was his sadistic pleasures that had made her leave.

He picked the photograph up and stared through it, to the time when it had been taken. He ran his fingers along the glass curves of her image as he remembered. She was grabbing a pillow to hide her camera-shy, yet perfectly photogenic face. Giving up, she had let the pillow fall and grinned sheepishly into the camera.

She was beautiful.

'Mr Griffen,' a voice said over the intercom system. 'There's a Mr Little here to see you. He says he is expected, but I don't have his name.'

Griffen placed the photograph and frame back on the desk.

'Show him through.'

Dwight had gone back to his office after speaking with Hasky, and had written a quick report outlining what had been said, only he put it all in his name. Less than an hour after faxing the report, Griffen had called the office and asked to see him as soon as possible.

I found that report very interesting, Dwight. I look forward to seeing you soon.

Dwight had immediately called Ellen and told her that he had to go to the city on business. Luckily, there was a flight departing from the small airport in less than an hour. On his way there, he dropped by Angie's office.

'Why does he want to see you?' she asked.

'It's pertaining to my report. He seemed pleasant enough.'

'It was probably an aide you spoke to. You didn't include that crazy insurance scam idea of yours, did you?' she asked belligerently, and could see from his expression that he had. 'Well, that's it then. He's going to can your ass. I'm in love with an unemployed bum.'

On the flight out all he could see was Angie's gorgeous face. There were no thoughts of Ellen, no room for her inside his mind. A strong passion for Angie ruled him.

It was as if Ellen did not even exist.

'You got something for me?' Jay asked through the booth window.

'Here you go,' Vinnie said, and passed him a piece of paper.

The face was in the middle of the sheet and took up about three-quarters of the page. It was a good sketch.

The face was round, but not fat, with average-length hair. The nose was straight and the eyes ... for some reason Jay was drawn to the eyes. There was something familiar about them – a mystic coldness in them that Vinnie had captured.

Pictures of killers never look like Everyman, Jay reflected as he stared into those smiling eyes. An inherent evil is always present, simply because we believe – especially the witness giving the description – that these people can have no decent human values. No redeeming features.

They are bad through and through.

At the bottom of the page Vinnie had made several notes.

five ten – six two
twenty-five – late thirties
blue eyes, dark hair, muscular
jeans and T-shirt, gym bag – Nike?
athlete? runner?
You need anything, me and Bobby are here for you.

Jay looked up as he read the last sentence, and Vinnie met his glance, nodding slightly. Although Caldwell would be against him going to Detroit, and he had no intention of asking permission, Jay now knew he would have almost immediate access to the computer and any files he might need.

'Thanks, Vinnie.'

'Don't worry about it,' Vinnie shrugged. 'Jay, you catch this bastard, you hear? He's a bad mother. You catch him, and kill him.'

Jay looked at Vinnie for a long time, and then nodded. *Kill him.*

Two words that filled him with a deep sense of confusion and fear. But at the same time he was certain it was something that must be done.

Before he left the building, Jay took a look at a departure schedule. There was an hour before the next bus to Detroit. Flying or driving would both be a lot quicker, but he wanted to travel as the killer had. He wanted to learn how the killer thought, get some kind of feed on how he lived. If he could get into his thinking process, he would be able to second-guess him, and then . . .

That always worked in the movies, although script-writers seemed to forget that to pull some of that shit off you needed a degree in psychology. But it had to be worth a try, because it was all he had.

For a moment he just sat in the car, picking at the battered leather interior, remembering the times Susan had been in it with him, all the times she had begged to borrow it so that she did not have to go on dates in her boxy Volvo. Once she had spilt a can of Coors all over the back seat. He had kicked her out into the pouring rain and made her walk half the way home before he calmed down.

He ran his finger across the faded stain.

'Who killed you, Susan?'

He licked his finger, and for a moment actually believed he could taste the Coors beneath the leather ... could hear her knocking on the window, and was afraid to turn in case her ghostly image was there, ethereal and soft ... *soaked to the skin, begging to be let in out of the rain ...*

He pulled up in front of his sister's apartment building, not even aware that he had started the engine and driven there through the Manhattan streets. There was only one squad car outside now, although he found it easy to imagine the confusion of automobiles that had been parked there much earlier on. The hustle. It was a scene he had been a part of too often. The criminal photographers, forensics dusting the apartment, un-doubtedly finding his own prints there. An ambulance, driving away slowly, not rushing as it had when arriving, when Susan's cleaner had called the emergency services, blubbering and panicked, when there had still been an inkling of hope, something to hold on to, to grasp tight in both hands and never—

Let it go, Jay!

She would not be back, and never could be.

It was pointless searching for something rational on which to put the blame. It was the fault of one person alone: what had happened would only ever seem right to her killer, and Jay would never understand. Even after he had killed that man.

He walked up the steps and pushed his way into the old building.

Going slowly up the staircase, he ran his hand along the smooth banister. No dirty back stairwell here, not like his place. She was too proud. But the doors still had those pathetic, cheeseball locks, and for all he knew they might have caused Susan's death as much as the killer himself. But Caldwell had told him there had been no sign of forced entry, which meant that Susan knew the man.

There was a uniform outside the door in the hallway, and Jay presumed that his partner was either inside or, more likely, had gone to get them lunch. Jay approached him with a confident air, like he had a purpose and was supposed to be there.

'I'm sorry, sir. This is the scene of a serious crime. Nobody can go inside without proper authorisation,' the officer said politely, but with underlying determination that nobody was going to get inside the apartment. The cop was young, his uniform pressed and clean. Manhattan's finest.

'I *am* authorised,' Jay said, and took his shield and identification from his wallet.

The uniform recognised the name and immediately stood aside. 'Sorry, sir. I did not realise.'

Jay stepped past him, into the apartment. He pushed the door shut and looked about the room, unchanged from the last time he had been here . . . the last time he'd ever seen his sister.

They had argued, shouting at each other, the noise a wild crescendo – until he had slapped her across the cheek. Tears had slipped from her eyes, as they did now from his, stinging her more than his hand ever could.

Get out!

Nothing about the room was different, yet there was something in the air – a scent he picked up on. He thought for a moment. There was no sign of a struggle. Caldwell's words were ringing in his ears. *She knew him, Jay.*

And then Susan was back.

How dare you hit me. The coldness in her tone had told him to leave.

How long ago was that? Two weeks . . . three? He had left then, believing there would always be time to apologise. Time to say he was sorry, never suspecting the end was so close.

How long had she known the killer?

The room was tidy, but everything was covered by the

dust left by the forensics team. He knew that everywhere would have been searched thoroughly – Hopkins and Deacon were good men, and he was sorry for what he had said about them to Caldwell. Everything searched – an invasion of her dead privacy. Her closet, every drawer, all her clothes, every nook and cranny, in an attempt to find anything that might help identify her killer. If Susan had any dirty secrets, they had been unveiled to the world this morning, unless they were locked in her mind. If that was so, they had died with her.

They had searched everywhere, and found nothing.

Everywhere ... except one place – where was her diary? Caldwell would have said something if the police had found it.

Once, Jay had called around unexpectedly, and was sure he had seen her with it. She had hidden the book quickly, fumbling and panicking. She knew what he would say about the diary. He would tell her that it was stupid. That it was foolish not to talk to anyone about her fears and worries, but instead write them down in a book. So she had hidden it, and then tried to look as innocent as possible when he came into the room, with his usual complaint of the door being unlocked at such a late hour, and the locks not being worth a damn anyway. He came close and hugged her.

Only problem was, he was a cop and could see in her eyes that she had been up to something. Nothing illegal – but something she did not want him to know about.

Back then, if he had been certain of the diary, he would have reacted just the way she expected him to. But now...

Where would Susan hide her diary? Where would she put it so that even the police did not discover it?

He was surprised by his choice of words. He was thinking of the police as a separate entity from himself, even though he knew he would always be a part of the whole they represented. They were tied down by procedures, rules, regulations. His emotions, his mourning for Susan, had cut him free from those bonds. Unlike the police, he was ready now to cross the fine line between right and wrong. He was prepared to become what he had always despised, if it meant finding Susan's killer.

And if he had not crossed that line by the time he found the man, he would when he killed him, as ruthlessly as he had murdered Susan.

Jay did not want to go into the bedroom, knew what he would find there, and did not want to see it.

So instead, he kept Susan alive in his thoughts, with prayers to the past. Her graduation ... how she had calmly stepped off the long pedestal while other students reacted with unabashed jubilance; her first job, working as a typesetter for the *New York Post*; the first, and only, article she had ever sold – for the standard rate, although a small note sent by the editor told her she had great promise...

I'm not a dreamer, Jay. I could never live like that ... but if only she had lived, if only—

If he went on like this he would go insane before he

even reached Detroit. His sister was gone – no amount of ifs and buts would bring her back. There was nothing he could do to change what had happened.

To avoid the bedroom, he found himself studying her video collection. The tapes were all classic horror and science-fiction movies, both old and modern, all except one – an out-of-place thriller called *The Drowning Pool* starring Paul Newman.

Susan had nearly drowned when she was a child. That had been the time Jay had saved her life. Surely it could not be this easy? Jay rubbed his hand on his unshaven chin in contemplation. It could be ... It even made sense for the diary to be hidden there, in an ironic kind of a way. She hid the diary because she believed he would despise it, yet the hiding place would always remind her of him.

He reached up and took the cassette box from the shelf. He hesitated, then quickly opened it with a sharp click. The book fell forward, and he caught it, dumbfounded but in a way not really surprised. It was about the size of a video tape, slightly smaller, and was thin with many pages.

At first unsure, he took off the elastic band that held the book closed.

There were at least fifty blank pages left; blank – as they would remain for ever. As he flicked through the diary he saw that most of her writing was compact and neat, utilising as much of the paper as she could. At the front, the handwriting was young, the spelling haphazard. She was a child, the writing style continually changing, entry to entry, as she searched for the one that suited her best and would become her own. The dates were in sequence, but the book was not written in every day.

Before he could stop himself, Jay searched for a specific date. The entry – just two sentences – had a page to itself.

My brother saved my life today.

He remembered her tortured hand just out of reach, and that final fear when he believed he would never get her to the surface in time.

Beneath the first sentence was something that surprised him. It seemed too mature for the five-year-old who had written it. It touched him deeply, explained more to him than he could ever know, and he knew he was forgiven for slapping her.

He read the sentence over and over.

I love you, Jay.

'You OK in there?' the uniform called from outside the door.

Jay shut the diary and hid it under his sweater before he opened the door and left.

'I'm fine.'

But he did not look fine. Tears were falling, and his face was tired. The only life in his eyes was anger and hatred, burning bright and strong.

* * *

After making a brief stop at his own apartment to throw some clothes into a bag, Jay returned to the bus depot. The scene was less hectic, now, but he was prevented from entering. The whole area was sealed off.

He was losing sight of what was good, losing focus. He was beginning to see these people as animated objects in his way.

Vinnie was not there, so he walked the streets, the bag on his shoulder, daylight shining, until he found the bus's first scheduled stop.

He waited, and prepared to lose himself in the world, as the killer had done . . .

Chapter Three
Dreaming

The dream, which he had not had for so many sane years, had always been the same.

Only now did it change.

In it he was a boy again, only eleven years old, young and innocent of the realities in the world. Only eleven, a full lifetime ahead of him.

Two months later his mother and father would be killed in an horrific car accident which also claimed the lives of five others, including two children. He and his sister had been with their Grandma ... but she was a part of the good times, stolen in the night by the killer.

She did not belong in the haunting vision with which he now slept.

His sister, all blonde locks and bubblegum, with the pout that all young girls are gifted with – cute or sickening, there is no middle ground here; you have your opinion, and that is all. His sister, Susan, was only five.

It was a reasonably warm day, cooled by a stiff breeze, and the water of Lover's Lake – where no lovers could be found unless you were to journey to a past generation, when linked couples were in teenage abundance – held an uncharacteristic chill as summer approached.

Susan liked to wade, too young to care about the depths or the currents . . . *just like you eat, huh, Jay?* . . . that could pull her under, drag her from the world without warning. The fact that she could not swim, yet sometimes ventured into deeper waters by accident, did not scare her. She was young and restless – nothing scared her.

Nothing.

Except, perhaps, for one thing . . .

The fish.

The horrible man-eating fish which, her brother told her, fed on humans, pecking away at their flesh, preying on innocent swimmers . . . and little girls who waded. And when there were no live people left, they swooped down to feed on the festering bodies at the bottom of the lake. Old meat, but good enough until something fresh came along.

'You'll catch a cold in this weather,' shouted Jay, a small, fragile-looking child, almost frail. He was carrying a stick in the way he will brandish the M-16 rifle in Vietnam . . . but that time is distant, and it too does not belong here.

'I don't care about colds!' Susan screamed. Unable to judge the distance to her brother, her screech was a lot louder than it needed to be.

74

'Hush!' he warned, afraid that her incessant chatter might give his position away to the enemy hiding in the trees across the lane. Then, in a quiet voice: 'But what about *the fish?*'

He liked to frighten her – it was part of the fun in having a younger sister. But it didn't stop her from going into the lake's cool water. Jay himself harboured an irrational fear of water ... *scared yourself silly about the fish? his friends joked when they swam during the hot summer days that were so near* ... which he could not explain. He could swim – his parents had taught him when he was a baby. But he had a distinct memory of being unable to breathe, of choking, his lungs collapsing inward, with him somehow trapped beneath the surface – and that was where his fear was born.

A single transparent memory that haunted him.

A memory he had vanquished – until now – the day he had saved his sister.

Susan took two nervous steps back toward the pebble beach, and then stopped.

So what if she was scared of the fish?

So what?

The fear made the fun more thrilling. She turned around and went further out than she had ever been before, daring herself, determined not to give in to her brother.

Jay, hanging on the small bank above the shingle beach, watching for movement in the trees across the lane, provided a quiet commentary to chill his sister's heart.

'You see, in the shallow water you think you're safe, but you're not. They are still there, pecking at your feet. Ooops, there goes another toe! And you don't even know it until you come out of the water, missing some toes, missing a whole leg up to the knee.'

'Yech!' Susan said, as she continued to challenge herself. The water was up to her jaw now, and occasionally she could taste it in her mouth, cold on her lips. She knew it was foolish to go this far out, but refused to be beaten by her brother again. This time she would show him. 'That's gross!'

'Yeah, but true.'

Further and further she went out.

'I can see those fish now. Thousands of them.'

Deep and deeper ... a little further.

'Creeping up on you.'

One more step, just one ... and then, perhaps, one more.

'You're lunch, kiddo,' Jay sang, and turned to see the cowardly progress she had made; turned to see her way out of her depth, so far out she seemed a mile away.

'Susan, you best come back a little.'

Turned ... *to see her disappear.*

One second she was there, water washing around her neck. The next, she was gone, the only testament to her existence the circular ripples that went out for ever, and the drops of water, from the floundering splash she had made when she went under, that hit the surface and caused baby ripples.

Three boys came running across the lane, carrying their own sticks and making gun noises with their mouths. They came fast, firing, and surprised Jay, who was still looking out towards the lake, waiting for his sister to resurface. But she did not.

He fell back off the bank, a high cliff to an eleven-year-old, not believing he had time to climb down, and hit the stony beach hard. He grunted, the wind knocked out of him, and then rolled on to his stomach, looking to the lake once more.

Still no sign of her.

He stood, and quickly kicked his shoes off.

'You guys!' he shouted, and ran for the lake.

Each step seemed to take an eternity, and he was aware of the tiny cuts the ground was making on his bare feet as individual stones pulled at them, grasped them, held them and refused to let go. A horrible slow motion, and all the time he pictured Susan falling deeper and deeper in real time.

When he finally reached the water's edge he dipped his foot into it, as if testing its temperature ... testing his fear.

'Fuck it,' he said, and ran in, splashing.

The three boys, who would all die in Vietnam playing real wargames, stood at the top of the bank.

'Hey, Austin!' one of them moaned. 'You're supposed to be dead.'

'Yeah!' another chorused.

'Hey, hey, hey!' the third said, excited. 'Austin's in the water!'

And then lightbulbs appeared above their heads, clicking on bright as they realised what was happening.

Susan!

They took off their shoes and jumped down the bank, heading for the lake.

The fish ... they were coming ...

Susan did not understand that she was drowning, only knew that the fish were coming and that, however much she kicked, frantically, unco-ordinated, reaching up to the disappearing daylight – she was falling down to their lair, where she would join the rest of the rank, festering bodies.

Jay dove under the water at the position he had last seen Susan, or as best he could remember. If he was only a few feet out in his estimation, she might die...

He swam along the bottom of the lake as fast as he could, skimming across the bed which suddenly fell away, and he was certain that Susan was somewhere below. Instead of going up for air before making his descent into the dark abyss, he swam straight down.

As he swam deeper, the water became more cloudy and murky. Darker. He was convinced he would never see Susan again. His legs were tired, and he had to strain his eyes just to see a few feet ahead. He kicked harder.

And then, coming out of the black, there she was.

He could not quite grasp her outstretched hand.

He kicked harder than ever, and felt her fingers tickle

his, their tips just touching ... but she was always out of reach, so that he could not close his hand about hers and pull her up.

He could see her eyes, open and full of water ... the water of the lake.

Dead eyes.

'No!' he tried to scream, but water filled his mouth and flooded his lungs.

No!

Jay awoke sweating and coughing, his head pressed against the bus's large and dirty window. The choking feeling was now upon him, overwhelming, and it took him several seconds to remember where he was.

Outside, the dusty road sped by. He looked at the slow horizon, then leaned back in his seat and closed his eyes. He re-opened them quickly, for all he could see in the darkness of his mind was Susan's hand, forever out of his reach, and her cold, dead eyes.

Daniel Mabe.

He quite liked the way it sounded. So he signed the hotel register that way, writing the name in flamboyant style – as if he had been using it all his life.

He took the key from the clerk and waved him away. He did not need to be shown to his room. This was his chance to explore, to study his new surroundings. To familiarise himself with them.

He would never be captured, but there was always room for caution. When the monster took him over and he killed, he became irrational ... just for a few seconds, a minute maybe, during that high greater than any drug can induce. Greater than any orgasm.

During those few seconds, he is out of control and vulnerable.

Anything can happen.

OK, so it's high noon, thought Kirby McCaul. Or high three-thirty, at least.

As he listened to the teacher putting a close on the last-ever class before the summer recess, he could hear them talking, but couldn't quite make out their words. He knew they were doing it deliberately, to intimidate him.

He looked at the clock.

Ten minutes before the bell. Ten minutes before – well, if this were a movie he could go on forever describing the clichéd scenario, but unfortunately it was *not* a movie. And he did not want to think about what was coming his way. They probably already had some people on the exits, and when the bell sounded—

But the bell had not gone yet.

Eight minutes, and Miss Harper was facing the blackboard with her back to the class. Slowly he raised his hand.

'What the fuck is his problem?' Johnny whispered, a little too loudly because Miss Harper turned and looked at the class suspiciously. It might be the last day of school, but she would not have language like that in her room.

'Was that you, Johnny?' she asked sternly.

Seven minutes ... and Kirby let a small smile play across his face. The dumb shit had made Miss Harper turn around. If he had not, she might have faced the blackboard until the end of class, and then it would have been too late. Kirby wanted to reach out and shake Johnny's hand.

'Me? No, Miss Harper,' Johnny replied innocently.

'Yes, Kirby?' Miss Harper asked.

'I need the toilet,' he lied, feeling like a smaller child than he was.

Miss Harper was the only teacher who saw the truth in Kirby, and often helped him when he was in trouble with the Principal. He did not like lying to her.

'Can't it wait, Kirby? There are less than ten minutes left in class,' she said.

... six ... close to five ...

'I need the toilet, *bad*.'

Johnny and his pals, two rows behind Kirby, were too stupid to realise what was going on. They tried to make fun of Kirby, sniggering between themselves.

Yeah, that's right, assholes. Laugh it up.

'Gross out, Miss. He's going to drop one in his shorts!' Johnny shouted, and the whole class erupted in laughter.

... four minutes ...

'Johnny!' Miss Harper scowled, and the whole class was instantly silent. She turned her attention to Kirby.

... three ...

'OK, Kirby. Go now. Take your books, and don't forget your homework. Have a good summer.'

Kirby heard their jaws drop onto the table behind as they realised what had happened. He turned and smiled as he packed his books into his bag. Expressions of dumb comprehension covered their faces. Kirby wanted to wave them goodbye or say something cool, but he knew that if he did, Miss Harper would suspect something and hold him back. So he smiled, and that was enough. His smile was so big – radiant. He could not contain himself.

Now their expressions were evil sneers, the type only children can produce. Kirby knew what they were thinking, but for now he just wanted to laugh. They would try to get him during vacation, and he would have to stay frosty if he was going to make it through the summer unscathed. But that was all in the future, and now was his moment.

His victory.

He marched out of the room with his head held high, two minutes of class left. He walked out of the building and across the small yard. And then, as the final bell rang, he passed through the gates and left them all far behind.

In the elevator Daniel was alone until the third floor, where the doors slid apart and a glamorous woman in her mid-sixties stepped gracefully inside. Rich, from the look of her. He found himself attracted in a way that no toyboy could ever comprehend. Creeps like that would cling to every word and notion of a woman like this, perform any sexual act, simply *for her money* – something he did not regard.

It would be so easy to kill her. In one swift movement he could pull the blade across her sagging, perfumed throat. Too easy; the reward too slight. She would be the only one to feel the pain; there would be no aftermath, no grieving relatives, just greedy ones as they waited for the will to be read.

Nobody cared about a woman like this. It would be crueller to let her live.

'I haven't seen you in the building before,' she observed. 'I would have remembered a guest like you.'

Was she eyeing him up – wondering what it would be like to have his muscled torso on top of her? Women like her were often attracted to his rugged good looks, Daniel knew, and lovers must be rare for her ... unless she paid for them, of course.

'I've never been in this hotel before,' he told her, and smiled – a cocksure grin telling her that he always got his way. Playing her game, even as he played his own.

At least make her think that you want her. That way, in a few days, or weeks, if he decided to kill her as an encore, his final farewell to Detroit *written in blood*, it would be that much easier to get into her room.

But first, he would do much better than her ... a gift of fear to the city.

Extract from the diary of Susan Austin.

23 April.

Today I met a man.

  *His name is Tony Elliot and we met in a bar called
Hot Nights, its sign in blazing red neon. I went with
Novelle, in celebration of the loss of my job – the loss
of the pathetic come-ons and passes made by that
snivelling shit Roger Card. The man is not unlike a
weasel. Anyway, we went to party, and we did just
that.*

  *Halfway into the night, I was a little tipsy.
Nothing to write home about and certainly not
drunk. This guy approached me at the bar and said
he was from out of town – those were his exact words,
just like a movie. And then he said something that
was so direct, so candid and honest.*

  But first, Diary, I must tell you what he looks like.

  *He wore a beat-up leather jacket, shirt and jeans.
The image did not particularly suit him. He is no
Mel Gibson, but very average-looking; not well-
built, not like Sly Stallone or Big Arnie, anyway.
But muscular enough so that he looks like he can
handle himself in a fight. But I did not want to fight
him, not yet. Excuse my sleazy mind, it is in the
gutter again.*

  *This is what he said to me: 'Where does a guy go
for a good time here?'*

  *Those words, after the devious advances of Card,
made me feel so wanted, but in a good way. They did
not make me feel low, or undignified, or any of that*

*feminist crap. I had gone out looking for a good time
too, and he had found me.*

*I told him to wait, not to move a single muscle.
'Don't even breathe,' I said. I found Novelle and told
her what had happened, and she said I had made a
good catch, and to get out of there quick before she
stole him away. It was so crowded in the bar that I
don't think she saw him too well, but was just trying
to make me feel good.*

Novelle is a great friend.

*When I got back to the bar, Tony was still standing
there, waiting, and I swear he had not even moved
one muscle. Not even raised the drink in his hand to
his lips.*

*We went back to my place and had sex like I have
never experienced. He made me feel so special.*

And when I woke, he was gone.

I hope I see him again.

Oh Diary, tell me he will call.

Please.

Jay looked up, turning the page back so that he could
check on the date of the entry.

23 April.

You're mine, you sonofabitch . . .

When he'd first begun reading the diary, Jay had felt
bad about violating his sister's most sacred and inner-
most thoughts. He'd read about her reaction to the death
of their parents, the fear when they had been separated
as children, the confusion of her first menstrual period,

her nervousness when she had been with a man for the first time ... all the private things. Her uncertainties and worries. All her fears.

But now – it had to have been worth it, just for this final entry.

Jay had checked into a room in the mean streets near the bus station in central Detroit. It was dirty, and he was surprised the management had the nerve to call the place a hotel. The bedspread on which he lay was stained, and he had thrown the pillow to the floor, not wishing to inhale its unwashed odours. The cheap black and white television had a meter on it; the table on which it rested was bolted to the floor. No doubt the television and table were connected in some inseparable way. And the walls were depressingly bare. There was no mirror, no wallpaper even, just plain white wallboard, chipped and dirtier than the sheets.

It was disgusting.

But it was what he wanted, what he had deliberately searched for. In his mind's eye he saw the killer, 'Tony Elliot' – although that could not be his true name – settling down in a room so similar it could be the same one. This was the way Jay would live until he caught the bastard. He had no way of knowing that while he bit into a cold chilli dog, the ketchup and mustard long since congealed, his sister's murderer had already eaten a lavish dish of veal simmered in brandy and cream.

He swallowed the last of the chilli dog in one gulp and rolled off the bed, careful not to disturb any sleeping germs. There was a payphone downstairs in the lobby, so picking up his wallet he left the room.

The lobby was small, the payphone bolted to the wall next to the front counter.

He searched his pockets for change, and came up with several coins that the phone would accept. He let them drop into the slot, and dialled Ray Province's home number. By the fourth ring there was still no answer, and he was about to assume that Vinnie was out when he looked at his watch. Eleven, in the p.m. He decided to let the ringing continue, reasoning that enough time had already passed to wake Vinnie, if he was sleeping. He was probably in a groggy state right now, rubbing sleep from his eyes before reaching out for the phone.

'Yeah? Ray Province.'

The voice was gruff, and nothing more than a whisper. Obviously Vinnie was doing his best not to waken his wife.

'It's Jay. Sorry, Vinnie, I never knew how late it was,' Jay apologised.

'Jay? Jay, is that you?' Vinnie asked quietly, still half-asleep.

'Yeah. Listen, Vinnie, I need a big favour and—'

'Shoot,' mumbled Vinnie. 'Just say the word and I'm on it.' He switched on his bedside lamp, making a hollow 'click', then eased open the top drawer of his night table, rifling through its contents until he found the pen and notepad which he knew were there.

He picked up the receiver again. 'OK, Jay. What do you need?'

'Get me anything you can on a guy called Tony Elliot. Anything, however inconsequential it might seem. Also, go to the Ellis Building on Second. Speak to a woman named Novelle Tourment. She's a ... *was* a friend of Susan's, a well-known fashion designer. Novelle should be able to give you some kind of description of this Elliot guy. He picked up my sister at a bar called Hot Nights on April twenty-third. I think Susan fell for him in a big way. You get all that?'

'Yeah,' Vinnie said, still scribbling frantically. A few seconds later he finished: 'Jay, just because he—'

'Don't mess me around on this, Vinnie,' Jay said. 'If you have something to say, just say it. Please don't dance around my feelings. Not now.'

Shit, Vinnie thought.

'Listen, Jay, it's just – well, just because the guy was putting the stones to Susan, that doesn't make him the killer.'

There was silence on the line, and Vinnie knew he might have gone too far. But the words had to be said.

'You think this is him, don't you?' Vinnie asked.

Jay contemplated the question for a moment. There was no solid evidence to say that Tony Elliot was the killer, other than the fact that Susan had obviously fallen hard for him the night they met – and four weeks later she was dead. That was all he had, and deep down, it felt right.

'Yeah, I do,' Jay replied tonelessly.

He could not afford to let his emotions loose, for should that happen, he would be out of control. He simply had to avoid thinking of Susan's death, however impossible that was.

'I'm on it,' Vinnie repeated. 'How are you holding up?'

'Great,' Jay said sarcastically, and regretted it immediately. Taking his anger out on his friends was wrong, way out of line. Especially Vinnie. He should save his anger. *For him* . . .

'Listen, Vinnie, I'm sorry. I—'

'It's OK. Jay, I don't think you want to hear this,' Vinnie began, knowing that what he had to say would upset Jay, but knowing too that he had to hear it. 'Hopkins and Deacon found photographs at Susan's place. And Shelby found more at the bus depot. Sick, frightening photographs, taken by the killer.'

'Thanks, Vinnie,' Jay interrupted, running from the facts. 'I'll be in touch.'

'Wait,' Vinnie said. 'Do you still think about the boy?'

'The boy?' Jay said. Three years ago, if he had been quicker, he might have saved the little kid. 'Do you mean Billy Rogers?'

Ever since, every time he looked in a mirror, he wondered why he had not gotten to the house in time, and failed to save the child.

'Yeah. We finally got a break. Some prints taken at the bus depot match some partials found at the Billy Rogers home. The sketches back then were by Southern, pretty rough, which is why I don't think you recognised him in my work.'

It was all coming back to Jay now.

He had been too late. Taking the steps two at a time,

his gun out, the woman staggering out of her room, her nightgown awry, her hair a mess. He had pushed her out of the way and kicked open the door to the boy's room, but he had been too late.

The man ... *Susan's killer* ... had been standing at the open window, his back to Jay. The man glanced quickly over his shoulder in the dark room. Jay lifted his gun and aimed, but the man jumped to the ground as he fired several useless shots. He rushed to the window, looked into the vacant night. Nothing, only curtains billowing gently around him in a slight breeze, the hot night suddenly cool. Toys were scattered across the floor, and the boy, Billy Rogers, was dead.

'You best pull the file,' Jay whispered. 'He's back.'

Chapter Four
Red's Tavern

'You're out late,' observed Red Comber, of Red's Tavern fame.

The man himself was a cliché. He was as big as a bear and, as some of the many women with whom he'd slept in his time would testify, he was just as hairy. A huge beard covered most of his face.

'Gettin' ready to close,' he told her. 'You best get home to your husband.'

'Is that why they call you Red?' she asked with genuine curiosity, pointing in the general direction of his face, which was hidden by a field of red hair.

It was a common mistake, and since it was a beautiful lady making it, he let it pass.

'My real name is Red,' he told her.

'You're kidding?' she giggled.

She was amazed. How could anybody call a baby 'Red'? It was a colour, like black or green, only worse. He had to be joking. Red could only be a nickname.

'Yes. Really. Would I lie to someone as pretty as you?'

It was friendly banter, that was all. In his day he had been a wild man, a party animal, but now he longed to be home with his wife.

'Listen, if you need a ride home I can call you a cab. Or there's always the lonesome stranger over there. He's been looking at you all night. I figure I best make the play for him, before you walk out of his life for ever.'

She turned and stared at the man, not trying to hide the fact in her drunken state. He noticed her watching and averted his eyes. Daniel looked down into his drink. He liked her, that was for sure. But it was Red he was gunning for. He was simply waiting for the woman to leave.

The two of them were Red's last patrons for the night, and Red mistakenly believed they were both drunk. Daniel was cold sober. He had drunk a lot less than Red believed – he had made his presence known, but not overstated it. And he had looked at the woman, even though he was watching Red.

In Red he saw a good fight. A challenge. A nice way to settle into the city. If he satisfied the monster early it might forego more bloodletting, give him the chance to meet somebody and truly hurt people. Give him the chance to feed off a family's misery and pain.

But Red was trying to hustle them out together so that he could close. Daniel shuffled in his seat, acting an unfamiliar role – pretending to be nervous because an attractive woman was watching him.

Red was doing a good job of ruining his plan.

Maybe he should let the monster have them both.

'He is kinda cute. But do you think he can satisfy a girl like me?' she asked in earnest.

One of the two men would have her tonight. Red did not seem interested, so that left one option. As for her husband – well, fuck him. He had his dope to keep him happy and she was tired of his arrogant beatings.

She hitched up her skirt as she got off the barstool, and walked over to the table where the man sat, brooding.

Red smiled. It was going great. He figured they would be out of here in ten minutes, and inside each other's pants before fifteen were up. He was going to be home within half an hour.

Hammer, his loyal German Shepherd, pulled impatiently on the tight leash that held him behind the bar. Red kept him there just in case there was any trouble. He saved money on labour that way, and liked having the dog at his side.

He stroked Hammer softly.

Come on, baby . . .

She reached the table and looked down at the man.

'Hi. My name's Gale Anne Hurd. What's yours?' she asked, her legs slightly apart, pulling the tight skirt tighter.

'Fuck off, bitch,' Daniel whispered harshly under his breath, so that Red would not hear. It was the anger of the monster as it unlocked its cage and clambered out.

'Oh,' she said, surprised. She began walking back to the bar, speaking out loud. 'So you like to be rough with women, huh?'

When she reached the bar, the man was next to her.

'You like to slap women, don't you?' she asked. She had been slapped more than enough in her life.

In that moment, all that was Daniel retreated, and he let the monster seize his mind. There was no point in fighting it. They were *both* going to die.

He jumped on top of the bar, and grabbed the baseball bat which hung above the bottles on the other side. He could feel Red trying to grab the bottom of his legs, but he was too fast, back down on the customers' side in less than a second.

Everybody was still, and Daniel slowly spun the bat on his fingers.

Red stood on the other side of the bar, surreptitiously trying to loosen Hammer's tether, silently asking himself how these tensions could have escalated so fast.

He braced himself, waiting for the drunk to strike.

The woman watched, bemused.

Suddenly, Daniel pulled the bat back and swung it hard. It hit the woman smack in the face and left the polished wood stained with blood. She stumbled back and fell over a chair, hitting the floor with a dull thud.

'Yeah,' Daniel replied calmly. 'Sometimes I like to hit women.'

Red had been expecting trouble, but not for the drunk to hit the woman. He looked at her unconscious body.

Her bloody mouth was twitching, red lips quivering. To hit somebody that viciously with the Peacemaker, you meant to do some permanent damage.

He was shocked, but over the bar damn fast.

From the way the drunk was holding the bat, he knew that his intimidating size would not be enough to warn him off. And that was just how Red wanted it. The man should hurt for what he just did.

Daniel took a step back, the bat still spinning on his fingers, like a slow propeller.

'You want a piece of this?' he sneered.

Daniel knew that he could not frighten Red, but his confidence and lack of fear might unnerve the big guy a little. In a way, he thought, his role was reversed from the previous night at the bus depot. Now *he* had to act confident and arrogant, sure of himself, as the kid had been.

This was it. All he had yearned for since the death of the kid ... and he was not disappointed. The monster was a vicious and cruel beast, angry and unpredictable ... yet it made him feel *oh, so good*.

He swung the bat, but it was wild and loose. Red ducked down and dashed forward beneath it, ramming into Daniel's chest. Red forced him back and pushed him against the wall. Daniel felt his back groan, and the bat fell from his hand.

He had completely misjudged the other man's speed and agility. He had expected a battle of pure strength, yet here he was, pinned against the wall, his wind knocked out of him.

Red punched him – three quick, sharp jabs in the chest, then pulled him back, just to ram him into the wall again. This creep was a pussy. Sure, he was tough when he was hitting women, and when he had the Peacemaker in his hand. But look at him now . . .

Daniel groaned again, recovering.

Red, relaxing slightly, stepped back from the wall, giving himself room to manoeuvre a real punch – one that would knock this sick fucker into the middle of next week.

Daniel slumped against the wall, but managed to stand upright, tired, his breathing heavy. He ducked quickly when he saw Red's fist coming in, and the big man cried out in pain when his hand crashed into the wall.

Daniel came up fast behind Red and hit him in the kidneys with all the power he could muster. He punched him again and again in the same spot, and Red moved away.

Hammer growled softly as he used his sharp fangs to gnaw his way through the leather that held him behind the bar.

Red landed a punch and his assailant fell back, grasping the edge of the bar so that he did not fall to the floor. Red was aware now that the man had never been drunk, but a couple more punches like that one would put him on his ass for the rest of the night.

Daniel flinched as blood ran from a cut into his left eye, and it flickered reflexively.

Gale Anne Hurd was slowly regaining consciousness.

Clinging to a table leg, she managed to pull herself to her knees. She would have stood, but did not want to draw attention to herself, afraid that the man might attack her again. She could taste blood in her mouth ... a coppery taste. She had once read that description but had never believed it, until now.

She was about to crawl from the tavern, leaving the two men to duke it out, when she spotted the bastard leaning on the bar, and Red advancing fast. She smiled, not realising that one of her back teeth was missing.

Red was kicking his ass.

Then Gale Anne saw something which Red could not see.

At his side, hidden by the palm of his hand, the man held a small knife.

She was about to shout a warning when the man suddenly moved forward. She was left speechless as the knife entered Red's gut. It was a smooth motion, like a liquid flowing. She felt her stomach heave as he twisted the blade, and pushed it harder.

Hammer chewed and ripped at the leash, somehow aware of how long it was taking him to join the fray.

Red staggered back, grunting in pain. He felt weak. A fistfight was one thing, but he had never been stabbed before. He was not sure he could handle it. Overcome by nausea, he was about to pull the knife out when the man reached in quickly and did it for him.

He felt warm blood on his hands as he clutched the

open wound, and looked up in time to see the man lunge forward, the knife cutting quickly.

Red fell back, dead before he hit the floor.

Daniel smiled, feeling warm and comfortable inside as the monster slowly departed. He could see it clambering back into the cage of his mind, licking its bloody lips.

He bent and wiped the blade clean on Red's jeans, and then turned for the woman.

She was gone.

He looked around uncertainly, and let out a scream of rage. He picked up a chair and threw it at a large mirror on the wall. The glass shattered and one of the chair's legs snapped off.

'Fucking bitch!' he screamed into the empty room, only the night listening. '*Bitch!*' he barely whispered.

He walked over to the jukebox and wrestled with it, before he managed to rip it from its socket, finally silencing the lazy ballad that had been playing all through the fight.

'Whore!' he screamed.

He was overcome by rage, and for a few minutes set about destroying the place. He went behind the bar, and that was when Hammer snapped at him.

Daniel jerked back, startled, fear engulfing him. He remembered what he – *no, it was the monster, the first time the monster became him* – had done to Ritz when he was a little boy, and he froze with terror.

Hammer growled.

A part of Daniel wanted to reach out and pet the dog. Daniel realised that he had never grown up, that he was still that little boy, and he longed for Ritz to be back among the living.

Then Hammer barked, and all Daniel could see was Ritz, baring sharp teeth and coming back from the dead to chew him up.

Daniel Mabe did not like dogs.

He killed this one quickly with the knife, as he did all he came upon.

Photographs . . .

The word, and all the images it brought forth, hung in the air about him. Poor Billy Rogers. He'd forgotten the nightmare, yet was being given a chance to redeem himself, now that only those close to the boy remembered.

Back in his room, Jay opened Susan's diary at the entry dated 23 April. He went through it again and again, and felt cold tears rolling down his cheeks, set free from his eyes at last. Before he could stop himself, he began to sob wildly, the book shaking in his hands . . . his grief dampening the white page, turning it a dull grey.

'Why?' he managed with a shaking voice.

He read the account one final time through blurred vision, and then closed the book.

'Why, you bastard?'

Slowly, he found the police frequency on his radio and set it up beside the bed. He listened as messages and codes flitted on and off through a haze of static, clouds . . . dark and grey . . . the water, dark and grey. Sleep had him, and with it the nightmare. He restlessly rolled over, sweating in the cold night, pulling the sheets tight in his grasp.

When he woke he was screaming.

All he could see was Susan's face, underwater. Only, instead of the face of a child, it was her adult face, horribly bloated. Her outstretched hand was, as ever, tauntingly just beyond his reach.

Darkness engulfed him, and he strained his eyes to see clearly, to see the real world where the nightmare could not touch him. Where the nightmare began . . .

He sat there and waited.

Waited . . . until the call came in. Homicide. *Red's Tavern.*

He took the gold shield off his belt where it was attached, and looked at it. Then he clicked the room light on, and sat on the edge of the bed for minutes, studying every detail of the badge, thinking of all it stood for. The shield reflected the light onto the walls and ceiling.

He climbed off the bed.

His anger was building up inside, gathering pressure and momentum, waiting to explode. He could no longer block out Susan's death. He accepted it, welcomed it with all the grief and desire for vengeance that were a part of the package.

He snatched up the shield and threw it into the open Nike bag which contained all the clothes he'd brought, as well as his gun. He grabbed the holster, and slipped it on, shrugging into a baggy jacket to conceal the weapon.

He zipped the bag shut.

The badge was there if he ever needed it, but for now he was Susan's brother, *no longer a cop*. He acted on feelings alone and could do anything, no longer trapped within the boundaries and restrictions of the law. These were zipped up in the bag, along with his badge.

He was outside the law.

Like the killer.

When Gale Anne Hurd woke up, she was not sure where she was.

After crawling to the door of Red's Tavern, she had fled – but with no intention of going home. She would never go home again, for there everything was paid for with drug money – including herself, she now realised. Red's death had opened her eyes to the violence with which she was living, the violence her husband advocated. It was a place where fear alone awaited her: a place she no longer wished to be a part of.

She had run down dark alleys, splashing through dirty puddles, heels clicking and echoing in the silent night. She ran with no sense of purpose or direction. All she knew was that she had to get away from the bar ... away from Death, and the man who carried it with him in his pocket, held it in both hands, had Death coursing through his body like blood.

She had often been afraid of her husband when he was in one of his chemically-induced rages, but here was a man of whom to be truly afraid. This madman had killed without pity or remorse, without provocation or motive. He was not some teenage punk who had gotten carried away by the intensity of the moment. He had arrived at the tavern with the intention of killing.

Nobody was safe from this man.

She'd run blind for nearly twenty minutes, choosing direction randomly, without thinking. Occasionally she would look back, convince herself that he was following, and run faster ...

... and when she finally stopped to catch her breath, she looked up to see where she was going, and was surprised to find herself in the classy neighbourhood of Bloomfield Hills, where her older sister lived. But Gale knew now that her subconscious mind had guided her here, from the moment she had left the tavern. Here, to the home of Karin Hurd and her orthodontist husband, Joshua O'Bannon.

While Gale had grown up wild and feisty, fuelled by fire, Karin had always been in the library, studying for exams and reading, even if she did not have to. And while Karin was at the library, she – Gale Anne – had been out getting drunk and meeting all the wrong people. While Karin the bookworm, whom Gale Anne had hated so much as a teenager, was busy passing exams, she had been busy flunking out.

As she sat up in the unfamiliar bed, Gale envied her sister more than anybody else in the world.

They had grown up on completely separate tracks.

Karin had settled into a comfortable home with a loving husband, while Gale had lived in a cold mansion, surrounded by security fences, with a man who liked to hit her as much as love her ... and then she discovered that the love was not even genuine. She had been bought and paid for.

She sighed, mourning her lost life. She might as well have been walking ... *working* ... the streets for the past twenty years. You could not call it living.

Gale Anne realised she was crying as she looked about the room, weeping over the wasted years of her life, sheets clenched in her fingers. She missed the stability which her sister had found, even though she had never experienced it.

When she raised her hand to wipe her eyes so that Karin would not know that her tough, hard sister had been crying, she felt the gauze bandage on her nose. It was rough to touch, and the pain there was incredible, especially now that the sedative she must have been given was wearing off. In fact, she could feel a searing pain all over. An aching throb. There was also a thick bandage on her left arm, and her mouth felt slightly numb.

'Jesus,' she whispered. *What the hell happened to me?*

The door opened suddenly, startling Gale. But it was only Karin, a familiar bounce in her step which Gale was surprised she remembered ... and missed.

'Oh,' Karin said, surprised. 'You're awake.' She reached down, switching on a soft lamp beside the bed, and then tried to fill the empty and difficult silence.

'I have no idea what happened to you. When Joshua opened the door late last night, you just fell in. There was blood all over the carpet. We took you to the hospital, and they fixed you up, told us to take you home. I . . . don't . . . it's been so long I don't know where you're living, so we just gave them our address and brought you back here again. There is a police detective downstairs who would like to talk to you. I didn't want to send him up if you were still asleep. I'll go and get him, shall I?'

Karin was about to leave, doing her best to hold back the heavy tears which were threatening to burst out, when Gale grabbed hold of her arm weakly. Karin looked down, and in that moment their eyes connected.

A rift that had opened during their childhood closed, the wide gap coming together.

'I love you. I'm so sorry,' Gale cried, and Karin bent low to hug her.

'I've missed you,' Karin said. She was also crying when she came away. 'Jesus, you look terrible,' she laughed pathetically.

'I'm fine now,' Gale said. Finally she was away from the drugs and the dealers, the wars and the gangland killings. She was safe. Even though she hurt, she felt good . . . felt *at home*.

Karin smiled. She had once looked upon her sister with no respect or liking – the drugged-out floozy she did not want to know. Yet lying before her now was a young girl she had not seen since they were both small children. Karin stood there, caught in a moment of time, afraid to move for fear of losing it – knowing that already it was becoming a memory.

She looked into her sister's swollen, bloodshot eyes.

'I love you,' Karin wept, and leaned forward, kissing Gale softly on the cheek.

Gale pulled her sister close and hugged her tight. It felt so good she did not want to let go. Ever.

Karin laughed and cried at the same time, surprised by Gale's sudden strength.

They both laughed for a long time.

'I'm Detective Caan,' the man said after he'd knocked and entered the room.

Gale sat up with her back against the pillows and wished all the pain would go away.

Even though her face was puffy and bruised, her nose broken, Gale still looked attractive to him, in a pair of Karin's satin pyjamas. He saw the potential that was hidden behind the mask of pain. The moment he walked into the room, the lost soul that was James Caan finally found a home. He did not even know the woman – the *victim*, he thought, trying to stay detached and keep his perspective – but what he felt was something far beyond regulation sympathy.

As far as clothes went though, at that moment he had absolutely nothing in common with Gale. He came from the outdated school of dress as endorsed by Columbo, the TV detective. He wore a dirty trenchcoat, scruffy shirt and tie. His hair looked uncombed, and he had not shaved.

'You're not Detective Caan. You're Peter Falk,' Gale said, and smiled.

He shut the door and sat in the wooden chair which had been placed at the side of the bed.

'I've never heard that before,' he lied, and as he spoke he rolled one eye. For a second he really *was* Columbo.

She laughed, then gasped in agony. 'Please, no jokes,' she said.

'I'm sorry. And I'm sorry for how I look, but I'm pulling a double-shift so I hope you can excuse me. Now, ma'am, I don't want to end our little banter here,' he said, reluctant to bring up the subject of his visit, for he felt he could talk with her for ever, laughing and joking, learning everything about her – but he could not. He had a job to do. 'The reason I'm here is that you told the hospital you were witness to a particularly brutal homicide in the bar known as Red's Tavern, just hours ago. We need a description of the killer, something to go on so that we can get it over the radio. There is always the possibility of a patrol picking him up on the streets. I'll need a statement, and you will have to look through our files. But all that can wait until later, when you feel up to it. For now all we need is a brief description.'

For a moment her expression was blank, a stone wall.

'Oh God!' she cried, and tears began to run down her cheeks. Although it comforted her that she could not envision his face, it also frightened her. She was afraid of the repercussions . . . the deaths she might cause. She felt his hand squeeze her arm gently, urging her to remember. 'I'm sorry,' she babbled. 'I don't remember. I don't know if I want to. I can tell you everything that happened, every word spoken – backwards. But I can't see him. I'm sorry.'

Caan had seen this kind of thing before. It was something many victims have to overcome.

'Take it easy,' he said, and held her arm firmly.

When a victim or witness of an attack or violent crime has been particularly traumatised by the event, they have a tendency to block out what frightened them the most – usually the perpetrator. They figure, using a kind of comforting childlike logic, that if they can no longer see the criminal, then the criminal can no longer see them.

Unfortunately it does not work like that, not in the real world.

'OK, don't worry,' he soothed, hoping she would see something downtown later that would jog her memory. 'Don't you worry.'

Hesitantly, he moved his hand from her arm to her covered thigh. It was an innocent gesture. He had fallen for her in a big way, and would testify that he had never felt anything as special as this ... *like a goddamn teenager getting laid for the first time* ... since he had lost Kelly.

'What if ... what if he finds me?'

'No way,' Caan said confidently. 'I've put a twenty-four-hour watch on you, and tomorrow evening we'll move you to a safe house. No need to worry. He's probably out of town by now.'

He might have only been doing his job, but Gale felt as if he genuinely cared. His wandering hand put her off slightly, but it did not offend her. It was comforting after the *'Fuck off, bitch,'* and the baseball bat coming at her. The detective was scruffy, and she had seen a lot of better-looking men, but he was kind and gentle – *special*. She liked him.

'How do you feel about going back to the site?' he asked.

'OK,' she said, with a degree of trepidation. 'I'm still a bit shaky but I'll be all right. Let me dress.'

The aftermath.

Not the true aftermath, of course. He could never be close to that – the grief of the family, the funeral, the torment and the pain. The agony. He could never be close to any of that ... never feel it.

This was his aftermath; and from a strictly analytical point of view it was a small, yet important part of the other one. Because here, in the cold heart of the monster was where the true aftermath began, at the scene of his work.

With the end he had brought about a new beginning, a new chapter in the lives of all the people close to Red Comber. His wife and his children, the runaway daughter he had not seen for a month before his death, she would come home only when she saw his healthy ... *oh, the picture would look so healthy compared to his pale corpse's face* ... red cheeks burning and bushy beard never looking bushier, on the local news. She would sit there, cold tears forming in her eyes, and she would call her mother and they would cry for hours, their mutual sorrow wiping out all their differences. Others would be affected, too – the regulars at the Tavern, all his friends, even the beer companies. All these, and more, his death would affect.

Daniel Mabe stood near the front of the crowd, which he had watched form over the past fifteen minutes, people from everywhere sensing death, and wanting to see it from a place of safety.

The pushing crowd was held back by a brace of police officers.

It was a dangerous place for him to be, but he knew the woman was gone, never likely to return, not even in the hands of the imprudent police. Yes, it was a dangerous place to be, but as he rubbed shoulders with the people who feared what he had done, he felt safe.

The camera around his neck was different from the cheap one he normally carried and had last used inside the bar. This one was special, with a powerful zoom and focusing equipment. With it, he took a lot of the pictures he wanted to keep and treasure in his personal collection. Those pictures had to be the best.

The camera was also a gift, a gift from Melissa. There had been a celebration, and they had taken many photographs of each other long into the night.

Oh, Melissa.

The door of Red's Tavern was shut, but using the zoom he managed to get quite a good view through one of the windows.

Heads bobbed, and there seemed to be a lot of movement, a lot of action to capture. One cop even stood at the bar, drinking a beer like it was a night out with the boys. A superior approached him, and they both disappeared from view. The drink was left on the bar – the glass to be dusted for prints by forensics in a distortion of the truth.

Very amateur, Daniel smirked.

Even though the clicks and whirrs – each one representing a tiny moment of time which would be framed on celluloid for ever – were not taken in rapid succession, he had soon gotten through a roll of film.

He slipped another roll in and looked to the window once more, and that was when he saw her.

Gale Anne Hurd.

Caan guided Gale across the alley and down some small steps. He opened a door and confidently, like he knew where he was going even though he did not, led her through the cellar with all its dusty barrels and bottles. This must be where Red gets ... *used to get* ... his deliveries, his mind mused.

They came up a ramp and through another door. This led into the Tavern proper, and they found themselves behind the bar – which looked so different from this side. It was easy to imagine crowds dancing and pushing and ordering drinks, and she saw Red, keeping them all patient.

'Watch the glass,' Caan warned as he led her to one end of the bar, away from the dead dog. He wondered about the mess under the sheet, and was glad he had not eaten any breakfast yet.

Glass was everywhere. Bottles and glasses. Smashed and shattered.

She watched as at least fifteen cops milled around the room performing various duties. And there were more outside, she noticed, as they walked by a window, holding back the crowd. Parasites, thriving on other people's misery, she thought grimly. A camera flashed, and she remembered reading a book once which had used something like this as its opening scene.

Gale was amazed by the damage. Even though the fight had been brutal, when she had left the Tavern there had been nothing near this extent of destruction. The killer must have been in a fury, and went about destroying this place, as he had destroyed Red.

Occasionally a cop would move her to one side as he, or she, walked by, and Caan would gently hold her out of the way.

All the time he was watching her. As he explained the procedures which were taking place, pointed out various objects which might or might not jog her memory, he watched her face, studied her expression – looking for the slightest kindling in her eye, anything other than the bland confusion and fear he saw there now.

Then they rounded a table, and he knew that he had lost her – possibly for good.

About five feet ahead of them, a cover pulled back as a bespectacled man prodded and poked at the fatal wounds, was the stiffening corpse of Red Comber. Caan turned her away quickly, but it was too late to prevent her from seeing.

Gale gagged, coughing violently.

'Jesus,' Caan moaned. 'I was told the body was gone.'

'Don't know who told you that, buddy, but they were wrong. This here,' the medical examiner said, casually digging in the wound, 'this here is definitely a body. Who's the chick?'

'The chick,' Caan whispered angrily, 'is an eyewitness! And you might just have lost us a perfect description of the man who did this.'

Caan turned to Gale. 'Come on,' he said softly. 'I'm sorry. It was a mistake to bring you here.'

She was here.

The woman ... a phantom, an apparition who passed by the window in less than a second. But that was all the time he needed to recognise her ... the woman he had hit with the baseball bat.

It had to be a ghost. She could not be here! But he felt it deep inside. It *was* her. Gale Anne Hurd.

Daniel was no longer aware of the people around him, pushing and clamouring to see the outside of the building, inside which Death slept, ignorant of the fact that the Keeper of Death himself stood beside them, walked among them, was one of their number.

He admitted he had not expected the police to bring her back. They must be desperate, he smiled. They had obviously smuggled her in the back way, unseen by everyone – as she had been when she passed by the window; an elusive spirit only he could see, only he could recognise.

As she could recognise him . . .

She had to die, he decided as the sun made its first appearance in the dark morning.

The boy inside him cowered as the sleeping monster was aroused. He was the innocent heart and soul, the tortured victim at the hand of violent and inhumane masters.

The death of the woman was a necessity, but the monster wanted it anyway. Had wanted it in the Tavern, earlier.

'. . . *a brutal and horrible crime, yet one without motive. The police have no clue to the killer's identity—*'

He looked to his left, and slightly behind him.

A newswoman – he did not recognise her so she must work for one of the local channels in Detroit – looking decidedly glamorous and out of place here, led her cameraman through the crowd, rehearsing her report and searching for a vantage point from which to film it.

He took a quick photograph of them and turned away. How little you know, he thought. How much I could show you, and the world.

He would go to the back of the building and wait for Gale to leave. When she did he would follow her, find out where she lived, then kill her when he was good and ready. He decided he would play with her a while, torture her. She deserved that, the bitch-whore, for making him go to all this trouble – for making it personal.

He was nearly free of the crowd, claustrophobia spurring him on. He still felt uneasy at the woman's presence. Suppose she had seen him from the window, and silently alerted the police?

But he felt lucky.

Slowly, calmly, he made his way out of the crowd.

A man blocked his path as he made for a space he'd spotted. An accident, of course, but Daniel could feel an untypical feverish panic overcome him.

Relax, it was nothing . . . Pure coincidence.

Annoyed, Daniel looked up to see who had got in his way, and when he did so, their eyes locked.

In them Daniel saw much of himself. He saw characteristics that were usually only evident when he stood before a mirror. These eyes were cold, calculating. The man behind them had a unique logic all of his own, much like himself. They seemed disconnected from the electricity which buzzed through the crowd, and Daniel knew that the man had not come here to see a puddle of blood.

Perhaps he was a regular at Red's Tavern and was surprised by the gathering but no, that did not seem right. There was something else in those eyes . . . and at that moment, Daniel's fear of recognition suddenly became a chilling reality, for it was that which he saw . . .

Recognition!

Daniel suddenly knew he had to get away from this place, fast. A cold sweat broke out on his forehead, and he could feel the monster thundering at the bars of his cage in an orgy of violence. *Oh please, not yet, not here . . .*

He pushed the man roughly aside and walked by.

He was about fifteen paces from the crowd, walking fast now, and breathing a sigh of relief. The man had failed to capitalise on what he had seen. He was safe.

'*Hey!*'

Daniel froze.

He sensed the whole crowd looking at him as they turned as one to see who had interrupted their morbid pleasure. A thousand eyes were on his back. They knew ... they all knew what he had done! They all recognised Red's slaying as his work – but one pair of eyes in particular, drilling into him.

Daniel shivered, as he felt the monster seep through every pore in his skin, slipping silently into the world.

Jay smiled without pleasure, not believing his luck. It all seemed to fit. The description, the looks, even the camera round his neck. *Photographs ... the eyes ... eyes that had stared at him across a dead boy's room.*

Susan's killer was less than twenty feet away.

He should not have shouted. Now, Jay would not see him again; this incredible opportunity messed up. He should have crept up and jumped him from behind, or, better still, should have just shot the bastard in the back of the head – and then explained to the authorities why he had done such a terrible, terrible thing.

But the man did not move. He remained frozen on the spot, as if riveted to a stage by a bright spotlight.

Fear ...

Susan's killer was afraid.

The crowd had already lost interest, and turned back to witness the removal of the body.

Jay continued to approach the man, who still had not moved.

Closer and closer . . .

Only five steps away now.

Move, you fucker!

Four . . .

Make a move. I want you dead.

Three . . .

'Take it easy and everything will be just fine,' Jay said calmly, although his heart was beating so fast he thought it was going to explode. He planted a hand firmly on the man's shoulder.

You're mine . . .

116

Chapter Five
Making News

Daniel spun fast, the short blade in his hand.

The motion took Jay by surprise, but not as much as the knife. He jumped back, just in time to avoid the man's swing. He felt the blade skim across his arm and rip his sleeve, but it didn't leave a scratch.

Jay's quick reflexes had saved him, but in dodging the knife he lost his balance and stumbled. By the time he recovered, the man was already away, running down the street ... chasing freedom.

Jay was off the mark fast, thinking about what Vinnie had written: *maybe an athlete, maybe a runner*, and sure enough, the sonofabitch was faster than a hare. But he had not gotten too far ahead: half a block at the most.

As he was running, Jay tried to pull his automatic free from its holster but his hand snagged on something inside his jacket and by the time he had the gun out the man was gone, out of sight at the intersection. Valuable seconds lost.

The newslady saw all this, although she was not sure what was happening.

'What the hell's that?' she pointed, on live television as the studio cut to her.

Mason Adams, her cameraman, turned and saw Jay running around the corner at the end of the block; he zoomed in close, focusing for a second on the gun in Jay's hand – an image broadcast into thousands of city homes.

'Come on!' he shouted. 'Get my jeep!'

Two cops on duty outside the Tavern also saw what was happening and broke clear, allowing the tide of people to surge forward. They took off in the direction they had seen Jay running.

One of them unclipped the radio from his belt as they ran, causing him to lag behind; his partner was already naturally faster.

'Foot pursuit. Requesting back-up on East Eleven!'

The immediate response was shrouded in static. 'Are you guys joking me or what? You got the whole Precinct crawling about down there.'

'This is no joke, dammit!' the officer panted, as his partner raced further ahead.

A gunshot rang out and echoed back.

'Get us the back-up!' he snarled.

He replaced the radio and withdrew the police issue .38, as his partner had already done, and they rounded the corner together. There, at the end of the block, stood the man with the gun, aiming down the next intersection.

'Freeze, fucker!' bawled the slower one of the two.

Jay turned, and in that moment knew he had missed his chance to bring the bastard down. When he looked back, the killer had disappeared.

'Shit!' he cursed.

If he waited for the cops, explained the situation, it would mean an orchestrated search with an army of manpower, but before that happened he would have to convince them of the truth, and without his shield that could take valuable time, hours maybe.

The cops were only half a block away now, one slightly behind the other.

'Don't move!' the same cop repeated, and stopped to take careful aim, while his partner continued to approach fast.

That's just great. Nice going, Jay.

If he did so much as twitch a muscle now he would be history. These two would blow him away and the truth of who he was chasing would never come to light. Not for a long time, anyway – when it was too late. It would be the end of everything. So Jay did not move. He imagined himself as he had seen many criminals ... as a bead at the bottom of the sight. He did not think the uniforms would hesitate if they had to pull the trigger.

The other cop was coming up fast, and the one who had stopped shouted again: 'Drop the gun on the ground!'

They were brave, coming up in the open like that.

Brave – and foolish. Especially the one running closer; he seemed particularly naïve. If Jay was not a cop himself but some scumbag drug-dealer high on crack, he could have taken them down right there and now. But he was one of the good guys. He had to remember that.

'Drop the gun or we'll shoot!'

Jay crouched down, ready to place his gun on the ground. He was overcome with dismay. He had been *that* close to getting the fucker, yet had let him slip through his fingers – again! He groaned in rage.

Then the other cop stopped and aimed. 'Do it – now!'

An alarm bell rang out suddenly, shrill and startling. Jay realised the killer must have broken into a building. Bad move – one that might prove his downfall. With luck, the cops would surround the place and catch him. Then, before long, his true past would be revealed. It was not a fitting end, not the one Jay wanted, but it would be good enough.

'Do it now!' the second cop screamed again. He was young and inexperienced; he should have fired a warning shot by now. If Jay had not been willing to drop his gun, this might have turned into a very dangerous game.

A loud screech distracted all three. A Renegade jeep was racing towards them, its tyres squealing.

Jay saw his chance.

Not missing a beat, he sprang up and grabbed the younger cop who was less than ten feet away, wrestled the .38 from his hand and threw it across the street. He then delivered a hard punch to the cop's jaw that left him crumpled on the sidewalk. He sensed the other one running towards them, unable to get a clear shot, thanks to the jeep moving between them.

Jay raced toward the end of the block, moving as fast as he had ever moved in his life, all the time waiting for – expecting – the bullet that would rip through his spine.

But it never came, and when he chanced a glance back, he saw why.

The jeep was about halfway up the block, still impeding his pursuer. The cop could not see him to get a clean shot off. He let out a small explosion of laughter and disappeared into the next street, searching for the door that must have been forced open.

The cameraman was leaning out of the Renegade, a small remote unit clamped to his shoulder.

'Yeehah!' he shouted.

He had been cooped up in a studio for far too long. *This* was why Mason Adams had become a news cameraman – the thrill of the chase, the excitement and adventure, the discovery of a new story, a scoop which the rival channels could not touch. Adrenaline pumped through his whole body, and he let out another shout.

'You get all that, Slick?' the newslady asked. She was at the wheel, concentrating on the street ahead. She had only just missed running down the first cop, and now she saw his partner, scrambling to his feet on the sidewalk ahead.

'I think so,' he said, fitting a different lens to the camera.

As the younger cop clambered to his feet, he spotted the gun he'd lost lying across the street and quickly retrieved it, dodging the vehicle approaching that swayed a reckless course through the street. Were it not for these morons, he and Steve, his partner, would have had the perp' by now. And his jaw would not feel like a painful balloon as it began to swell up.

Fucking nuts! They could both have been seriously hurt by the crazy bitch at the wheel.

He reached the end of the block and saw the gunman running carelessly down the middle of the road, occasionally moving to the buildings on either side, apparently searching for means of escape. Well, escape he would not, the young officer thought grimly.

The few early morning pedestrians had sensibly retreated off the street, and he was free to fire. He aimed patiently, and slowly applied pressure to the trigger.

The jeep skidded around the corner, the newslady grabbing the wheel, nearly ejecting Mason out of the vehicle. And there, looming closer and closer, was a young police officer, aiming a gun.

'Shit!' she screamed, slamming on the brakes and the horn, and pulling the wheel sharply to the right.

Before the cop could get his shot off, a loud blasting sound filled his ears from behind. He whipped round in terror, just in time to see the careening jeep only feet away, bearing straight down on him.

He danced to the side, and was about to dive ... *gonna make it, gonna make it* ... when something sharp caught him on the head.

Mason tried to pull back inside as the cop's face came up fast and filled the camera lens, but the jeep was moving too fast. The cop's head hit the camera in a death-dealing collision, the impact throwing Adams back against the woman, who lost her grip on the wheel.

The cop watched the wheels skid away through blood-filled vision. At first he believed he'd been shot, but as he slipped from consciousness, he knew that could not be right. The gunman was running away from him, and had never even looked back. There had been no shots ...

The jeep was out of control. It bounced up the kerb and hit a wall head on, pitching both of its occupants forward and then stalling, its engine finally dying. The woman's head hit the dashboard and she was knocked unconscious, but Mason was lucky, sustaining only a sprained wrist.

Without wasting a second he grabbed a small, light camcorder from the back seat, quickly checked it over and found no substantial damage. As he looked, he examined the camera he'd been using with a live link to the studio and wondered if they had cut to commercial yet or whether, much more likely in today's voyeuristic society, they were exploiting the situation.

The camera was dented and bloody.

Adams pulled the newslady's head back, and got a shot of it on camera. Through the viewfinder he saw a thin stream of blood trickle from a cut into her eye, waking her, groggy and confused. She was going to be OK.

He opened the door and almost fell out, his legs like jelly because of the crash. At first he thought he was going to collapse, but then he managed to get a hold of himself. He focused the camera on the cop lying huddled on the ground, on the young officer's face. Nausea washed over him at the sight of the mess. He lowered the camera, fully aware for the first time of the horror their pursuit had caused, the havoc for which they were responsible.

'Oh Jesus,' he whispered, in a state of shock as he half ran, half stumbled down the street in search of the gunman.

'Hey!' the other cop shouted as he reached the scene of the accident and saw the cameraman staggering away.

Before his appalled eyes was the wrecked vehicle, rammed up against a wall, its front crumpled inwards, a dazed woman inside rubbing her head. He took a step towards it, but then spotted his partner, lying in a gathering puddle of his own blood . . . and the automobile was forgotten.

'Hey, you reckless sonofabitch!' he bawled after the cameraman. Then, as he came up on his partner, he saw how bad the injury was, how still his body. 'Oh fuck!'

He fumbled for his radio and almost dropped it in his

panic. 'I need an ambulance on ... shit, on East Nine. Fast! I've got an officer down!'

He dropped the radio and fell to his knees. Gently he lifted his partner's hand and rested it in his own, sticky with the young man's blood.

'Hang on, Rob. Hang on in there,' he whispered frantically, but knew that he was already holding a dead man's hand. 'Hang on, goddammit! You have a wife and kids ... you can't leave them!'

Officer Robert Parker was young and full of energy, and he left everything behind. His partner wept for the unnecessary death, and for the years of mourning that his family – especially his wife, Julie – would have to endure. He thought of the phone call that would soon interrupt Julie's day, and shuddered. He would try to inform her himself.

'No ...' he cried, gripping the young man's lifeless fingers.

'*No!*'

Daniel Mabe ran down the dark aisles of the derelict store. Its high, dirt-encrusted windows afforded little light; the shelving was high and the aisles narrow, cutting out most of the glow. He found himself shrouded in shadow, and although he was grateful for the darkness, it also frightened him ... *admit it* ... because it would hide his pursuer equally well.

But it did not matter because he would soon be out of here. All he had to do was find some sort of exit, and he would be back on the streets.

Free...

But first he had to get out – and fast, because his break-in had undoubtedly been noted, and the police would be here soon. They would find him easily, would close in around him, tighten the net so that he could not escape. He would be trapped within the department store, running down its long aisles like a lab rat trapped in a maze. Once the cops got here he would have no chance.

All this fear, this diabolical horror of being captured, was because one man had recognised him, recognised his work. Once, he had been untouchable. Unseen and unnoticed, he could pass like a shadow, not attracting anybody, and not asking for any special attention. But suddenly things were getting difficult... laborious.

If the opportunity ever came about, he would kill the man who had recognised him.

Tonight...

That was the monster, awake again and heralding the duel, the final showdown. It had slipped out of its cage, surprised by the unexpected freedom and smiling gleefully. It held him tight.

Tonight...

Then Daniel heard two shots.

At first he pushed against the shelving at his back, tried to melt into it so that he could not be seen, like the Claymen in the old Flash Gordon serials he had watched as a child. He tried to become one with the shelving, tried to shrink into it...

Then, as old cartons jittered and danced at his touch,

he cursed his clumsiness. If even one of the cartons had fallen, his location would have been given away. He put his hand on one, even though it was now steady, just to reassure himself that it was not going to fall.

He could keep the monster at bay no longer, and as he gave into its yearnings for the hunt, he prayed that it would get him out of here alive.

Silently, he moved along the aisle, back the way he had come.

Jay fired down the street to warn the cameraman off, and then entered the shallow darkness of the main floor of the department store, through a side door that gaped open. Jay knew what he was walking into – a game of death with a ruthless killer. He had seen what this man was capable of doing. *Susan* ... she had felt it, had been in his killing hands.

Jay longed for some kind of assurance that the cameraman would not follow. The cameraman knew nothing. He probably did not even know there was another man in the store. He would come in after Jay, trying to play the hero, and be easy pickings for the killer. As well as watching his own back, Jay was now burdened with the other man's safety – a distraction he definitely did not need.

'Jesus,' he whispered, scanning the aisles. All was in darkness. He figured he was at one end of the store, which was in the shape of a long rectangle. He inched along the back wall, looking down each aisle, straining his eyes in the gloom to see as far as he could.

Nothing.
Not a goddamn thing...

Mason, the camera held tight on his shoulder, crept into the building a couple of minutes after Jay. He looked both left and right, but could see nothing in the greyness. He itched to use the camera light, a sharp beam that would show him everything, and for the first time questioned the wisdom of what he was doing.

The shots in the street had made him hesitate, but he'd been in worse jams than this and had come out alive. This was nothing he couldn't handle.

For just a minute he wanted the light, though – and his finger caressed the button which would fill his surroundings with a bright glow. It was tempting, but would give his own position away, make him an easy target for the gunman.

He walked with exaggerated stealth; each time he came to the end of an aisle he peered down it, waiting impatiently for the shadows to shift, for the gunman to reveal himself.

But that never happened, so he jogged quickly across the open gap and stood behind the next wall of shelving, his breathing loud in his ears. When he looked down the fourth aisle, it was exactly the same as the first three. Adams was growing restless. The footage he was getting on tape was boring as hell, and he had just decided that the gunman had left the store, when—

—something moved.

He searched the gloom, but could see nothing. Were his eyes playing tricks on him?

He did not know what to do. He was thinking, and that was bad; at times like this you should depend on gut-level instincts and stimuli. He should not be hovering behind the shelving, uncertain of himself.

Then, thinking no longer but obeying a deeper instinct, Adams jumped into the aisle, simultaneously pushing the button on the camera so that the narrow passage was filled with light.

And there he was, leaning against the wall of shelving, hoping he was still unseen.

But Mason saw him ... and he was *not* the gunman.

Suddenly Mason knew why he was here, why he had dared to follow the gunman. It was to save this man, hiding and praying that he would not be hurt.

'Hey!' he whispered, and began running toward him, the camera bouncing on his shoulder. 'You have to get out of here, my friend. It's not safe.'

It never crossed his mind who this man might be.

Jay saw the light from where he stood on the metal walkway, above the aisles and along one wall of the store. It was a good vantage point, but now he ran for the spiral stairwell, urgency flooding his body, the hard, grated metal vibrating under his feet.

The light could mean only one of two things: either the cameraman had come onto the main floor and immediately put his light on, which would attract the killer like a moth to a naked flame, or he had found the killer and foolishly believed him to be some kind of innocent, with Jay as the gun-toting maniac.

Daniel emerged from the shadows, slithering out as easy as a snake. He knew he had been seen, but did not know who the cameraman was, or why he was here, only that he was a new pawn in the game.

His game.

A new witness to his fury.

'I don't know who you are, or what you are doing here, but there is a guy with a gun and we have to get out,' Mason warned him.

The voice drifted up to Jay as he descended the stairs almost stumbling twice in his haste, grabbing at the rail to prevent himself from falling.

Daniel took a couple of slow steps forward, gathering slight speed and momentum as he walked. For now, he kept the knife hidden at his side.

Jay reached the bottom of the stairwell and did his best to orientate himself. His grip tightened on the rail, and rusty brown dust pushed into the palm of his hand.

'Come on,' Mason hissed urgently, 'I know the way out.'

You stupid fuck, Jay thought, and began to move along the back wall. *Get away from him!*

Mason grabbed the stranger's arm and was about to lead him out to safety, where he'd be hailed a hero as he had been many times in many different countries – usually thanks to his award-winning tapes – when Daniel's hand came up fast.

Mason did not even know what had happened as the blade pushed deep into his side. A terrible pain began there, and then ascended as Daniel savagely pulled the knife up in that direction.

Mason screamed and gurgled, and Jay moved faster. *No* . . .

Daniel twisted Mason around as he fell to his knees, and looked straight into the camera still held by the dying man. His face was a picture of calm, only his voice betraying the anger of the monster.

'This is for you, motherfucker, for starting this. When I find you, I'm gonna rip your fucking guts out!'

Jay listened, chilled, as the words rose above the dying man's moans. And then he heard the laughter. Loud, happy laughter . . . and he saw the man standing above Susan, laughing that laugh . . .

No!

Daniel grabbed the camera and, as if finally released from its burden, Mason collapsed to the floor. Daniel chuckled as he filmed the man, writhing and dying, pleased as he jogged back a few paces and placed the camera on its side, on the floor, so that it captured the whole of Mason's body, his death throes, the anguish on his face.

He quickly wiped his prints off.

He felt so good.

And then a gunshot rang out, silencing his laughter, and he remembered where he was. Daniel saw the muzzle flash at the end of the aisle and several cartons exploded above his head, raining down around him.

Daniel straightened, and there, his gun held out straight in one hand as he ran down the aisle, not bothering to aim, simply firing, pulling the trigger over and over, wild and crazy, was his pursuer.

Who are you? What have you started?

Daniel ducked into the next aisle. Jay pointed the gun at the shelving and fired five more times before he reached the cameraman's still body. He ignored it.

Halfway down the next aisle, the killer was zigzagging looking for an exit, laughing to himself again, as if he believed Jay would stop and whimper over the dead fool. But there was still another fifteen feet or so to go before the end of the aisle.

Although it was dark, Jay, a breath away now, could see just fine. He thought again of the killer grinning as he cut and tortured Susan, but pulling himself free from the swamp of evil imaginings, Jay knew he had time to get a final shot off.

A shot that would count for something.

End it.

He aimed patiently, not rushing. The man was a perfect target at the bottom of the sight. The man was dead: it was over.

He pulled the trigger.

The gun clicked, the magazine empty. The sound was hollow, and he heard it echo through the chambers of his mind. All the time the killer was laughing, and when he reached the end of the aisle he turned and winked.

Their eyes locked.

Jay charged down the aisle, screaming in anger. No

words, a primal cry. He would kill him with his bare hands! He must not be allowed to escape!

Daniel spotted a door and ran to it.

The wink had been to lighten his fear. He was scared. The monster had left him high and dry, retreated to its cage after declaring war on this poor sonofabitch.

He could hear the police sirens now, cutting through the early morning air, and if this door did not open, he knew he would be captured by his charging Nemesis.

But the door did open, out of the store and into a filthy back alley. Within seconds he had darted down it, scrambled over a chainlink fence and had reached the anonymous safety of a network of streets, a wakening city. The hotel was only a few blocks away and he began to walk casually, his cool returning.

He was safe.

He was free.

Free to kill the man who had recognised him. For somehow, Daniel Mabe knew he would never be safe again until the man who pursued him was dead.

Jay saw the open door and ran out, straight into the flashing lights of three squad cars. Suddenly, the five cops who had answered the emergency call for back-up all ducked behind their vehicles.

'Freeze, mother!'

Dazed, Jay remembered the Beretta in his hand – complete with a new magazine – and realised how he must look to them.

'Drop the gun, fucker!'

'You don't understand—' Jay began, but was interrupted by another of the cops.

'Yeah, that's right. And if you don't drop the fucking gun, we're not going to get the chance to.'

There was no way they would believe he was a cop, even if he had his NYPD badge and shield. And the killer was long gone by now. He might, although Jay did not think so, be heading on out of Detroit, as he had moved on from Manhattan, only this time he would be extra careful to leave no trail. No obvious trail – but there had to be *something*. Jay could not lose sight of hope altogether, or he would go insane. There must be a way to find the killer ... there *had* to be.

It would never be over.

Jay let the Beretta swing on one finger, placed in the hoop of the trigger, then he slowly placed it on the ground. He took a couple of steps back.

'You look like you've done that before, pal,' one of the cops grunted as he came forward, his 'cuffs already out. He grabbed Jay by the arm and pushed him roughly against the hood of one of the cars. 'I guess you know this part as well. You have the right to remain silent. You have the—'

And on it went, but Jay heard no more. He knew his rights. Hell, he had recited them more times than he wanted to remember.

I'm a cop, I'm a cop. I am a cop ... he told himself over and over. He had to stay sane, otherwise he would be behind bars faster than he wanted to think about. When he explained all this he had to keep his emotions under control, because if he came over all crazy they would surely lock him up and throw away the key. And yet, oh God...

...the man who had killed Susan had escaped...

In the back of the car he screamed loudly and angrily, a long cry to the rising sun, and one of the cops jabbed him in the ribs to silence him.

'Hey! Shut the fuck up.'

...and would kill again.

Chapter Six
The Lost Boys

Daniel Mabe sat on the edge of the bed in his hotel room, leafing through the pages of his journal, searching for one particular entry. Occasionally, a picture or note would catch his eye and he would pause to remember. Yet some of the photographs were distant and foreign to him, some of the writing so unfamiliar that it might have been written by a different hand, or in a different language during a different lifetime.

But it was all his work.

They were all his victims.

The children, the men, the women. The animals, all the pets ... *the dogs* ... they were all his own.

He couldn't even remember half of them. Taking their lives was as inconsequential to him as crossing the street, and that dismayed and discouraged him because the destruction he had caused, the pain and grief he had enjoyed so much at the time, no longer stirred the slightest emotion within him.

137

A waste of my talent, he thought.

But other photographs brought back chilling memories. He was sweating as he sat there, unconsciously and gently rubbing his erection, reliving the horrors ... *the pleasure*. He looked at the photographs, and saw himself through the eyes of his victims.

He was a lover, a father-figure, a friend or a neighbour. And while his role varied, the end result was always the same, when seen through his victims' eyes: betrayal.

As he turned the pages, each one a record of misery, he wished they could be more understanding, see things from *his* point of view. He was not the Angel of Death or the Grim Reaper, nor the Devil Himself with a pointed tail and sharp trident. He did what he believed was good, what the monster told him to do. Daniel Mabe was the real victim. He was afraid ... and he wished they would acknowledge that.

There it was, the entry for which he'd been searching. He scanned the page, and read it over to himself.

... and it was a warm night. To cool the house of the almost relentless heat, several small windows had been left open. The smallest of all, the bathroom, was the most accessible, so I crept stealthily to the wall and scaled the drainpipe, squeezing myself in through the window and lowering myself head-first into the bath tub. With its smooth plastic surface, a soft peach in colour, this is the tub of a woman. Not the colour I would choose, but that does not matter

because I am not the one who will spend hours soaking in tepid water, weeping, dreaming of suicide, grieving over my lost son.

The only light is a faint glow coming from a street lamp; once out on the landing I am surrounded by dark. That does not concern me because I am familiar with this house, with every creak of its floorboards. I know what is depicted in the six paintings that line the walls, three on either side, even though I cannot see them. And I know that this first door is only closet space, but the next, that is the boy's room ... because I have been here before, often.

I push the door open, listening to the hinge squeak, and think how I should have fixed that before I came tonight. Inside is a room typical of any six-year-old. Toys are scattered across the floor, clothes thrown on a chair and about the room with abandon, not folded or put away. There is no care or responsibility here. The closet door is slightly open to guard the boy from any marauding night creatures; and for added protection a bright light shines inside it, filtering through the slats in the wood, throwing patterns of shallow light across the room. I walk towards the bed, careful to avoid the toys, and watch the boy roll beneath the covers. He is not bothered by my soft, night sounds. I reach the bed and stand above him. It is not often that I feel this powerful. In my hands I hold Billy Rogers's life, and I think how easy it would be to kill him. He is completely defenceless.

When I was here two days ago, I slept with his mother for the third time and she professed her love for me. I answered her accordingly. That night, I told the boy there are no monsters in this world, no real monsters. But I lied. I gave him a false sense of security so that he would not fear this night. There are monsters in the world, and sometimes they hide within the person you least suspect. Silently, I pull the hunting knife from inside my jacket and . . .

As he read what followed, he remembered the night he had killed the boy, his death painless and quick. He did not like hurting children, but sometimes the monster demanded it of him.

He was preparing to leave from the boy's bedroom window when a man . . . *him* . . . had kicked the door open. He had a gun; their eyes locked for a brief moment, less than a second.

Then, as he dropped from the window and let the dark shadows claim him, the man was squeezing the trigger, the sound filling the night.

Who are you? Why have our paths crossed before?

He tried to forget the man, and thought instead of the boy's mother; he wondered what had happened to her. She was a sad woman, a parasite, feeding off her son's – and his – joy, in order to forget her husband's death in an industrial accident. Parasitic in turn, he fed off her misery.

There were no dates in the journal. He had realised

early on in life that time did not matter. When the
monster stole his innocence, he had a lifetime ahead ...
and at that moment, his body engulfed by hot adrenaline,
he knew that he would never be hurt, and that time
would never touch him.

He would protect the monster, and it would protect
him.

They would die when they were ready.

He found the next blank page of the journal, and
began to write.

*I do not want to kill the woman, but it must be. I
know the monster will take care of it when the time
comes ... and that it will want to work fast. Do her,
and get out of Detroit.*

I will obey the monster ...

I can already hear it calling.

*There will be police protection, and it will be
difficult.*

*It will mean a massacre ... a bad time for
everybody.*

Except the monster ...

It is not my way.

*I like to hurt people, make them feel pain without a
knife or gun. Death is my weapon; the aftermath
what I seek, what I need.*

The killing is for the monster.

They had a perfect image of his face on video tape. There
was probably a national All Points Bulletin out on him.

The police have had his description before, although fingerprints would not help to identify him because, unless you went a long way back, and dug deep into a dead town's history, there was no record of his existence. Fingerprints would only match him to other murders, in other cities.

One of his eyes was bruised a slight black and blue from the fight with Red. The cut above his eye had clotted, and he scratched the thin scab away. His stomach looked the worst: the bruises there were turning a horrible orange-yellow.

He read again what he had written.

Who was the man in the derelict store?

The man from the crowd, who chased me ... we know each other.

I'm not saying we're best friends, but I do remember him. He is the man from the room of Billy Rogers, but it is more than that.

We share a past.

He's familiar. There's something in his eyes ...

It will come to me.

We are soulmates – I could see that in his cold gaze, the wild fire and anger that burn in his heart. He also knows the monster.

It owns me, but he has tighter control. Can use it, and unleash its wrath whenever he likes.

We are brothers ...

The summer recess was always a hard time for Kirby, and

particularly so this summer, with Johnny Whittingham out looking for revenge.

He was up early and had his papers delivered before his parents even woke. That gave him time to grab a quick shower and wash the newsprint away, turning the water a dull grey as it fell from his hands.

And then he was out, with a little money from his hidden savings to keep himself from getting bored. He wanted to buy something, and as reading was what he loved doing most he decided to treat himself to a good book. He could always go to the library, but sometimes it was satisfying to buy something because it made it your own, It would be your possession for ever, something nobody could take away.

First, he'd stop by the Baskin-Robbins and then go say hi to Leigh at the library, see what new books he recommended.

Of course, there'd always be Johnny Whittingham . . . chasing him, waiting for him on street corners, his lack of success making him even angrier. There would always be the thrill of that, of the danger.

All his schoolwork was done, so the coming weeks were his own.

A time of joy and adventure!

Kirby liked the vacation.

Sunlight filtered through the pale blinds as Ellen Little ran her hands through her soft hair. She sat on the couch, tears in her eyes, staring into the cup of dark coffee before her. She was grateful that she could not see her tired reflection in its surface. Then she looked up at Jodie Kershaw who sat opposite on a straight-backed wooden chair.

'You got anything stronger?' Ellen asked, knowing the answer already.

'Now, you know I don't drink. Won't have the stuff in my home,' Jodie said, looking at the sad woman before her. Ever since her husband had died an alcoholic nearly fifteen years ago, Jodie had never even looked at a drink, and never would as long as she lived. 'I figured you came around here to talk. If you want to get drunk and drown your sorrows with the first man you meet, then that's just fine with me. But mark my words, Ellen, you will regret it.'

'I know. I'm sorry,' Ellen apologised.

Jodie Kershaw had lived her whole life in Haddonfield, and ever since she was sixty had held a job at the local library. Before that, she had worked there as a volunteer while she taught English at the school. At seventy she still loved reading, especially the classics, but it took longer now to wade through a book. The print was so small, her eyes strangely dim these days.

Jodie was like a grandmother to the whole town; she had fulfilled that function longer than anyone could remember. She was there for them all.

'Now, you know I work with Leigh Nichols down at the library, who moonlights as Chief of the Fire Department. I've heard him talk, and it sounds to me as if this arson business has got Dwight under a great deal of pressure. Why not speak to Dwight about your doubts, straight out. Have you tried that, dear?'

Ellen looked dismayed and sipped her coffee. It was not nice – too strong and leaving a bitter taste in her mouth long after she'd swallowed, but she did not say anything. Jodie had been like the mother she'd never had. As a child, for many years, she remembered going to Jodie's house and climbing up on to her knee, listening to the stories she told. Stories Jodie's mother had told Jodie, and if Ellen ever had children, stories she would tell them.

Right now, though, it was looking doubtful whether she'd ever have children ... would ever have anything at all.

'But it sounds so silly. What if I'm wrong?' Ellen could feel the tears growing heavier in her eyes. But what if he *was* having an affair, sleeping with another, sharing his love? Who would love her then?

'Tis better to have loved and lost than never to have loved at all ... Whoever said that was out of their mind. To have loved was not worth this much pain and insecurity. She felt old, alone.

'You obviously don't trust him,' Jodie replied gently. 'Speak to him about it, honey. Confront him with what you suspect.'

A lifetime of experience was in these words, yet Ellen still found reason to doubt them.

Confront him. The phrase was hard and it frightened her. She did not know if she could do that.

'He never even called before he left, never kissed me

goodbye,' she mused, surprised that she missed his wet lips on her cheek so much. That hurt the most: he had left for the city without telling her why he was going. *Or who he was going to see out there.*

'Then he no longer loves you,' Jodie said with finality, her old-time values and beliefs guiding her judgement.

And that was enough for Ellen. The tears were finally released.

Jodie knew she might have been a little blunt, but there was no point in hiding from the truth. She held out her withered hand and Ellen clung to it, like it was a rock in the middle of the ocean and she was stranded there.

'Confront him,' Jodie urged again.

He never even kissed me goodbye, Ellen mourned, then wondered how long it had been since Dwight had begun to just peck her on the cheek on his way out. How long it had been since he'd *really* kissed her.

Images from the mist.

Number Eighteen, rushing in and charging like a bull. He pulled his arm back, dodging after the snap, ready to make the pass but then, as Eighteen hit, before he could release the ball, he was falling, falling so far. He landed on his leg, hard, heard bones crack ... seconds passed and the mist cleared. Coach was looking down. 'You're OK, kid. You're OK, kid.' He did not feel OK. He saw a bobbing stretcher, punches being exchanged ...

And then the mist ...

When Officer Bobby Roberts woke from the millionth

replay of his final football game, his first rational thoughts were not of revenge, of his shattered career or his leg that had been broken in four places, but of Dawn Taylor, his girlfriend.

He looked at the phone and wanted to call her. Dawn was currently working on a documentary in England. He missed her so badly, and was counting the days until her return, wishing he had listened when she'd asked him to take some time off.

They had met when she was filming a programme about life in the police academy (the production abroad was a similar feature about British law enforcement), and Bobby had impressed her with his story of a shattered dream, when she inquired why he had joined the force.

Some things did not make the final cut.

They had gone out to dinner, and talked about ambitions and secret hopes, the childhoods that had shaped them. They predicted each other's futures ... they made love.

That was over a year ago.

He looked at the phone, ached to call her, but knew he should not. His phone bill was a testament to his love. Slowly, he rolled off the bed and went to take a shower, washing the sleep away.

It was Saturday, and Bobby had a rare day off. The kids would be at the park today playing tackle football – *his* kids, the ones he had saved from the streets. He decided to go down and watch them for a while, maybe even join in a couple of plays.

Bobby liked the children, and knew that they liked him back. He had experienced a lonely childhood, his parents always moving from city to city, dragging him with them. As a schoolkid he barely had time to settle, never mind make friends.

He was feeling lonely today, missing Dawn, so he went to them. They were too young to understand the pain of missing a person, but would understand that he was hurting, and offer him their own brand of comfort. They wouldn't mock him, or try to fix him up with an easy lay, or ask prying questions like his colleagues did.

Bobby stuffed a bag full of Coke cans from the fridge and left the house in jogging pants and T-shirt. He was not in bad shape, but ever since Dawn's departure half a year ago, his workouts had become less frequent, and a lot less strenuous. As her return became imminent, he knew he would have to work hard to look good. He could easily lose a few pounds, and could always use more exercise.

'Hey!' one of the kids shouted as he spotted Bobby, interrupting the play and pointing. 'It's the cop man.'

As Bobby approached, the game came to a slow and lethargic halt. The teams gathered together and met him as a group.

There were twelve of them, two more than the last time, the newcomers curious, resentful of this adult's interference in the game. He could see it in their eyes ... but it was a couple more kids off the street. Perhaps a couple more lives saved.

He dealt out the cans, tossing them towards the kids, who caught them confidently. One of the kids whom he'd got to know well after these past few months, was Ron Locca, aged twelve, who had been caught in a gang of teenage muggers, carrying a .357 Magnum. Bobby had busted him, but instead of taking the kid downtown and then on to Juvenile Hall, he'd told him to be at the park the next day.

'And if you're not there, I'm gonna bust your ass,' he'd threatened, speaking a language he knew the kid would understand.

The next day Bobby had walked into the park, not really expecting the kid to show up, but there he was, and they spoke for a while, Bobby pursuing every angle he could think of in an attempt to elicit a real response from him. Finally, resorting to his last plan, he threw the boy his much-cherished, personally obtained, Dan Marino signed football.

The boy had laughed at the gesture and called Marino a pussy, but Bobby could tell it had touched him somewhere.

Ron Locca had never been given anything in his life before then.

Pretty soon they began to talk about the game as they threw the ball to and fro. Bobby knew that he had gotten through to the kid.

Gene Siskel was another one he knew well.

Similar story really, only Gene was thirteen and had been dealing dope in high school. Bobby had told Gene to be at the park, and out of curiosity the boy turned up –

establishing his status, as they all did, by being late. When he got there, the boy saw something that made him cry when he was alone in his crummy room at the slum apartment – a group of children running around, throwing a ball and shouting. A group of children being ... *children*.

The following week Gene returned, running with the rest of those kids, smiling and happy. And when all the other children had gone, when Ron had taken the ball home, when he was alone with the cop and could not be branded a snitch, Gene told Bobby everything he knew about a low-life drug-dealer by the name of Frank Nolan.

It had felt good to Bobby, to put the scumbag away, and it proved to him that the kids were more intelligent than most people gave them credit for. He was their friend, as they were his.

Unfortunately, new kids sometimes only came once, and were gone the next week – back to a life of petty crime which would develop into something bigger as they got older.

Sometimes they turned up on their own, and sometimes established kids talked their friends into coming along. And occasionally, Bobby would persuade a new child to come, and invariably it was these who needed it the most.

But one thing was for certain. When Bobby had told Ron Locca to be at the park, he didn't think he would still be coming here himself nearly six months later. He felt a need to watch over the children, to make sure they

were staying out of trouble. He genuinely liked and
cared for them ... and knew that the feeling was
mutual.

If he ever missed a week, even if he didn't drop by
while he was in uniform for a few minutes, he would get
phone calls from them asking if he was OK. The
children had his number in case they were ever in
trouble. He was a leader to them, a mentor. All he could
do was accept it, and be proud that he was making a
difference.

'Who's winning?' he asked.

'Gene took an early lead, but we're catching up,' Ron
told him. 'Right, guys?'

There were various cries and shouts from half the
children, while the rest basked in the glory of their lead.

'You playing?' Gene asked. 'They could use a ringer.'

'Yeah, maybe I will.'

He had joined in three plays, deliberately running
slower than he could, throwing shorter, holding back,
when he saw the police artist from the bus depot
walking across the short grass towards him. The man
was wearing a long, thin coat even though the sun was
shining bright and there was no chance of a shower.

Bobby faked a throw and handed the ball off to Ron.
'See you later.'

Then he walked out of range of the game in the
direction of the police artist. Like a mother looking after
her brood, Bobby did not want the children to overhear
anything that might corrupt them, anything ugly. No
mutilated bodies or bank robberies.

'Ray Province. You can call me Vinnie,' the newcomer said, offering his hand.

'Bobby Roberts,' he replied, and took the hand with good heart. The artist seemed easy to like, and his shake was strong. 'How did you know I was here?'

'I haven't been on the streets for a while, but I still know how to pick up a scent,' Vinnie said, and looked about the park, watched the children playing football.

He didn't want to beat around the bush. He needed a yes or no answer as soon as possible. Vinnie was not here to make new friends, he needed help: *double the manpower, halve the work*. And that also meant that he would be ready the next time Jay called in the middle of the night. If Bobby was not in, then he would do it alone. It would take a little longer, that was all.

'Listen, Bobby. The guy who killed those people at the bus depot also killed Jay Austin's sister. He's gone to Detroit to—'

'I'm not blind,' Bobby interrupted, with a little more attitude than he'd intended. 'From the moment I saw him at the depot I knew he was seriously pissed at something. I did some homework, and figured he might need help. I was going to put in for some vacation time I got coming, see if Jay needed the company.'

'Why?'

'I don't know, it just seemed right. My girlfriend Dawn's in England and I'm really missing her, you know?' Just saying that felt good inside, telling somebody that he was hurting, even if this Vinnie guy didn't understand. 'Especially now that she's nearly due home. I really need to get my mind off her, and I figured this could be the way. Only thing is, I never got the chance to check it out with Austin.'

'Well, I've known Jay for a long time, and he wouldn't have wanted anybody along for the ride,' Vinnie said soberly. 'Besides, you're no Dirty Harry – I can see that much looking at you. You're no vigilante cop who gets his kicks from chasing people halfway around the world and blowing away bad guys. This is where you're a hero, Bobby – out here, on this field. You're changing lives here,' Vinnie said, then checked himself, suddenly aware that he was making a speech. He took off his sunglasses. 'Listen, Bobby. You want to get off traffic duty, and I need your help. I think we could use each other here.'

'What did you have in mind?' Bobby asked.

'Like I said, me and Jay, we go back a long way. I know how he thinks, and I figured he would be heading for Detroit. I let him know I was here if he needed any legwork doing. Now, I've been keeping my ear to the ground, and I've heard that some serious shit has just gone down in Detroit – Jay was a big part of it, apparently. Caldwell is kicking ass all over the Precinct, and he's asked the Detroit PD to hold Jay for a few days, give him the chance to cool off. So, if you do help, nobody should know what we're working on.'

'I got time to change and shower?' Bobby decided quickly.

'I was counting on it,' Vinnie grinned, sniffing the sweaty air between them.

* * *

Novelle Tourment sat in the office section of her apartment. It contained two drawing boards – one she used for sketching, which was where she was sat at the moment, and the other for working out the best colour schemes and fabrics.

Novelle had her own factory where her designs were exclusively manufactured. The drawing offices there were better equipped than her home, but sometimes she woke up and could not be bothered to put on her office persona and go out. And on occasion, but very rarely these days, she'd wake up with a picture of a design in her mind that was so unique and special that she'd have to get it onto paper immediately, lest she forget the smallest detail.

She looked down at the very rough sketch in front of her now; it was one that not even a student would be proud of. She picked it up and crumpled it into a small tight ball, launching it across the room so that it landed neatly in the empty waste-paper bin. Empty, as it always was. Novelle had taught herself never to throw any designs away, however preliminary or pathetic they might look at the time. One day, leafing through her extensive portfolio, she might see one of those sketches, and in it, the potential she had failed to recognise at the time of drawing.

But the rules had been broken, and she did not care for that particular sketch, nor for any of her work.

All the rules were broken now.

Her life did not matter any more. She was rich,

famous in the world of fashion, had been on the cover of *Time* magazine, and appeared on every breakfast and talk show there was in New York, and now she had lost her best friend.

Violently, she scooped everything to the edge of the worktop – her pens and pencils, crayons and charcoal, paper and erasers – everything – and then let them fall off the end.

She ran her hands through her long, soft hair, tears streaking her make-up. Yes, she had everything, but none of it counted. She would sacrifice it all so that Susan could have life once more.

She walked into the living area, with its expensive furniture and designer decorations. Objects, that was all they were. They could be worth thousands – millions – but in her heart, in her life now, they held no value and she wished they were not here. Occasionally, her eye rested on some small item she had purchased for herself, out of pleasure, pure and simple.

The dancing ballerina, forever frozen in a pirouette.

The small, porcelain angel, carrying the dying soldier in her arms. Susan had liked that angel, saw the story it told. A soldier who had loved a woman very much, and then lost that love when he died on the muddy field of battle. The angel would carry his love and pass it on to the mourning widow, who would come to understand her loss better, and learn to live without him.

She went to the fridge and pulled it open. The wine bottle was still there, as she knew it would be. The one Susan had given her a week ago. She would drink it now, taste its flavour rolling down her throat, lose herself in its sweet fragrance.

Look after it for me, Susan had said. *Keep it, and one day, if he breaks my heart, we can drink it together.*

Did he give it to you? Novelle asked.

Now she wondered: *Did he break more than your heart, Susan?* Novelle wished an angel would come to her, the bearer of Susan's lost soul.

She reached in, her arm passing from shadow to light as it entered the fridge. Her fingers were about to clasp the neck of the bottle when she remembered...

Did he give it to you?

Yes, Susan said, staring dreamily into the eyes of the angel, then the dead soldier. She looked at Novelle. *I never want this to end*, she said. *I want to live for ever.*

Novelle snatched her hand back before it touched the bottle. If Susan's lover Tony Elliot had given her the bottle, then his fingerprints might still be on it.

'Oh my God,' she shuddered, and was about to call the police when the door buzzed. She walked to it, looked out the peephole.

When he realised somebody was looking out, Bobby Roberts held up his golden badge so that it filled her vision.

The cab driver pulled up at the entrance to the Detroit General Hospital. His fare was a tall, lean, well-groomed man who wore what looked like an expensive suit. As he climbed from the cab he tipped generously.

'Thanks, man. Hey – hope your sister's all right,' the driver said, pulling away in search of his next fare.

But the man did not hear him. He was already strolling across the roadway, just as an ambulance set off to some unknown, bloody destination, its sirens cutting a path through the afternoon traffic. As he approached the electronic doors they slid apart with a whispering hum.

To his right were several booths, three with their curtains pulled across. Urgent voices filled the room.

'Shut it down! Shut it down!'

Behind one of the curtains, several doctors and nurses were obviously fighting to keep somebody alive.

'Don't lose him!'

'He's getting away!'

There was a long silence.

'Let it go.' A quiet whisper.

'No!' A painful, anguished cry.

'Come on – let it go! He's gone. He's the first one you've lost, but there will be more. You have to let him go.'

A curtain pulled back suddenly, clattering on the rail, and a young doctor emerged, his face streaked with tears. A nurse followed him as he hurried across the floor, then down a corridor.

The man turned his attention back to the booth. As the curtain was tugged across from the inside, he caught a second-long glimpse of the bloody mess in there. He felt no revulsion . . .

He watched after the young doctor until he disappeared at the end of the corridor, and wondered how much he was hurting. He took a slow step towards the booth, listening.

'All right, let's get this mess cleaned up.'

'Can I help you?'

The voice had taken him by surprise. Turning, he saw a small orderly, a wet mop in his hand.

'I'm looking for Admissions.'

The orderly thought about this for a second. It was only his third week on the job, and he was still getting lost in the labyrinthine corridors.

'Well,' he said, after a moment. 'You want to go down that corridor, take the first left, and . . .'

Five minutes later, Daniel was at Admissions. There was a waist-high curved counter, behind which stood a young blonde-haired nurse, sorting through several files and placing them in various pigeon-holes.

'Hello,' he said sombrely, remembering that he was supposed to be here searching for his injured sister.

'Oh, sorry, sir. Didn't notice you there,' she apologised.

The man looked good, probably about ten years older than herself – but what did that matter? She smiled, showing him her perfect teeth. Ever since her boyfriend had left her nearly two months ago – for another nurse on the floor – she found herself assessing every man she came into contact with. This one rated real high.

Her eyes ventured down to his hands which he had placed on the counter. No ring. She looked up to his face again, his blue eyes as deep as oceans and hypnotic.

'How may I help you?' she asked.

'I'm not sure you can. My sister was brought into the hospital last night. I wondered if you could tell me her room number, or at least her status if I am outside regular visiting hours.'

He was well-spoken and polite, and he seemed to respect her, not like most people who treated her like some bimbo receptionist, ignoring her hard-earned qualifications.

'What name is it?' she asked, smiling.

'Kevin Hurd,' the man said, and then looked away as he realised his mistake. 'Sorry. Gale Anne Hurd.'

She smiled. He sure was cute.

Daniel smiled back, charmingly.

The nurse worked fast, typing the name into the computer, which faced away from the public, and waiting for a second before a file appeared on the screen from the database. She read it, then turned and gave the man a professionally reassuring smile.

'Your sister's OK, Mr Hurd. She has a broken nose, a few stitches ... she also lost a back tooth. Nothing too serious. She'll just be a little black and blue for a while, that's all. She was never actually admitted. We just patched her up and sent her home.'

The nurse was not aware of the criminal nature of Gale Anne Hurd's injuries, but was smitten by her brother.

'Really? I wonder if you could do me a big favour. Gale and I have been out of touch for a while, and I do not have her current address,' he said, his fingers wandering to hers and dancing a tango with them on the edge of the file. 'Perhaps you could give it to me?'

She had seen this coming and was ready for it, but had lowered her guard. She knew she could be fired for giving him the information, but did not want to disappoint him. Not only because it had been so long since he had seen his sister, but because she wanted to please him.

The nurse knew that in her wounded state she was easily susceptible to charm, and that this gorgeous guy was using her, but in a dark way she liked that – and the attention he was giving her.

'It's confidential. I might lose my job,' she offered mechanically, hoping he would flirt with her some more. It was an interesting game.

Daniel took her hand in his, palm up, and made small circles on it with his finger as he spoke. 'I would make it worth your while.'

'Oh,' she said dreamily, losing herself in his attraction. 'Two Sycamore Avenue, Bloomfield Hills. You better call me.'

She closed her hand around his finger and clasped it tight, digging one of her nails into it. A trickle of blood was set free and she let go, sucking the blood from her nail.

'I will. You know I will.'

Chapter Seven
Childhood

Jay looked around the bare room. It was just like every interrogation room he'd ever been in, only now his perspective was reversed, and he realised how effective the bleakness was.

His face was bruised badly; one eye swollen, almost shut. His ribs hurt, his whole torso ached.

Driving back to the Precinct building last night, a call had come over the radio about the death of Officer Robert Parker, and Jay had known then he was in trouble. Before reaching their destination, the cops had taken him down a desolate side street and proceeded to beat the crap out of him while he was handcuffed, watching out all the time for intruding citizens with video cameras.

Back home in Manhattan, if circumstances were similar, the same thing would have happened. Cops watching out for each other, angry at the death of a brother.

He was booked ... and if anybody asked, he'd resisted arrest.

There was a table, long and wooden, and two chairs. Jay sat on one of them, his right hand cuffed to it. He knew that this chair was bolted to the floor, while the other was loose.

Captain Kamski sat on the end of the table, towering above him intimidatingly, looking down at the lowlife before him ... and Jay wondered how many times he had assumed that position. Along the wall to his left was a mirror, and Jay could feel a thousand pairs of eyes hidden behind it, watching.

'It's like I told you,' Jay repeated, irritated that Detroit's finest continued to cover the same ground over and over. All they had to do was make one call to Caldwell to confirm everything, for Chrissake. Or check the apartment he was staying in. 'I'm a cop.'

Kamski thoughtfully stroked his silver-grey beard. He was tall, and his face bore an uncanny resemblance to that of Dustin Hoffman.

'Why didn't you identify yourself as a police officer at the scene of the arrest?' he said sternly.

'I did – in the car. No one believed me,' Jay said ironically, referring to his damaged face.

'Heard you resisted,' Kamski shrugged.

Jay sighed. He was tired, and bored with the questions, couldn't believe how long this was all taking ... how far away the killer was getting. That was how he measured time now. It was late afternoon, nearly twelve hours since Tony Elliot – or whatever his name was – had escaped from the store.

'Something like that,' he said flatly.

'You never showed any proof of your ID. Why didn't you produce your shield?' Kamski asked, his hand moving up to his slightly darker moustache.

'I told you a thousand times, I'm on vacation. Do you take your shield when you go on vacation?' Jay asked, feeling good that he had turned the tables on Kamski for just a second.

The killer had gotten away, it was as simple as that. And he could blame nobody but himself. *He knew, the fucker knew I was out of bullets*. He had to make the best of the situation at hand, and was aware that he would not do that by pissing off the Detroit PD.

Relax...

'No, I don't. And I don't take along a cannon like that,' Kamski said, indicating Jay's handgun which lay – *sans magazine* – on the table's scratched surface. 'What the hell is that, anyway? A Colt?'

'Beretta nine mill'. Holds fifteen in the mag, and one up the spout,' Jay said with a degree of pride, and then smiled. He knew that he was getting his movies mixed up, but he squinted and lowered his voice to a raspy whisper. 'At this range, it could blow your head clean off.'

Kamski stood, ignoring him, and silently paced the room, thinking as his hand moved faster on the beard.

'What are you doing in Detroit?'

'I'm on vacation.'

'I don't buy that. It's bullshit, and you know it. People want a new car, they come to Detroit. They want a vacation, they go to Disneyland.'

Kamski stopped pacing and looked down at Jay, deciding to cut him some slack.

'Does it have something to do with your sister?'

'You sonofabitch!' Jay exploded, and stood, tugging at the chair, but it was useless. He pulled violently at the titanium alloy which bound him at the wrist before relaxing, frustrated. 'If you knew about it, why am I cuffed to this fucking chair?'

'I've got a dead cop, and a dead civilian! If this was just about you and your sister, I might have cut you loose hours ago.'

'I don't see that crazy bitch driver in here!'

'That is because *that crazy bitch driver* is the mayor's daughter. If I haul her ass down here, not only will I lose my job, or get busted into the file room, but it will make headlines. Bad press for the mayor will mean that he will lose the upcoming elections, and he's the best thing that has happened to this city for a few decades. It's a matter of politics.'

'Fuck the politicians!'

'And,' Kamski continued, 'she's down at the General, recovering from a concussion.'

'So you hold me for involuntary manslaughter and murder, neither of which I had anything to do with.

That's great, man, fucking great! And while I'm in here, the killer just walks away.'

'You were the catalyst,' Kamski reasoned. 'If you hadn't been running around the streets like Mel fucking Gibson, neither of those people would be dead!'

Silence.

'How did you know it was him?' Kamski asked calmly.

There was no way to describe how Jay had known it was the killer. He had no solid proof, no corroboration, just an exceptional sketch, and a very poor description which came down to little more than what the killer had been wearing at the bus depot.

And little Billy Rogers . . .

It had been instinct.

He had looked into the man's eyes . . . *those eyes of ice* . . . and Death had stared back. As the woman at the bus depot had warned.

How could he explain these feelings to Kamski?

Then he remembered the photographs that had been found at Susan's place. He had never seen them, never wanted to. But they gave him an idea – something that might offer final confirmation that the man who had killed Susan had also killed Red Comber. He hoped it would be enough to satisfy Kamski.

'Did you find any photographs at the bar?' Jay asked.

Good move, kid, Kamski thought. He had been informed by Caldwell about the photographs that had been found at Susan Austin's apartment. Kamski had never known the woman – to him, she was just another victim. He could offer his sympathy to Jay, but knew that he would not appreciate it.

They had a job to do, and that was all that counted. 'What photographs?' Kamski asked.

'I don't know, I didn't see the fucking things,' Jay said without patience. 'Pictures of the body. Blood. The damage he did – anything! But you found them, didn't you?'

Kamski nodded, and reached into his pocket. He dropped five photographs onto the table, then bent and uncuffed Jay.

'Thanks.'

'You can handle the pictures – they're clean. This is one evil bastard, isn't it?'

Jay did not want to answer the Captain's question. They both knew he was right.

Jay massaged his wrist where the titanium had left a sharp red mark. He picked up the photographs, but let them fall as soon as he laid eyes on the first. He had seen dead bodies before – victims of shotgun blasts, and much worse. But he was not prepared for the freezing brutality of these pictures: it was their gloating depiction of death which shocked him.

The first one must have been taken at Red's Tavern, and the only reason to explain the killer leaving the others was narcissism: a criminal conceit. He wanted to show Detroit that he had killed before, and would undoubtedly kill again.

But they already knew that now ... without the evidence of the photographs.

The first picture was of a dead dog, its body cut up bad, lying behind the bar.

He killed the dog. Somewhere, deep inside and far away, Jay knew that was significant.

Why did he kill the dog?

The animal had been tied to a rail behind the Tavern bar. There was no way it could attack him, so why?

'Jesus,' Jay whispered, drawn to the other photographs like an iron filing towards a magnet. He did not want to see them or experience them, but knew he must.

And in each picture he saw Susan.

...They were only children, although more mature than most, because when their parents had been killed, Jay and Susan had lost their innocence. In front of them lay a grown-up world that neither of them wanted to face. A world full of fear and uncertainty, without the magic of youth. One they were too young to understand.

Even so, they were still together – and that was enough.

They lived in a Home, a place that had been especially built for children like themselves, with two play areas, rolling fields everywhere, a games room, a disco once a week, and its own small – yet adequate – school. The teachers and adults here cared for you as if you were their own children. The home had no strict rules, and there was little need for discipline. In the most genuine sense, it was a home away from home.

But it was the Home's perfection which brought the cold, harsh reality to Jay. He and his sister were not on vacation; this place was not a holiday camp ... *it really was home*. This was it, all there was left now that their parents were gone. He finally, truly comprehended the hard truth, which he had refused to believe, when he had been told it four months ago.

Their parents were not coming back. They were gone for ever.

As the eldest, the truth hit him harder than Susan. He had to be strong, to always watch over his sister and show her the right way to go. But first came the depression ... the time he'd tried to take his own life. If it had not been for one of the guardians trying to make out with her boyfriend, a paramedic, Jay would surely have died.

He still had uneven scars across his right wrist to remind him of that time; now they served to remind him of something else. If he had died then, Susan's life would have taken a completely different course and she would be alive today.

He sat in the interrogation room, unconsciously rubbing his wrist, staring bleakly at the photographs. He blamed himself for Susan's death. Somehow he managed to convince himself that it *was* true: if he had died that night, when he had stolen through the dark corridors to the kitchen where there was an array of sharp knives to choose from, then Susan would have grown up in a small town called Canberra, safe from the killer. She would probably not even have seen or heard of his victims in the news.

She would have regained her innocence.

'Susan,' he had said, distracting her from a game of table tennis – the bouncing white ball the most important thing in her young life at that moment.

'Susan, listen to me for a second,' he said desperately, and she turned, her attention captured by his tone. 'Mom and Dad are never coming back.'

'I know,' she said, resilient and resourceful as only very young children are. And then she went back to her game.

It was true, of course. Their parents never returned, except for the memories, haunting and sad, and the sweet dreams. The brother and sister slowly began to learn to live with the truth, and their almost idyllic lifestyle at the Home continued.

Sometimes a married couple seeking to adopt children would express an interest in one of them. But it was always one or the other, never both. And that was not the way it worked. They were a team, partners, inseparable. You couldn't have one without the other – they were a package deal.

And it stayed that way for a long time.

But then something bad happened in the adult

world. Children started to disappear from the Home – not one by one, but in huge groups of ten and fifteen. Friends left without warning. There was no time for tearful farewells, no promises to write.

Although Jay never learned exactly what had happened, it was easy to guess now. The funds had dried up. Soon after that, the Home was forced to close, operating on a skeleton crew until places could be found for all the children.

Jay was one of the last to go, and he remembered walking the corridors at night there, listening to the shrill, long-lost voices that would haunt the passages for ever. The voices of his friends, all of them gone. And without their abundant joy, the place seemed so lonely and cold, like a graveyard...

The next morning, Susan was gone too.

He held no malicious feelings towards the guardians at the Home, not even that first morning when he'd run into her room to find it empty. Their separation could have been caused by anything, even something as insignificant as a typing error which would have given them both different surnames. Anything ... but the split, he knew, had not been deliberate.

Susan found a new home with a young couple in Canberra, while he was packed off to a place nearly 500 miles away.

It was closer to a prison than a Home. He couldn't imagine anybody calling it a *home* – except, perhaps, the sadistic adults who worked there, without love or compassion. Jay became a statistic like all the other kids there – nothing more than a number on a piece of paper. All the rooms were the same. All the meals were the same. Preferences were discouraged.

The children were obliged to work in the field for six hours a day, two on Sundays, and one boy, the eldest there at sixteen, once told Jay a story he would never forget.

'A kid – he had only been here about a month – dropped in the west field. He was only nine years old, and real skinny. They took him to the infirmary, and he was never seen again. At first we were all optimistic. I was only fourteen, a little older than you. My parents sent me here for stealing cars. I had been here two years at the time, and I figure now that as my parents had another kid, my brother, who turned out better than me, they just kinda left me here. Forgot all about the skeleton in the closet. Back then, I still missed my parents, was counting the days I was away from them. We all hoped that the sick kid's parents had done the smart thing – come to their senses and returned for him. Either that, or for some reason, he had just been sent back into the real world. We all hoped good things for him, but that boy was not so lucky. Two nights later I discovered the truth. A rainstorm that had been brewing for the past few days finally came down, and I could not sleep. I listened to the rain pattering on my window, and the wind blowing hard like a savage animal. I stood at my window and looked out, thinking how wonderful it would be to run in the falling rain, to feel the cold wet

171

on the nape of my neck, to run my hands through dripping hair. The rain rivulets formed bars on my locked window and as I stared between them, losing myself in empty dreams, I began to discern figures moving outside. There were two of them – and they were carrying something between them. I couldn't tell for sure, but I thought it might be the boy who had been sent to the infirmary. I watched them walk out to the fields and dig, and as lightning filled the sky I could see rain running off their clothes. It lit up the large sack they had carried, a rough sack that was the coffin of a nine-year-old boy, and I watched, helpless, as they pitched him into the muddy grave and covered it over with earth. A week or so later I saw a kid wearing the boy's jacket. He said he had picked it up in storage for five bucks. They buried him in the very fields where we work.'

Jay did not know whether to believe the older boy. He asked him why he stayed on at such a terrible place.

'To help kids like you. To teach you to escape.'

That was the first time Jay ran away. They caught him, on galloping horses, *carrying rifles*, before he was even a mile away from the main dormitory building. They incarcerated him in a dark cellar with another boy, who was suffering from malnutrition. Cold meals were brought down for Jay, but nothing for the other boy, so he shared his food. In return, although he asked for nothing and expected nothing, the boy gave him a rough map of the area, including the sewer system through which he had once tried to escape.

'Go north. You'll find a garage about twenty miles from here. The guy there offered us food and water, said we could stay the night there if we helped him clean the pumps. When we woke up we were back here. The bastard must have called them and turned us in,' the boy moaned. 'Unless we had been dreaming.'

The next day he was let out of the cellar and Jay never saw him again.

Two days later, Jay also came out into the sunlight which was so bright it blinded him.

Susan got a far better deal.

She was sent to live with a young couple who cared for her and loved her.

A child of their own had been their dream, but after two miscarriages they decided it was not meant to be. They had been warned it was dangerous to try again, fatal even. But they loved Susan, and she loved them back – although she missed Jay unbearably and sometimes found herself upsetting her guardians with her sadness.

Then Jay came for her.

A month after he'd been let out of the cellar, with a store of fruit and other food he'd been able to hoard, and having memorised the map, he slipped into the smelly underground drainage system – a journey he would never forget – and made his way to freedom.

He did not come to save or rescue Susan.

She liked her new home and guardians.

He simply came one night and spirited her away. She left her foster-parents a rambling explanatory note telling them not to worry, that she would be fine, and that her untimely departure was not their fault. She could not express that sentiment deeply enough. She promised to be in touch, and a tearful reunion lay in her future.

Until she met them again, Susan was rarely free of the guilt she felt for leaving them so heartlessly, those kind and trusting people.

When Jay told her his tale, about life at his home, he painted a dark picture, but not nearly as dark and bad as it had been in reality. He made life there sound almost comic, and the escape like an exciting game.

Along the 500-mile trek to Canberra there had been a couple of close calls, but try as they might, the guardians could never capture him. His love for Susan would not let them, and it was this love which had driven him on, fuelled him during the hard times. The real reason he had escaped was so that they could be together again.

And for Susan and Jay, that was how it should be. Always.

'The dogs,' Jay whispered softly.

'What?' Kamski asked. He had been sitting, listening quietly, as the young cop with the haunted face relived a powerful part of his past.

'The kid ... in the cellar,' Jay remembered slowly.

'He said he was down there for killing the dogs. A week or so earlier a couple of dogs had been slaughtered with a knife from the kitchen. He said he'd done it. Do you—?'

Kamski was already nodding. 'It's worth checking out. I'll get someone on it.'

Jay had been pouring his whole life out to Kamski, his whole relationship with Susan, and now he knew why.

Was it possible that he and the killer – as children – *had lived in the same place?* That he had known him as a boy, and they had been friends, companions in a dark place? That they had shared dreams and food in a dark cellar, alone?

Jay was shaking his head slowly, the idea disgusting him.

'What's wrong?' Kamski asked, but Jay was silent, lost in these new disturbing thoughts.

Was it possible that they were both victims of a brutal society, only Jay had adapted a little better, survived with his soul intact? That one had grown up good, the other bad ... and they were destined to live parallel lives, their paths occasionally crossing?

As they would cross once more.

'He killed her,' Jay whispered, tears slipping out silently.

He had taken his sister's free and kindred spirit – just talking about her somehow kept her alive – and destroyed it.

Susan was the best there ever was...

'I'm sorry, Jay,' Kamski said, and placed a hand on

his shoulder. 'You have to believe that. But I cannot cut you loose so that you can catch up with this psychopath in another city, and shoot up their streets. Caldwell asked us to detain you, for your own good. I hope that one day you will understand that.'

'But he's not *in* another city,' Jay argued, beginning to think like the killer – a sadistic sonofabitch who killed for the thrill, for the rush, like a primitive addict. It did not matter who he killed, so long as he did it, and for the first time ever, the bastard had a motive. Twisted revenge.

'He's still in Detroit,' Jay persisted. 'You've seen the tape, and I was there in the store. *I heard him*. He's pissed off at the cops, and he wants me. I think he knows it's personal. He's still in Detroit, and he will kill again. Trust me on this, will you? He owes us, and as far as he's concerned, it's payback time.'

'I don't think so,' Kamski said, unsure.

Jay sighed, defeated. What did it take to convince these people? They were dealing with a man who killed for pleasure, who found joy in other people's pain and misery. A sick, *sick* man ... And he was out there, stalking the people of Detroit.

What did it take to convince Kamski of that?

'He's out of the city – as you will be in a couple of days. Back in Manhattan.'

'No way, Captain,' Jay said firmly, shaking his head. No way.

He would be following the killer, always following ... until their final confrontation. Until it was over.

Chapter Eight
Dangerous Love

When Detective Caan approached the house in Sycamore Avenue later that day, about five-fifteen as the air was beginning to cool, Gale did not even recognise him. His hair was combed, or at least washed which was a start, and he was clean-shaven. He wore a white shirt and a fashionable tie, and a pair of black slacks. The only thing that marred this new image was the Nike running shoes. Gale had absolutely nothing against Nike, but leather shoes would have been more fitting.

Unaware of Gale's secret appraisal, James Caan looked down the street to where the black and white patrol car was parked. It would have been closer at the end of the driveway, but deep down he knew that the end of the street was the best place for it, especially since it was only three houses away. He raised his hand, and Officer Shue returned the wave.

Shue laughed, and then watched with subdued amazement as Savoy, his much younger partner, managed to put a whole doughnut in his mouth.

'Caan's dressed up for a wedding,' Shue observed. 'You're disgusting, do you know that?'

The answer was a long time coming. Savoy tried to reply immediately, but as soggy morsels of doughnut fell from his mouth he only succeeded in cracking himself up, so that it took even longer for the words to emerge.

'That's right,' he laughed.

Most of the doughnut was still mashed up in his mouth, and Shue turned away. 'How did I ever end up with you for a partner?'

'You're just lucky, I guess.'

'Yeah ... the worst kind of luck.'

Savoy had been his partner for just over a year now, and they respected each other to the highest degree, the idle banter never getting out of hand. They were good friends.

As Caan knocked on the door, he thought about the man at the back of the house.

Alan Hawkins.

An ex-Vietnam weapons expert who was an outcast at the Precinct, Hawkins was regarded as an oddball by most of the cops, and they did not like working with him. Kamski usually kept him locked away in a closet, out of sight of the public, because when he let him out it was like unleashing a beast. You did not assign him cases, you let him loose on them.

But Hawkins was good at what he did do, and often his experiences counted for more than just disturbing memories.

Times like now.

Hawkins was situated in the trees at the back of Karin's house, at the bottom of her garden. It was not a forest, nor even a small piece of woodland; it was about forty trees, and that was more than enough to hide Hawkins among the leaves and brush, camouflaged and sweating in the heat.

He had drowsed fitfully for a few hours in the afternoon, sleeping light, and was waking now, as the sun began to near the horizon.

Caan was confident in Hawkins's ability to remain unseen until the moment was right. No matter what happened – if anything – they would always have Hawkins, their ace in the hole.

Karin opened the door and let Caan walk through the small hallway into the living room.

'Hello, Detective,' she said. 'Gale's sleeping upstairs. I'll go wake her.'

At this, Caan almost jumped out of his seat. 'Oh, don't bother. This was just a social call, nothing important. I just thought, you know, that maybe ...'

Caan found himself shuffling his feet nervously, unable to find the right words. He felt like a kid, a nerd, trying to ask the prettiest girl to the Prom.

Karin laughed. She found it amusing that a mature man, a *cop*, was struggling to pluck up the courage to ask her little sister out.

'After all this, I think it can only do her good,' she told him.

'You and Joshua better grab some clothes too. I'm moving you out to a safe house,' Caan told her, confident now that he was back on his own ground.

'Why? I thought you said we'd be safe here.'

'I don't want to take any chances,' he told her, and smiled. His look was soft and gentle, but with firm determination behind it. She felt reassured, and nodded, before making her way up the stairs to wake Gale.

Caan paced about the room, sweaty-palmed and nervous.

The plan he had formulated during the afternoon was not the reason for his discomfort. It was clever, and he was confident that it would go smoothly. Officers Kerwin Dubois and Cindy Williams were already here, having slipped in unobtrusively about an hour before Caan. They were waiting in the basement until Karin and Joshua left. Then they would come up and play their roles to perfection – move about the house, watch television. All the excitement of a young married couple – well, not quite *all*.

About nine they would retire to the bedroom, where they would wait, and wait – until morning if necessary, and then repeat the routine through the next day and night.

Some time after nine, Caan would return with Detective Laura Irving. Thanks to the wonders of make-up and a good wig, she was the twin Gale never had.

They would retire to the other bedroom.

He smiled, a part of him, a small molecule hiding in the back of his mind, hoping the killer showed tonight.

They were ready, the plan perfect ...

It was the date with Gale that made him nervous.

Caan looked at the various pictures that lined the walls, and the knick-knacks – especially an attractive collection of delicate dancing horses – that were everywhere. The room was awash with the objects that make a home, not like his own untidy apartment. He wondered how much time Karin and Joshua actually spent in here. To him, living like a slob as he did, the room seemed almost like a museum, everything having its place, and remaining there.

Yet he could remember a time when he, too, had lived like this ... and with tears in his eyes he took out his wallet and removed a small, ripped photograph of Kelly. He looked at the happy, bubbling curves of her face for a second before replacing the picture, hating himself for everything that had happened to her ... *her face bleeding, the pain as they raped her, the anger as they cut her, all the time the gun pushing on his throat, his hands tied, the horror and hatred as they murdered her* ... he wiped the tears out of his eyes and returned to his study of the room, observing, because that was part of his job.

Most of one wall was a huge French window which led out onto a stone patio. Caan walked over to the glass and looked out at the gentle slope of the garden, at the bottom of which stood the trees in which Hawkins was hidden.

Caan could not see him.

'Hawkins, you sonofabitch,' he whispered.

Hawkins watched Caan through the compact binoculars he held and smiled because he knew he could not be seen.

From the low branch he sat on he had a perfect view of the back of the house, and also along the left wall. Through the different windows – using the binoculars – he could also see a large percentage of the interior. When Caan turned from the window, Hawkins replaced the binoculars in the green rifle bag.

If the police knew of the personal armoury he had brought with him, Hawkins would probably be spending a large part of the rest of his life growing old in a dirty cell.

In the bag . . . was the M.16 assault rifle, with an M.40 under-over grenade launcher attached to it, and the Colt .45 longslide, boasting a laser sight for pinpoint accuracy. Just put the red dot on what you want to hit, and pull the trigger. Boom, baby! There was also a nightscope inside for when it got dark, and a Mach 10 machine pistol. Finally, clipped onto his belt in a sheath, was a large hunting knife.

Everything, even the blade of the knife, was painted a dull black so that it would not reflect any light and give his presence away.

Hawkins was not a cop, he was a survivor. He had taken all they had taught him in Vietnam, and adapted his particular skills to the society in which he now lived. Rules and regulations meant nothing to him. He never investigated cases – he closed them.

Hawkins got the job done.

He had heard some pretty bad shit down at the Precinct. Sick rumours about the guy they were after. He had even killed a cop's sister. If he got the slightest opportunity, Hawkins was going to bag him.

'Caan wants to take you out,' Karin told her sister.

They giggled like schoolgirls as she told Gale how shy and nervous he was, this macho cop who could not even ask a woman out to dinner, however unusual the circumstances.

'Do you mean it?' Gale asked.

'Yes,' Karin replied, and then put a serious face on, repressing her laughter. 'He really likes you.'

Gale laughed wildly, and then began searching through her sister's closets for something to wear, and look good in. But then she caught sight of her reflection in the mirror.

'Oh my God. Look at me,' she complained.

'He obviously has,' Karin joked, then realised that her sister was genuinely upset. 'He really does like you, I mean that. He won't care how you look, so I don't think you should, either. I think you could weigh three hundred pounds and have five chins, and he would still have fallen for you.'

'Get outta here,' Gale giggled, and resumed her search for something nice to wear.

'I mean it. He's acting like Joshua when he first asked me out – a bag of nerves. I virtually had to do it for him.' Karin smiled as she remembered the moment. Even the word exquisite did not seem good enough to describe it. She brushed sandy hair away from her face. 'Look what happened to us.'

While Gale took a quick shower, Karin made herself a cup of coffee and gave Caan a Coke from the icebox. In some ways, he seemed like an innocent child at heart. A lost child? No, not lost; the man must have a map or some kind of guide, because he survived so well in the world of violence and brutality that he chose to inhabit.

Angie was excited when she saw Dwight's car pull up outside her house. When he opened the car door, she could see his bag and knew that he hadn't gone home yet. This was his first port of call. She had good news for him, and the fact that he had come here before seeing Ellen made her doubly pleased.

After only seven weeks on the market she had managed to find a buyer for the expensive and difficult Gleason property, and she'd only had to bring the price down 5000 dollars. The property was out in the middle of nowhere, a couple of miles from the edge of town. A doctor believed it would make the perfect retirement home for him and his wife. They were a sweet couple, scented by nostalgia.

There was a knock on the door, soft and gentle, yet firm like his touch. She walked into the hall, barefoot and naked except for the extra large T-shirt she wore with the motif *When You Got It Up, Keep It Up* emblazoned across the front ... and when she was around, she knew that was not difficult.

She put the chain on the door and opened it slightly, just enough to peek out.

'Yes?' she said, pretending that she did not know him.

'Quit fooling around,' he replied, and pushed at the door – roughly, considering his soft touch.

She had to be quick to flip the chain off, but she did it before it pulled taut. Dwight walked in and quickly shut the door. Perhaps he was nervous about coming, about being seen with her here.

'Relax,' she eased. 'We work together, remember?' She wrapped her arms about his neck and reached up to kiss him on the mouth.

As they went into the living room he still seemed preoccupied, and she decided it had to be more than being at her home.

'How was your trip?'

He walked to the drinks cabinet and poured himself a straight vodka, filling the glass. 'Fine,' he said.

She led him to the sofa by his tie, and then pushed him onto it, spilling some of the drink. She was eagerly anticipating the love they were going to make, but first she had to ease his mind, lay his worries to rest.

'I have some news,' she said. 'I found a buyer for the Gleason property.' And she laughed happily, her mouth breaking into a huge grin.

Dwight did not share her excitement. He raised the glass to his lips, and even though his hand was not visibly shaking, she could see the drink trembling on the surface.

'What's wrong, honey?' she asked, pleading with him

to trust her, and tell her what was troubling him. She felt a foolish twinge of jealousy, that he would tell Ellen what was wrong as soon as he got home. That if she pushed the subject, she would lose him to Ellen.

But that would not happen.

If he told anyone what Griffen had said, it would be Angie – especially since it almost concerned her. But certainly not his wife – Ellen, he corrected – with her practicality and sensibilities. He could not tell her because she was too plain, and would not understand what he was doing with Griffen.

Angie would understand.

And she could be persuaded to see that what he was doing was right.

But not yet...

'Nothing.'

His response was bland and flat, and she did not believe him. However, she decided to drop the subject for now. She had to distract Dwight from his problems, make him forget what was worrying him. And she knew the perfect way to do that.

She took the glass, recalling how the vodka had trembled at the mention of the Gleason place ... now that had instilled fear in her heart. She leaned forward and found his mouth with hers.

They made angry love on the sofa, and then moved to the bedroom where they slept.

It was nightfall when Dwight woke, drowning in darkness.

He had to get back home to end all this.

He was basically a good guy, but he could feel a rottenness slowly eating away at his insides. Taking all the good away.

He rose silently, making sure that he did not disturb Angie. He wanted to be back before she woke, sleeping at her side. He did not want to have to explain where he was going, or why. It was going to be difficult enough as it was.

He had to end it now.

'There are two men waiting for you at the end of your garden, just inside the tree-line. They are Detectives Wright and Slater,' Caan explained to Karin and Joshua. 'They look mean, but actually have hearts of gold. They will take you to the safe house.'

Karin hugged her sister, tears in her eyes. After finding her, Karin suddenly had a bad feeling ... that she would never see Gale again.

'See you soon,' Gale told them brightly.

'Let's go,' Joshua whispered, nodding to Caan and softly taking his wife's hand.

Gale watched them walk down the garden. As they reached the trees, they turned back and waved. Then they were gone ...

None of them saw Hawkins watching, looking down from his perch.

The battleground was clear.

'Adios ...'

Gale did not know what to expect. She wasn't even sure

why Detective Caan was taking her out, but she was glad that he was. She didn't really care whether he was attracted to her or not. For all she knew, although she seriously doubted it, he might be using her to draw the killer into the open.

She was just pleased to have somebody out with her. Somebody she didn't really know taking an interest in her welfare, taking her mind off what had happened, however closely associated with it they were. If Caan was not here now, she would no doubt be at the safe house on her own, moaning about what had happened and crying herself to sleep.

He didn't tell her where they were going, although they were both dressed for something special. She wore one of Karin's dresses. Her sister was fourteen pounds heavier, so it had been a case of finding something that fitted reasonably well and looked OK. Gale had discovered a red dress, simple in design, pretty but not too revealing. For once, Gale was not flaunting herself, as she had done so often in the past. Besides which, being too big, the dress kind of hung on her and was not as tight as it should be. With it, she wore a pair of red heels, and a leather jacket over the dress.

All through the drive she had worried about how she looked, but Caan told her she was fine. Perhaps she was hoping for something more than *fine*, but taking into account her facial injuries – with the make-up doing a poor job of hiding the bruises – Gale knew that anything more, like 'gorgeous' for instance, was not really possible.

She hoped they weren't headed for some upscale restaurant, but did not say so in case he'd made reservations and she destroyed his surprise. She was afraid that people would stare at her. She did not want that kind of pressure. She just wanted to let her hair down and have some fun. Have a good time, so that she could forget who she had once been, and what had happened...

The car stopped unexpectedly.

'Here we are.'

She looked around. They were nowhere. The car was parked halfway down a dirty block, with shoddy buildings that looked like they were about to fall down.

'What is it?' she asked, afraid to get out of the car.

'A movie theatre.'

She couldn't prevent the surprised laughter that escaped her lips. *A movie theatre?* It wasn't even one of those flash multi-plexes with twenty-one screens or more. It was ... she did not know what it was. The façade under which they had parked was scummy, and there were no posters advertising what was on.

She was pleasantly surprised when they walked off the street and into the theatre lobby. It was clean and smart, and her original doubts were soon replaced by a sense of wonder.

Instead of posters advertising current or future programmes, the walls were lined with elaborately-framed stills from classic movies. Gale was fascinated. This was no ordinary movie theatre – nor was it anything as simple as a revival house.

This place was something very special . . . somebody's dream.

Everything about it had a personal touch, and as she wandered through the lobby she stopped to look at glass display cases of all sizes, containing what must be original props and costumes.

'I had a buddy at school,' Caan explained as he followed her around. 'We were like, real best friends, you know? Nothing traumatic ever happened between us, but we were always there for each other. Anyway, until I met him, the movie theatre was just a dark place to go with a girl, but he taught me to love movies, and to appreciate them. He was a real movie buff. We would have conversations, and until he told me later – even though everything fit into what we were talking about – I would never realise that everything he'd said was taken from one movie or another. This place is his, Gale. It belongs to him. He's responsible to nobody but himself, shows whatever movies he likes, whether they are popular or not, and there is always an audience. As he used to tell me, usually after we had sat through some trash: "Remember, every film is somebody's favourite".'

'This is incredible,' she breathed. 'This whole place, it must have cost a fortune.'

'Not really.'

The new voice surprised her, and she turned to see a man who must have been roughly the same age as Caan, yet who looked so much younger. Obviously, being a cop, especially a good one, must be an incredible strain.

All the trauma, the midnight phone calls, the long days and longer nights – it all extracted a toll from the human body, and mind.

The man had dark hair which he left long. He was tall, with a confident air about him. He was sure of himself. Sure that he could do no wrong, and that others would do no wrong while in his presence.

'I inherited the place from a relative so distant I didn't even know he existed. He probably heard of my infatuation with the movies, and figured I would do more with the building than just have it boarded up. When I got hold of it, this place was a mess. I pumped a lot of my own money into it, and turned it around. Now, although it looks bleak from the outside, I have enough regulars to keep the place open and cover my costs. It's just a hobby really, like the movies have always been,' he said, and then introduced himself, leaning forward with graceful flamboyance to kiss the back of her hand. 'Bruce Truman.'

'You always were a charmer,' Caan said, and it was Truman's turn to be surprised. He hadn't realised his old friend was there.

Gale was grateful that Truman had made no reference to the condition of her face. She was beginning to forget what had happened, and to enjoy the date. She watched with marvel as the two men slipped into an easy banter.

'You know,' Bruce said, 'I was just telling a girl I'm seeing about how I know James Caan. At first she asked who the great James Caan was, so I told her he was Paul

Sheldon from *Misery* – she's a big Stephen King fan ... and she refused to believe me.'

'They never do believe you,' Caan sighed. 'Do you want me to give her my autograph?'

Gale watched and laughed, at first hesitantly as she wondered if what they were doing was legal, while he signed a photo of James Caan – the actor, not the cop. It was a private joke she had been let in on – one they had been performing for as long as either of them could remember.

It only worked in the beginning, anyway. Sooner or later the fans wanted to meet the star, at which point the truth was always revealed. There had never been any hard feelings.

'On your gravestone, it's gonna read *James Caan – But Not The Actor*,' Bruce joked, and they all laughed.

'He's not dead yet,' Gale said, and placed her arm around Caan's back.

She held him tight and did not want to let go. She felt good in his company, at ease after what she'd been through. She wanted him to hold her close ... wanted to be with him.

'Salty Ashbrook said you have a print of *Miracle Mile*,' Caan said, and tentatively placed his arm around Gale's shoulder.

Miracle Mile was his all-time favourite movie – a love story set amid a field of horror as a musician learns by mistake that a nuclear war has begun and that missiles will hit the city in just over an hour. Caan had only seen it once. Paid fifty bucks entry at a trashy horror-film festival, and *Miracle Mile* had been the only movie he liked.

'I have,' Bruce replied, and smiled.

It was good to see Caan with a woman again. Ever since the death of Kelly he had been an emotional corpse. It was good to see him learning to live again.

Gale really enjoyed the film, having not been to the movies since she was a kid. She had been frightened in all the right places, and by the end was appropriately in tears.

Afterwards, they decided to stop for pizza.

'How long exactly have you known Bruce? Since you were in grade school, you said,' she asked, hungrily eating garlic bread, not realising how starving she'd been.

'We go back a long way. There was a time when we drifted apart, but then came Vietnam, when everybody was your friend. By the time you came out, a bond was formed and shared by everyone who survived that hell.'

As he spoke, he stopped eating and looked thoughtfully into her eyes.

'Survival was all that counted then. Out there we all learned to appreciate how valuable life really is. Bruce pulled my ass out of the bush once. Some heavy shit went down that night ... fire everywhere. We were on regular foot patrol when the ambush hit us, and a lot of men went down early. Then our own air support hit us.'

She stared into his eyes and saw flaming napalm tears forming deep and slowly coming forward.

'We were all dead or dying. A lot of good men were lost

that night – napalm clinging to their bodies, bullets hitting them from nowhere ... from everywhere. I had been hit in the leg and could not walk – figured I might as well be dead. I watched them – the Cong – coming out of the ground, out of their tunnels and holes in the ground, and placed the barrel of my rifle to my mouth. Then Bruce found me. I did not know it, but he had taken a bullet in his arm and yet he still managed to haul my sorry ass out of there.'

As Caan spoke, his eyes had clouded over, and gone misty with remembrance. *The heat, the burning horror, the screaming and confusion.* It was a time he would never forget, yet one he would always want to. And that was the same for everybody who had been there.

It had been a nightmare come true.

She watched as silent tears fell from his eyes and down his cheeks, and to bring him out of the terrible past she placed a soothing hand on his thigh – under the table, out of sight – and rubbed gently.

He was the most compassionate man she had ever met. Nobody had ever opened up to her like that. With her other hand she softly touched his cheeks and wiped the tears away.

'Where do you live?'

As Caldwell came down the Precinct steps he saw that the streets of Manhattan were unusually busy, with cars pumping pollution into the atmosphere like there was no tomorrow. He watched as they crawled by, bumper to bumper, and decided it would be quicker to walk home. In the morning he could get a cab into work, or Teressa could drop him off in her station wagon.

The walk would also give him a chance to think.

An efficient, if irritable-sounding Captain Kamski of the Detroit Police Department had called him earlier, saying there had been some trouble in Detroit. Several people had been killed and, as Kamski put it, 'a rogue cop out of his jurisdiction' had been involved.

'Jay Austin,' Caldwell had said, the first words to pass his lips before he even thought about what Kamski had said. There had been a slow, silent pause and Caldwell could imagine Kamski nodding: 'So he is one of yours?'

The conversation had gone on from there, resulting in Caldwell asking Kamski to detain Jay. He would have preferred it if Jay was back home, out of harm's way, but there was still the unmentioned question of charges being brought against him. He was under arrest at the moment, and would have to be escorted back.

I don't think he will do anything now. He's intelligent, and a damn fine cop. I don't know how much he had to do with those deaths, but he will know he has gone too far...

When he reached home, Caldwell was in a quiet, contemplative mood. Teressa cooked him a meal, and a pleasant aroma rose from the steaming food, washing through his nostrils. But all he could do was take a couple of small bites, and then push the food about with his fork while he thought.

'What's wrong?' Teressa asked, slightly annoyed that she had cooked him a proper meal just to see him neglect it, and play with it like a child.

'Where are the children?' Caldwell asked.

He seemed to see them less and less these days, as his work became ever more demanding. Julian was sixteen in less than three weeks, and his parents still hadn't made arrangements for his party, or bought him any presents. The kids were growing up too quickly; long gone were the days of dirty diapers and waking in the middle of the night to the sound of a baby crying. Caldwell missed those times.

'Lorraine is at a party – an all-nighter at Nichola's. We discussed it last week, remember? We decided she could go so long as she called home first thing in the morning, and so long as she did stay at Nichola's home. Plus the usual – no drugs, no excessive drinking, no driving until morning.'

Caldwell did not remember discussing the party, but knew that Teressa would not have come up with such strict and rigid stipulations. Good times ... good times, and rock and roll. That was all being young meant these days – no responsibility, no real respect. Nothing learned in preparation for the outside world, on the edge of which they party, waiting to fall into it, unwilling ... frightened.

'I called them earlier,' Teressa continued. 'Sounded like they were having quite a ball. Julian's gone to watch a couple of movies with his friends. Said he would be back late.'

And that was going to stop soon as well. Caldwell thought. The streets of New York were worse than ever, and there was more scum out there than Caldwell had ever known. Nobody was safe, not even the cops. And his own son was out there, wandering the streets, coming in when he pleased. That had to stop.

But for now it was good that the kids were both out. They liked Jay, and he didn't want them to hear what he had to say.

'Jay's in trouble,' he told his wife.

She sat down opposite him, a cup of coffee in her hands, and watched as he continued playing with the food until she pulled the plate away. It had gone beyond annoyance and irritation. Her husband was in an almost catatonic state, beginning to scare her.

'What happened?'

'Do you remember Susan, his sister? You met her nearly a year ago when we had them both over for dinner, and then a couple of months later when Jay arranged that surprise party for her.'

'Yes, I remember. What is it, Alan?' she asked, her fear growing.

'Susan has been murdered.'

'Oh God!' Teressa exclaimed, shocked. 'Is Jay—' She placed the cup on the table, afraid she was going to drop it.

'No. He took it badly. I thought he would be OK, but that whore Cyndi has just left him, and he's . . . well, he's not too good. He's been drinking heavily, and the last time I saw him he looked pretty bad. He left for Detroit, believing that was where the killer has gone. Something bad happened there – a murder, a chase, a lot of shooting. People are dead, Teressa. Jay is in real trouble.'

Caan knocked twice and the door of the apartment safe home opened.

'Any problems?' Caan asked as he walked in.

'Yeah,' Slater grumbled. 'The pizza kid is late.'

'And the cable doesn't work,' Wright complained.

'Where are the O'Bannons?'

'Sleeping in the bedroom,' Slater said.

'Yeah, but they were making some noise earlier. Who needs cable?' Wright grinned.

'Irving?'

'Bathroom,' Wright said, and pointed.

Slater knocked heavily on the door. 'You about ready, sweetheart?'

Laura Irving walked out of the bathroom, and Caan whistled. 'Didn't I just leave you in my bedr—?'

'I don't wanna hear it,' she snapped, a small grin on her lips. 'I just don't wanna know.'

She was bigger than Gale, broader in the shoulders and hips. The red dress Gale had been wearing tonight would probably have been a good fit on the police-woman. There was a certain familiarity in her features and, of course, the clothes and make-up helped.

At a distance they would look identical, even though Caan could see differences up close, in the light.

'Let's go to work,' he said.

* * *

The evening dusk turned slowly to dark nightfall, and the grey clouds boiled, a heavy storm brewing. It was nearly four hours since Caan had left the house in Sycamore Avenue with Gale Anne Hurd.

Savoy looked bored as he watched the silent, empty street, drinking lukewarm coffee straight from the flask.

'That's disgusting,' Shue commented automatically.

'No, I'll tell you what's disgusting – the fact that Caan is out wining and dining that babe Gale Anne, while we're here drinking cold coffee. Answer me this – was she as hot as I remember?'

'Hotter. I could get in the sack with her—'

'*I'm* disgusting? Listen to you. You're married,' Savoy reminded him. 'I can't believe you just said that. You have a wife and kids.'

'I am married, and I do have children,' Shue confessed. 'But did you see her ass in that dress?'

'I did. I really saw it. I'm proud to have seen it. Having seen it, I think I can understand your slight infidelity and loss of ethics and morals,' Savoy joked, knowing that Shue would never be unfaithful to Maria.

'That's right!' Shue laughed.

They did their best to alleviate the boredom and eventually, their conversation drifted from the dimensions of Gale Anne's butt to other, less significant topics.

In the trees at the back of the house Hawkins had nobody to talk to, but he was not bored. As he sat looking through the nightscope, occasionally lowering it from his eye so that he could get a broader view of the house, he played games in his mind.

What would happen if the killer approached the house from the left end of the street? Or the right? What would happen if he came through the trees, and passed directly under Hawkins? What would happen if ... *it could never happen, you're too good for that* ... he discovered Hawkins? If he didn't spot the killer until he was already in the house? What if? What if...?

'There he is, there he is!' Savoy cried, like a child seeing Santa for the first time in Bloomingdale's, excited as Caan's car pulled back into the driveway.

They watched as their buddy climbed from the car, and jogged around it to open the other door, then stared in amazement as, laughing and smiling, the couple went inside.

'The horny bastard is actually going in,' Shue observed, grinning. 'I never knew Irving could look so hot.'

At the door, Caan leaned in and kissed Irving lightly on the cheek.

'Go for it, Detective Caan!' Savoy shouted, banging his fist on the dashboard like some kind of demented Neanderthal high-school football player.

The trap was baited.

Hawkins, alert, spotted the light flicker on at the front of the house through a door which was open a crack. Eventually they would come through and he would see who was downstairs. It was obviously not the killer, so he decided to call through to Shue and Savoy, see what they had.

Hawkins wore a small, thin headset which was a combination of both earphones and microphone; this came down the side of his face from his ear in a thin metal strip and then, at his chin, hooked around so that it was an inch from his mouth, ready to pick up the slightest whisper. It was an elaborate set-up, much easier than forever having to remove a radio from his belt every time he wanted to open his mouth.

He looked at his watch.

'It's nine-fifty. I got a light on at the front of the house.'

Shue pushed the speech button on the car radio.

'Yeah. Relax, Rambo. It's just Romeo come back off his date.'

Shue made no attempt to hide the contempt he felt for Hawkins. The man was not a cop. He was a deranged psychotic with a badge. Shue had only worked with him once before, on what should have been a routine bust. Thanks to the trigger-happy heroics of Hawkins, he'd found himself walking out of a massacre. He was dangerous, and Shue believed he should not be on the force. If he didn't carry a badge, the man would be living out his years in solitary confinement. He was a madman who believed you should shoot first and ask questions later ... only with Hawkins, the questions were irrelevant, since he shot to kill and rarely missed.

Hawkins sat in the trees, unfazed by the hostility he picked up in Shue's voice. If it ever did bother him, he could always lose the headset. But that would piss Caan off if he ever found out. It would be irrational and unwise to remove the headset ... yet.

He knew – ever since the Granger bust had turned sour, and possibly earlier when his reputation preceded everything he did – that Shue disliked him, maybe even hated him. But for now he had to ignore that because they were on the same team, and he personally had nothing against Shue.

If he was given a chance to show his unique abilities over the next couple of days, they would learn to appreciate him.

Ellen lay in bed, watching time tick slowly by on the small LED readout of the electronic clock which was the only light in the room. In the complete darkness and silence it was easier to think; with nothing to see or hear, there were only her thoughts for company. Nothing could influence them. They were all her own, and the darkness kept them that way. But if she switched a light on, then Dwight would be everywhere ... his book on the bedside table, his glasses, his clothes ... all these things and so much more could intensify the pain within her. Even now, she believed his scent lingered in the air.

She had called the airport and found out that there was only one plane due in from the city today, and that would be arriving about noon. At two, giving Dwight plenty of time to get home, she had called the airport again.

The clerk then ran a check for her.

'It landed at twelve eleven, a little late because it had to fly high to avoid a bad storm. Mr Little was booked in seat 34a, an aisle seat by request and yes, he was on board.'

She thanked the clerk and hung up.

An aisle seat – that was Dwight all right. She smiled at the thought of the storm. He was afraid to fly, afraid to even look out of the window. Unless he made a friend real fast, somebody to talk to and take his mind off the flight, he would have spent the trip sweaty-palmed, clinging to his seat.

He should be back by now.

And he was, Ellen supposed. He was at *her* place, getting a quick one in before he returned to continue his deception and lies. She wondered how long he'd been having the affair. It sickened her that for months, years even, his love had been nothing but an act, a lie, with no purpose except to fool her. She hated him for that, for not having had the courage to tell her.

Yet the truth hurt so much, and if she was going to believe it, she knew that she would have to be force-fed the information. It would have to be rammed down her throat, where it would cut deep into her heart. A wound that would never heal.

Twelve eleven ...

She looked at the LED readout, floating in a sea of darkness.

Twelve eleven ... and now it was midnight.

She was crying, but did not realise it. These were not

tears of sadness; she had already shed those. These were the bitter, angry tears of acceptance, the start of the healing process. With each tear a part of Dwight left her, another part of him was excised from her system.

She smiled through the tears because she actually felt better.

Suddenly, in the silence of the night she clearly heard the sound of a key working in the lock outside. He was home – no, she corrected herself. He was back. This would never be his home again.

She listened as he moved through the sprawling bungalow.

She made no effort to wipe the tears away. Let him see them. Let him see the hurt he had caused.

The door swung open ... *twelve twenty-seven* ... a moment of time she would never forget – and his hand reached in, instinctively finding the light switch. The sudden brightness caused her to squint, and it took a few seconds for her eyes to readjust, by which time Dwight was across the room and at her side.

'What's wrong?' he asked, genuine concern filling his eyes and voice. He reached forward to touch her softly, but she pulled away.

'Don't touch me.'

She looked into his eyes and deep, deep down knew that even though he no longer loved her, he still cared for her. It was a small consolation, and on the surface she could not bring herself to believe it. She turned away from him looking straight ahead, like a horse with blinkers on.

'Who is she? Just tell me – so I don't have to hear it from the gossips one day.' She refused to choke on the sobs she was fighting to contain, and spoke without emotion.

'Oh Jesus,' he whispered, and fell back. 'I'm sorry.'

She realised that even though she had come out of this the worst, a part of him was dying tonight too. She was the victim, but he was a victim to his own love for another woman. It did not matter how long the affair had been going on, just that their marriage was over, and that he was hurting too. He still cared for her, and she would always remember that as long as she lived. She had lost him, but it had been through no fault of her own.

He was crying as he hugged her. He pulled her close and tight. 'I'm so sorry,' he whispered in her ear.

'Who?' she begged. To her surprise, she found herself raising her arms and returning his hug. '*Who?*'

'Angie,' he whispered. 'Angie ... from the office. I'm really sorry, Ellen. I never meant for this, for any of this. For you to get hurt—'

'Oh stop! Please!'

Ellen did not want to hear his apologies or excuses. She was simply grateful that she did not know Angie very well. If they were close, she probably would have ripped her eyes out.

Why couldn't Dwight come to the phone all those times, Angie dear?

'Leave me,' she stated flatly.

It was a hard command, and he knew it would be best

for both of them if he left. But he hated to see her in this state, and he hated himself for causing it.

'It was my fault,' he told her. 'All my fault. You had nothing to do with any of it. I mean – you're a good woman, Ellen.'

Ellen was sobbing. She knew he meant well, and that he was being sincere. And she appreciated his honesty, grateful that he had not tried to deny her accusations, that he had not made pathetic excuses for his actions. It was simply something that had happened. But she could not forgive him. Given time the wounds would heal, but at the moment they were open and bleeding. One day they might be good friends, but not yet ... not for a long while.

Dwight knew he'd better leave before he started having second thoughts. He was already beginning to doubt what he was doing.

'Goodbye, Ellen,' he whispered, and let go of her hand.

He switched the light off as he slipped back through the door, leaving her in darkness once more, alone ...

Goodbye, Dwight.

'The kiss was a nice touch,' Irving smiled, as they walked into the kitchen. 'You want anything?'

Caan reached into the fridge and pulled out a can of Coke. It was virtually all he drank these days.

'That stuff must be rotting your insides,' Laura commented.

Caan smiled. It was better than the bottle.

'Probably be rumours all over the Precinct tomorrow,' she grinned. 'Especially with Shue and Savoy out there.'

'Yeah,' Caan said, lost for a second in memories of Kelly and thoughts of Gale. He was looking forward to returning to his apartment, where Gale was waiting ... where they would make love again.

'Wow!' Laura exclaimed. 'Fudge cake.'

Kerwin Dubois and Cindy Williams were not only partners. They had a close understanding of each other; an understanding that would be even closer for the fact that in three weeks they would be married and embarking on a two-month tour of Europe.

In the Academy they had been told stories by old and experienced cops of how relationships, friendships even, had failed because of the long, strenuous, and often threatening hours a cop has to work, because of the risk he or she is always under. Like many police officers of their generation, however, Dubois and Williams had found a relationship within the force, and although they were not perfect for each other – is anybody? – they were good together.

Cindy smiled, lying under the covers in full uniform, her husband-to-be at her side.

In three weeks they would be on their way to Europe – nothing but snow-capped mountains and old log cabins, with open fires burning. Nothing but dewy fields and Continental love.

The rain came down heavy, announced by loud claps of

thunder and bright flashes of lightning. Hawkins pulled a hood over his head, careful not to dislodge the headset, even though the branches above provided limited cover. Occasionally the rain would break through as the wind changed direction, and he listened to it dance and patter on the waterproof hood.

Hawkins looked at his watch.

Nearly midnight.

He panned the nightscope across the lower floor of the house, and then the upper. It was harder to see through the heavy sheets of rain, but it caused no real difficulty, just minor discomfort. No lights were on, and even though he could not see into the rooms with any detail now, he could see enough to know if anybody was moving inside.

The house was still.

He surveyed the back yard, and watched as the rain drained down the hill, and then looked up the left side of the building.

Nothing.

Midnight.

The wind changed direction again, and cold rain blew into his face. Freezing rain, biting into his hard skin. He began to feel uncomfortable, wondering why he was here.

Were he not, he would probably have gone fishing. He would probably have gone to the small town of Tanner, a place where more than fishing was on offer.

He remembered the second time he had been out that way, the time he'd met Tessa with her long, flowing red hair and burning lips which he touched so softly, her swaying hips and long legs. In the sweltering heat they had made hot love, and the fishing he had intended remained no more than a memory from his previous trip.

That had been six long months ago, and since then he had been back to Tanner nine more times.

And each time, Tessa had been waiting for him.

She was the first woman he had ever loved.

Before he had joined up to go to Vietnam, after hearing Kennedy's rousing speech, Hawkins had screwed around some, but only for pleasure, never commitment. It had meant nothing, and the women he had been with thought of him in similar vein. Back then, sex was plentiful, but true love was hard to come by.

He left the country unattached, sometimes envious of his fellow grunts who received letters from their loved ones; he was always there for them when the letters stopped arriving, when their girlfriends tired of waiting for them to return, or felt disgraced by their presence in this unpopular war, when only a year earlier they had been so impressed by their boyfriends' bravery.

Out there, sweating his life away in the jungle, Alan Hawkins had learned the sacredness of life, and sometimes wished there was somebody back home waiting for him. As his friends – not those puking college buddies who had skipped over the border or were back home protesting against the war – his *real* friends had fallen about him in fields of death and pestilence, killed in a foreign country fighting a war they did not understand, Hawkins had become an empty shell of a man.

Emotionless.

The last time he'd been out to Tanner was less than a month ago, and he had told Tessa of his love for her. She had spoken to him about moving to Tanner, about leaving the city behind and coming to live with her. For the first time since Kennedy had asked him to go out to some shitty jungle to prove his love for his country … for the first time since then, Hawkins had felt wanted.

And the feeling had been good.

When he had returned home from Vietnam, his country had rejected him, as it had so many. Hawkins had felt that betrayal deep in his heart until the day he had met Tessa … and that was the first day he really began to live again.

He wondered why he was here now, freezing his butt off, twenty feet off the ground, willing to kill somebody, or be killed himself – a very real possibility now – for something he no longer understood, or believed in. He slowly lowered the nightscope.

In Tanner there was none of this – none of the rotting disease that was eating away at society. In Tanner there were only two things of importance, two people – Tessa and himself. Life was simple out there, with no shades of grey to deceive and betray. Everything was black and white, good and bad.

Nothin' to do but fish and make love real slow.

In Tanner he was alive, no longer the killing machine he was perceived as being here, but a real man, with feelings and flesh, a wild sense of humour. His fellow police officers would not even recognise him out there.

Six months ago something had fastened itself deep into his heart, and only now was he comprehending the extent of the change it had wrought in him.

If he should die, Tessa would be out there waiting – for ever. If he should die...

Hawkins found himself falling from the spiritual level of readiness for combat at which he had lived for so long; and with this descent he lost confidence in his own ability to survive. If he should die, he would not be truly mourned. His funeral would be a lonely affair, attended only by cops; Tessa would not be informed of his death.

After the next forty hours or so, he was going to hand in his shield. He would do it right now, but couldn't just leave Caan a man short, without the chance to get something organised. It would just screw up the whole operation. He could wait a few hours, a couple of days perhaps... and then he would have the whole of the rest of his life ahead of him. Within three days he could be sleeping at Tessa's side, for that night and every night thereafter.

For the first time since climbing the tree, Hawkins prayed that the killer would not arrive. He was no longer sure of himself, thoughts of Tessa making him rely on caution rather than instinct... and that could be his downfall, his death and all that he feared could now become a reality...

Then, as he slowly played the nightscope across the lower floor, he spotted a quick movement in the living room, through the patio door. He pulled the scope away from his face but saw nothing. He hesitated, shaking his head.

He was becoming careful, and that was not his way.

He lifted the nightscope a final time.

Somebody was moving slowly up the stairs.

It was game time.

Chapter Nine
The Eye of the Storm

Hawkins grabbed the M-16 from the rifle bag and jumped from the tree. He hit the ground hard, but performed a controlled roll to ensure that he did not hurt himself. He stood, and began running towards the house, crouching low.

'I got a man in the house,' he whispered into the mike. 'Bottom floor, heading up.'

'All right. Let's do it,' came Caan's quiet reply from inside.

Hawkins reached the wall of the house and stopped for a second, repeating his message to Shue and Savoy.

No response.

'Fucking technology!' he complained quietly.

He gripped the M-16 tight in both hands and could feel his conviction returning. Caan and Irving were aware of the situation, as were Dubois and Williams. He could not waste any more time.

He thought of Tessa, of her fiery hair cascading down

her shoulders, and wished that Shue and Savoy were at his side. He would tell them this later, but already knew they would not believe him.

Shue and Savoy both sat in the patrol car, Shue behind the wheel where he had been all night. His head lolled back as if there were ball-bearings between his neck and shoulders. Shue's throat was cut, and it was his blood that dripped, splashing hollowly in a shallow pool on the radio unit as Hawkins's voice came through. Savoy had made a move for his gun, but then hesitated and grabbed at the radio to warn Hawkins. He changed his mind again, pulling desperately at the gun. It was not even clear of the holster when the bullet hit his temple.

Caan waited inside the empty closet of the spare bedroom where Gale had been sleeping earlier.

Originally, he'd had no intention of trying to make it with Gale, but they had found themselves returning to his place anyway.

He had not slept with a woman since Kelly's death and had been hesitant, but Gale had put him at ease with her playful attitude and sexy charm.

After the love, they had held each other for a few short minutes.

He was grateful that he felt no remorse. If Kelly was looking down from the heavens she was smiling, happy that he was – at last – managing to get on with his life.

At Gale's side he had felt perfect and right.

He'd found it difficult to leave, and smiled as he remembered her whispering after him as he climbed from the bed and left the apartment.

Be careful ...

He grinned. She had laughed at his Fred Flintstone shorts.

Some tough guy ...

And that was when Hawkins's voice came over the radio.

Daniel had checked the ground floor of the house for other cops before he began his cautious ascent of the stairs, aware that the slower he moved, the louder and more emphasised any creaks would be. But he also knew that, being unfamiliar with the house, he couldn't just go charging up the stairs and kick down the first door he came to.

When he reached the top of the stairs he went left along the landing and stopped at the first bedroom door. He placed his ear close to the polished wood and listened. He could hear the slow, steady breathing of two people.

The bitch had a husband.

As he pushed the door open he wondered about the strain this had placed on their relationship. She had been at Red's Tavern alone, looking for a man. By now, her husband would have learned this, either through her own admission or the police enquiry.

He walked into the room and stood above them. They each had their own side of the bed; each lay still.

Daniel raised the camera to his face, and pulled the blanket back with his other hand, the one holding the silencer-equipped .45.

Something was wrong.

In the darkness he could make out the vague shape of a handgun, held at the man's chest, pointing up at him. As his vision adjusted, he could see their police uniforms.

He heard the cock fall back on the handgun.

'Surprise, asshole,' Cindy said.

Daniel let the flash go on the camera, filling the room with white light that drowned their eyes. He was already firing the .45 ... the soft, sweet sound of death.

'Fuck!' Cindy grunted as she felt Kerwin's body jerk from the bullet impacts. And then – as she was about to fire blind – several more hammered into her torso.

Moving quickly now, Daniel ripped the picture off and left it on the bloody chest of one of the cops – registering for the first time that one of them was male, the other female. Then he was out of the room, not waiting to see how the picture developed.

He had figured the police might try to catch him when he came to kill the woman, Gale Anne Hurd, but nothing like this – a plan orchestrated to hurt him, as much as protect the woman.

He was angry, and could feel the monster taking charge, thirsty for the fight.

A fight the rest of Daniel did not want. But the monster was too strong, demanding he finish here in case the woman was in another room.

* * *

Hawkins looked through the patio window but couldn't see anybody inside. He ran quickly down the side of the house, holding the M-16 high in one hand while he reached for the front-door key from his pocket with the other.

At the end of the wall he hesitated, but only for a milli-second, before stepping out, the gun aimed and ready to fire. Nobody was at the front of the house, but there was no point in taking chances. He would be of no use to anybody dead ... especially Tessa.

For a moment his attention was caught by the patrol car. Its headlights were on, and from here everything looked normal enough. However, there was no way both of them could have fallen asleep, and no way either of them should have done so, which meant only one thing.

'Shue. Savoy,' he whispered harshly.

No response.

They were both dead.

Hawkins unlocked the front door and pushed it open, going in low. He knew he was not expected, so as long as he was quiet and gave no notice of his presence, he could afford to move fast.

He entered the living room, where he had first seen the killer, through the patio window ... *wished he had just shot the glass out and crashed through when he had first run to the building* ... and quickly checked it out, even though he was positive the killer was already upstairs.

Speed and instinct ...

He should have been up the stairs by now, but instead he was taking slow, cautious steps at the bottom of them, and it was all because of one thought, one person ... *Tessa*.

Hawkins reached the top of the stairs and looked both ways along the landing into the darkness and shadows. He spotted a door that was open a crack, and crept swiftly across the carpeted floor.

The rifle held steady and prominent in his grip, he pushed open the door, and saw the blood-spattered remains of Officers Dubois and Williams. Hawkins ran to the bed and saw the photograph, curled and sticky with gore, and was instantly thrust back to Vietnam, where a sick killer, a GI, had once run amuck, following orders of his own.

Jesus, no ...

It was happening again.

He reached out to touch Kerwin's chest, the glossy picture. The young cop's expression in the photograph was confident. He had not expected to die.

This was the violence he, Alan Hawkins, had brought home from Vietnam. Violence he had once used and advocated, but now wished he had never encountered. He wanted to leave this place and find peace with his love, but first, he knew that whoever had killed his colleagues must die.

Even though he sensed he had lost his own edge. Even though it could mean his own death.

Daniel saw two more sleeping figures under the covers.

This time, he fired several shots straight away, the .45 spitting muffled fire in the darkness.

Feathers drifted in the air as the pillows under the bedclothes exploded.

The monster in his mind screamed with insane rage, and Daniel began to collapse, confused and afraid.

A trap. It was all a trap!

Laura got up from her hiding position behind the bed. '*Freeze!*' she said, feathers decorating her hair.

Daniel took a frightened step back. She looked like the woman from Red's Tavern, like Gale Anne Hurd, but moved with a greater sense of purpose and strength. There was a gun in her hand, and she was about to aim it at him . . .

Daniel could not move.

Then the monster lifted his arm and fired, putting a bullet in her forehead. She slumped to the floor.

A closet door behind him slid silently open. He did not see it or hear it, but the monster's instincts were sharper than his own. It sensed the door shifting in the air.

Daniel turned as another cop stepped out.

The man never had a chance. He was raising his weapon to fire when the monster released a blaze of gunfire.

The first two shots hit him in the chest, knocked him back into the closet. The third hit his arm. The killer was reckless now, Caan certain he was a dead man. The gun had fallen from his hand, and a fourth shot shattered the door of the closet, sending splinters into Caan's face.

'Hawkins,' Caan moaned. 'Hawkins ... back-up.'

The monster grinned – a grimace on Daniel's face. *There was somebody else in the house.*

The monster moved towards the door. It was enjoying this, and Daniel felt small, as if he were the one in the monster's mind and not the other way around.

And slowly, the monster was taking him over – the rush, the thrill, the energy burning bright in the darkest hour, was enough to wash his fear away.

Daniel smiled in surrender to the monster.

At the sound of the voice whispering his name in his ear, Hawkins was certain that Caan was down, and Irving undoubtedly dead. Without thinking, relying on the instinct and reflex actions he believed he had lost, Hawkins fired through the adjoining wall as he ran for the door.

'Fuck ...' Daniel moaned as he dived to the floor.

It was a miracle he had not been hit. He crawled for the door as dust and plaster danced a white tango with the drifting feathers.

There was some serious fire-power in the next room – enough to blow a wall down, and some crazy bastard behind it with his finger on the trigger. It couldn't be a cop. Police officers did not behave irrationally like that; they had rules and procedures to follow. Regulations that were not to be ignored. And cops did *not* carry machine guns around with them.

Daniel reached the door and peered around it, his arm outstretched, aiming the .45 down the landing.

When Hawkins appeared, he wasn't expecting the killer to be waiting there for him; he believed his shots, at the very least would have panicked him. When he saw the .45, Hawkins zigzagged across the gallery overlooking the large sitting room below.

The killer wasted no time in firing after him. Hawkins considered bringing the M-16 up to return fire, but decided instead to vault over the top of the balcony, never even thinking about what might be below.

As he arced over, he took a bullet in his arm. It was only a flesh wound, the bullet passing through skin and tissue ... He tumbled the fifteen feet to the floor, the wooden rail above him exploding in a violent storm of splinters as the killer expended more rounds. He landed on a couch and quickly rolled over the back of it so that he was safely hidden under the gallery, at least for a little while. He lifted a hand to the bloody wound in his arm. Jesus, it hurt. He needed a tourniquet – fast.

Upstairs, Daniel ran to the chewed-up remains of the balcony and looked over the edge, smiling manically.

The crazy fucker was gone. There was no sign of him and, just for a second, the monster relinquished its tight grip on Daniel's mind. Then it started up again, thrashing its will against Daniel's, insistent and demanding. It wanted him to go downstairs, to find the man, pathetically trying to flee despite his injuries, probably crawling for the door by now.

Kill him, the monster snickered. *Go on – kill him, with his own fucking gun.*

Daniel's adrenaline was pumping fast, charging every molecule of his body, and his mouth lifted in a cruel sneer. Part of him wanted to go down the stairs, take the fight to the gunman. But it would be easier to run ... *leave now* ... while he still could, before more police arrived.

Hawkins stood under the gallery as still as a statue, trying to slow and control his ragged breathing so that it could not be heard and give his position away. Silently, he pulled off the sweaty rag he had been using as a headband and tied it around his bicep, wincing as he pulled it tight, then tighter, to prevent the bleeding.

He would have to chance moving again soon. Right now, the killer was probably climbing out of an upstairs window, jumping to the wet ground below and making his escape. *Go ... go!* But Hawkins found he could not move. As drops of sweat trickled down his tense face ... *he could feel the wet leaves of 'Nam brushing against his skin as he silently watched the gook patrol march by. He was alone, his platoon massacred, and a million miles from friendly ...*

Hawkins shuddered at the memory. He could not move even if he had to, even if his life depended on it. *He came out from the bush and suddenly, the night was filled with foreign cries ...*

Back then he'd moved too soon, and the enemy had hunted him for a week, never letting up, never giving him the chance to sleep. But whenever they came close, running a tight ship since he had little ammunition, Hawkins had shown those Commie bastards hell.

Daniel stood almost directly above, watching the dark floor for the slightest movement. Quietly, he slipped the empty magazine from the .45, and fitted it with a new clip.

The jungle receded, and Hawkins was brought back to reality when he heard that old, familiar sound. He looked up, striving to judge exactly where the sound of the new clip being loaded had come from. He waited patiently for a minute as lightning hit outside the patio window, then heard sudden movement from above as the killer ran for one of the rooms.

Hawkins darted quickly into the spacious living room, in time to look up and see the killer disappear through the door into Gale Anne's room, the room of the trap ... *Caan and Irving.* He fired quickly, hoping to get lucky, and pumped two of the grenades out. The walls around the door blew up, sending fragments everywhere.

He ran up the stairs, charging up them as he should have done the first time; if he had, there might still have been survivors up there.

At the window, Daniel was fumbling with the latch, taking valuable seconds to twist it. For half a second the room was filled with light from the explosions, and he felt dead eyes on his back.

The window unlocked, he pushed it up and climbed onto the narrow ledge.

Before he jumped he took one last look into the room,

dust catching in his throat, making him cough. He remembered everything – the dead bodies, the blood, but then ... *the crazy gunman was running in, and the other cop, the dead one in the closet, was reaching for his gun with a bloody hand* ... he fell from the ledge as the big man fired, the sound and muzzle flashes filling the night like the thunder and lightning. Deadly shards of glass showered down like spears, cutting him, and a bruising rain of bricks, as another grenade was launched.

When he hit the ground, Daniel was dazed, in pain from a twisted ankle. He had no chance of making it to the trees so he limped back to the wall of the house, and then stumbled along it.

Hawkins saw Caan and bent down to him. He ripped his shirt open to check the wounds.

Caan groaned.

'You're wearing a vest,' Hawkins said, surprised.

Caan grinned.

That must hurt like a mother, thought Hawkins. Broken ribs, for sure. But, excepting the wound in his arm, Caan was not bleeding his life away.

'You gonna be OK?' Hawkins asked.

'I'll live. Go get him ...'

Hawkins moved to the window, and leaned out. He spotted Daniel duck back into the wall where he was safe in a blind spot, then heard him running along the paved area. Leaning out as far as he could, Hawkins fired the M-16 loose in one hand. All the shots were wild and went wide of their target, and Hawkins could feel the gun jerking violently in his hand. He stopped firing, knowing the shots were useless and that he would probably break his wrist if he continued.

He paused, looking at the dead body of Irving, and then climbed onto the ledge, hung there and jumped, performing another controlled roll to stay off his injured arm.

Hawkins ran quickly round to the front of the house and looked both ways, predicting that the killer would head straight for Shue and Savoy's patrol car. If he did that, he would probably make it clean away: all he had to do was ditch the automobile a mile or so from here and walk away from the whole mess.

But the car remained where it had been all night, a coffin now, its headlights a lie – a sign of life. They threw golden tunnels of light onto the street, and the puddles and rain reflected it back into the night.

The street was vacant. Too late, Hawkins realised what had happened.

He turned back towards the house, his finger already closing on the trigger of the M-16.

But the killer was already firing from his crouched position in the garden, hiding in the shadows, where he had patiently waited for Hawkins to come racing out in pursuit; waited for him to turn so that he could see the shock on his face.

Clever bastard...

Hawkins took a bullet in his side but continued to turn, firing the assault rifle. Another shot hit his chest, and put him on the ground. His back groaned, and the gun dropped from his hand.

Slowly, as he watched the killer approach, dark unconsciousness swallowed him.

Chapter Ten
Advocation

Daniel sat in the nurses' home, his private journal of death open before him. The television was on, but he paid it no attention. Inside the room there was only the journal and himself.

The monster was sleeping.

There are two people living inside this shell.

Two people at odds with one another but who have no means of escape. Their boxing ring is without corners into which to retreat. Their torment is never-ending.

There is Daniel, and there is the monster. Daniel is afraid of the monster, but he lives under its rule. After all, it conquered him, and owns him.

But the monster knows it needs Daniel to survive. Without him, it cannot exist; without him, it cannot kill ... So, angry and unwilling, it must sometimes slink away, and sleep in its cage.

And there is a third entity in this dark hall – a thin splinter of intelligence, a naked thread of mind that survived the monster's takeover all those years ago.

I am the boy ... before my dark psychosis revealed itself.

Sometimes the pen is in the hands of Daniel.

Sometimes it is in the claws of the monster.

And, occasionally, I hold it, and savour its touch.

I am the innocence.

I am pure. My soul is clean.

I keep this journal and write these words so that one day people may understand, and pity me ...

Dumbstruck, Vinnie looked up from the pages of the magazine entitled *Here & Now*, and then let it fall from his hands. It had been lying on the table all day. If only he had flicked through it that morning, instead of now, as the night was coming to an end!

The article told of a chilling dialogue that had taken place on a Greyhound bus journey from Manhattan to Detroit, between the writer – a Peter Richards – and a man who could only be Susan Austin's killer. It pointed in the directions the killer intended to go, places he might visit next.

Vinnie paced the room.

Who was this guy? He was calling himself Daniel Mabe, but Susan had known him as Tony Elliot, and Billy Rogers's mother as Andrew Walker ... How many other identities did he have? *How many other people had he killed?*

'Are you coming up, honey?' his wife called from upstairs.

'Just a second, baby.'

He pulled open the window and leaned out into the cool breeze, swallowing the air, trying to arrange his thoughts into a coherent order.

He picked up the magazine and read the article again.

'Jesus...' Vinnie whispered thoughtfully to himself, and turned to the contents page, searching for the address of the editorial offices.

Chicago.

'Vinnie?'

'Yeah. In a minute, babe.'

He moved to the phone. He had to call Bobby, get him out there. If the killer read the article, Peter Richards might be in serious danger. He would also call Kamski in Detroit, put them on to the magazine.

Jay, old buddy, I think I just found our guy.

'You're very pretty, you know that?' Daniel asked the nurse as she took a shower.

He did not hear her response because he was distracted by the television news.

He was the lead story.

You have to get out of here. It's not safe...

Damn straight, he thought, as he saw himself on the screen, lurking in the shadows as the cameraman ran towards him, *stepping into the light.*

The image bobbed with each footfall, and Daniel

looked at the screen, stared into his own mind. National APB after this. His picture was going to be everywhere. On the news, in the papers ... *everywhere.*

Except for sides of the milk cartons – they would always be reserved for missing children.

The monster had been out of control ... needed discipline, he mused.

Hey! You have to get out of here, my friend. It's not safe. I don't know who you are, what you're doing here. But there's a guy with a gun, and we have to get out. Come on – I know the way.

It was his television début, but after only seconds, a minute at the most, the attention shifted off himself and onto the bleeding, writhing body of the cameraman.

This is for you, motherfucker, for starting this. When I find you, I'm gonna rip your fucking guts out!

... out of control ...

Watching himself now, he was actually afraid. Not of capture, but of the monster.

He shivered.

A gunshot rang out, and for a brief moment the cries of the dying cameraman were silenced. A caption at the bottom of the screen read – *Recorded Live.*

Sick bastards, Daniel thought, and envisioned himself ducking and running as more shots sounded. He could picture the man in the aisle now, aiming patiently, not realising he was fresh out of ammo.

The monster had known.

The monster wanted that bastard.

And on the screen, the cameraman still twitched in

his death throes, and Daniel wondered how many complaints had already been called in about the disgusting footage being shown to the public. He smirked, picturing relatives of the dead turning on to see this.

'What did you just say?' the woman repeated, shouting above the hissing water.

Well, fuck her. If she couldn't come out here and talk civilised instead of bawling her head off from the shower, she could go and—

Hey!

The screen faded to black, and a woman's bright and breezy voice-over – just like she was reading the weather – continued the report.

'Now, in tribute to our very own Mason Adams, we present a brief montage of some of his best, award-winning work.'

The screen came on bright and sudden as he was thrust into some shitty, Third World, war-torn country. In the midst of a gun battle, the screen bobbed, not unlike the way it had done earlier as Mason Adams ran, trailing behind a group of rebels, several of them falling as they were shot.

Shrugging disdainfully – although the monster acknowledged that Adams and himself were not that different; both living for the thrill of their work, the danger and the excitement – he turned away from the television and grabbed a magazine from the table in front of him.

The nurse was pretty, and as he thumbed through the magazine he remembered the delights her body had held – sucking and pulling, his erection huge and hard. As he thought about the sex, he massaged his penis, one hand tucked into the front of his jeans—

Something he read cut his thoughts off, and his hand stopped. He flicked back a couple of pages and looked again at the name he had just seen.

Peter Richards. It sounded familiar but he couldn't quite place it. He concentrated, but nothing would come from the dark shadows of his memory. He thought about his journal, and wondered if he had ever killed anybody of that name. He didn't think so.

'Well, what do you want to do now?' the nurse shouted, as steam and mist rose about her ... but he ignored her.

On the Greyhound bus from Manhattan to Detroit there had been a man. An inquisitive fat guy; he'd asked a whole bunch of questions ... had been very conversational.

Daniel read the article, searching for clues ... and he crumpled the magazine in his furious grasp. He thought about the bus and the fat man sitting next to him – and the fact that Mason Adams had stolen his limelight no longer bothered him.

They had been in the diner at first – some tacky roadside stop. And then on the bus.

Peter Richards.

'You dirty motherfucker,' Daniel muttered angrily, as he realised who the author of the article was.

The monster growled, enraged.

'What did you just say?' the blonde nurse asked as she

came into the room. She had one towel wrapped around her body, and was rubbing her hair dry with another.

'Enlightening article,' he said, and stood to face her.

'Oh yeah?' the nurse said, not that impressed. 'As enlightening as this?'

She let both towels drop onto the carpet, and he surveyed every smooth contour of her body, wet and glistening.

He took her angrily, pushing her to the floor and holding her down as he entered her. He smiled as they lay on the floor, and she fought against him at first. But then she relaxed as his body went through the primitive ritual of sex, his mind distracted by the images and commentary of a news-flash on the television.

There were long shots of bodies being removed from a house, police officers going about their business, crowds pushing.

'This was the scene of a mass slaughter last night, at the Bloomfield Hills home of Joshua and Karin O'Bannon. Although there has been no official comment from the police yet, it is believed that at least four officers were killed, possibly five, and another two were seriously injured. These murders may be connected with the death of Mason Adams, our very own award-winning cameraman, and the brutal killings at Red's Tavern. Speculation is that the police had a witness to that crime. A serial killer, possibly the same man who was captured on film by Adams, and widely shown on this channel, may be in our midst. We would like to warn the public to take care and—'

He decided to go to Chicago, the magazine's home base, and check out the editorial office – see if he could locate the home address of that fat fuck. He'd teach the guy a lesson that had nothing to do with magazine journalism, and after that, he'd move on to someplace quiet, where nothing much ever happened. Someplace where his killing would go unnoticed.

He slept for a short while, and when morning came, as the sun rose through the indistinguishable clouds and smog, Daniel quit Detroit, leaving the blonde nurse sleeping peacefully.

As Daniel was leaving Detroit, Jay was being escorted up from the cells to Captain Kamski's office. He did not wear handcuffs, but the uniform walked close, ready for trouble. As they marched through the Precinct, the unexpected silence put Jay on edge.

It was too quiet.

Something had gone down. Something big – and very, very bad. That much he could feel.

The uniform knocked on the door and Kamski waved Jay inside. He was on the phone. Jay sat down.

'How is he?' Kamski asked into the phone.

Jay did not hear the response, but the Captain appeared to breathe a sigh of relief.

'That's good. Thank you, Doctor Bale. I'll speak with you later.'

Kamski hung up and an uncomfortable silence filled the room. He stared long and hard at his desk. It was left for Jay to speak first.

'What's happened?' he asked quietly, knowing that it was something to do with Tony Elliot.

A minute passed before Kamski looked up.

'This is the situation. I had a witness of your killer, from the murder at Red's Tavern. Only last night, the killer found out where she was staying. We baited a good trap, but ... somehow it got fucked up.' He stopped and cleared his throat. 'I got five dead cops I have to bury. Two others are injured badly, but they're going to make it. One of them, Hawkins, was on the brink of retirement. Not a conventional officer, but damn good at what he did do. He destroyed the house, and nearly got the bastard.'

Jay could find no words to express his reactions. There was sympathy, of course, but guilt, too. He felt responsible for all these deaths, for all the victims and all the lives ruined. It was his fault for chasing the bastard here, for chasing him at all. If he had let the investigation go through the proper channels, as Caldwell had counselled, none of this would have happened. The killer might even have been apprehended by now.

Might even be dead.

Well, he soon would be.

Kamski sighed heavily. What sickened him most was the ruthlessness of it all. He had never seen anything like it. The man actually *enjoyed* what he was doing. Fed off it ...

Kamski looked at Jay, knowing he was the only person who could find the killer.

235

He decided to cut him loose.

Jay had already stepped outside the bounds of the law. To step further, deeper into the black heart of illegal activity could not hurt him. Kamski acknowledged that his whole perspective on Jay had changed.

He was no longer a rogue cop out looking for revenge.

He was the one man who could stop this evil.

The saviour of them all.

He's coming around.

The voice drifted to him from far away, yet it was close by. He wanted to reach out and touch it, but when he tried to lift his arm, he could not.

We shouldn't have woken him. You know that, don't you?

The voice still sounded distant, as if somebody had shouted and he was hearing the echo. But he could feel it, the texture – soft and firm. It was a female voice.

He wondered if it was Tessa, and was afraid to open his eyes in case it wasn't. For now he enjoyed the dream that she was here, at his side.

I know that. But this is police business. This voice was male.

Police . . . ?

Events slowly came back to him.

I am a cop.

I am in love with Tessa.

I am a cop, and I was shot. (The rhyme made him giggle like a child.)

I'm in love with Tessa, and she could be here.

He blinked his eyes several times, and the drug-induced grogginess began to wear off.

A woman stood above him. She had the same fiery red hair as Tessa, but she wore a white gown and a soft skirt. Hawkins had never seen Tessa out of Levi's.

He sighed, disappointed, and looked around. The bed next to him was occupied by Detective James Caan. He was grinning.

'You look like shit, Hawkins,' he said.

'Thanks, man. So do you.'

Gale was holding Caan's hand. The sight was beautiful, and Alan could not wait until he was out of the hospital so that he could find his Tessa and marry her.

'You got a visitor,' Caan gestured at an approaching figure.

'Five minutes,' Dr Bale warned, and left.

'Who are you?' Hawkins asked.

'I'm a cop,' Jay told him. 'Manhattan Police Department. The man you chased last night killed my sister.'

Hawkins looked away, and Jay saw the anguish in his face.

'What's wrong?' he asked.

Hawkins paused, thinking for a second.

'Over in Vietnam, it happened a few times. We would enter a village, and the people would troop out, waving sticks and protesting, telling us to go away. They were panicked, raving about a man with a painted face who came out of the trees while they were sleeping, and murdered one of them. "Painted Face", that's what they

237

called him. They said he was a phantom, an evil spirit. He would sneak in during the night, and take one of them out. He always left his mark – a photograph – but not of the victim, of a different corpse, to scare them so much that they could never sleep soundly again.'

Hawkins paused before continuing.

'It turned out he was a soldier ... a fucking American, painting his face with green and brown camouflage, and leaving the camp at night while the rest of his unit slept. A fucking grunt! One of ours. He may even have been in my unit.'

Hawkins felt a cold snake touch his spine and settle there. He finished dully: 'I may even have shared a watch with him.'

Jay nodded; he knew how Hawkins felt. Years ago, when he was a child in a dank, dark cellar, Jay might have given the killer food.

The thought made him nauseous.

'You have to end it,' Hawkins whispered, exhausted, and hurting. 'Finish it ...'

Jay finished reading the article and then passed the magazine back to Kamski.

'You think this is our man?' Kamski asked.

'It's all I've got,' Jay said.

'I was put on to it by a friend of yours ... Ray Province. Told me he was checking out a couple of leads for you,' Kamski said.

'Did he have any information for me?' Jay asked.

Kamski pulled a notepad from his desk. 'He said they

ran your sister's boyfriend's name through the computer – and I did the same. Tony Elliot, isn't it? We both came up blank. He also spoke to a woman named ... now, let me get this right – Novelle Tourment. At her place she had a bottle of wine Tony Elliot had given your sister. From this they got a partial, which matched some of the stuff we found at Red's Tavern. They also got a positive ID. Province thinks the killer might go after the writer of the article in Chicago. I'm inclined to believe it, after what he did last night.'

'I'm going to Chicago,' Jay said, and stood.

'Wait a second.' Kamski held up a hand. 'Vinnie told me that one of your colleagues, Officer Bobby Roberts, is going out there to interview the writer, Peter Richards, see if he can give us any new leads. That's all. I'll tell Caldwell I've got you here, if he asks any questions. And I'll let your friends know where you're heading. Check in tomorrow. I should have some information about the children's home by then.'

Kamski turned away from Jay for a moment, and looked out of his window at the dirty Detroit skyline. When he turned back, his eyes were cold and intense.

'You find him, Jay. And when you do, forget the questions, forget the warning shots. I want this guy dead. You don't arrest him, you hear me? You kill him.'

PART TWO

Haddonfield

Chapter Eleven
Life and Death

Officer Bobby Roberts walked up several flights of stairs in the apartment building; the lift was out of order, and his leg was cramping. He had to stop twice and rub life into it.

When he reached the third-floor landing, he walked down the corridor until he found Richards's apartment, having gotten his address from the editors of *Here & Now*. They did not seem particularly fond of the writer. He was too arrogant, thought he was too clever – always pushed his deadline to the limit. Although his writing was the best, they said, the decision to run the controversial article was a close call – the one not to call the police, or the lawyers, before it was published even closer.

Bobby knocked, and waited for an answer.

Dawn would be home soon. OK, there were still some weeks to go, but with his life suddenly full of activity instead of routine procedures, the time was flying by.

He knocked again, wondering how much Peter Richards really knew about the man they were chasing, and how much of the article had been speculation to make it more interesting ... to sell more copies of *Here & Now*.

He waited, then knocked again.

The door suddenly opened.

It was him!

The monster grabbed the man's hand. As he pulled him inside, he brought the blade up and cut his throat.

Bobby, his hand rising to the wound as the killer let go, pulled his gun out as he stumbled forward and fell. He saw another man – Peter Richards? – tied to a chair, his naked body marred only by the small bullet-hole in his head. It was a remarkably clean kill.

He dropped the gun, and his blood soaked into the carpet as he collapsed forward.

'Dawn,' he managed.

Dawn.

Daniel had been to Chicago before, but it was only now that he discovered why it was called the Windy City. Even though the sun was blazing, and the sky was a mesmeric blue, the fast breeze that blew about him off Lake Michigan chilled the air so much that he was glad of the warm jacket he wore on top of a sombre suit.

He walked across the churchyard, trying to remember where her grave was located. He hadn't visited it for over two years, and since then the burial ground had expanded, become cold and unfamiliar. It sprawled across acres, so big and beautiful.

He studied the bright flowers he carried – a huge bouquet of reds and greens, yellows and violets, all the bright colours. The colours of life, contrasting with his dark surroundings. The flowers represented all the optimism in the world, while the churchyard was a place of ultimate doom, and this feeling permeated through his whole system.

This was the place were Death lived. Brooding and menacing, with Its thousands of markers. Thousands of millions ... all the people It had ever claimed. All the victims.

He stroked each petal of the flowers softly with his finger.

It was time to say goodbye to the one person who meant anything – the only person who had ever really cared for him. He had to speak with her, because soon he believed they would be together again, in her dead world.

The monster was becoming more and more out of control. Daniel was afraid – felt there was little he could do to keep it in his charge.

He felt a strange desire – no, a compulsion – to find the man who had chased him through the streets of Detroit. It was time to take the fight back to him, time to stop running and face his ... destiny.

Was it destiny which had brought him here?

Daniel wondered whether he would be here, feeling so bleak and depressed, if the monster had killed the man who had chased him through the store. He thought not. If his pursuer were dead, Daniel wouldn't care. He would go on living, go on killing – two purposes that were one.

But the man was alive! He was a real threat – and perhaps he had survived for one reason – to bring Daniel to *his* destiny.

They knew each other. Their paths had crossed before.

The man had recognised him – looked into his eyes and seen who he was, all that he had done. Deep in his heart, Daniel knew that the man would always be following, one step behind. And then one day, he would catch up, and the streets would run with blood.

The man was on his level: Daniel had seen that in his eyes. For whatever reason, he was primed and ready to kill. Yes, Daniel knew they were alike, in more ways than one, ways that would scare his *brother* if he knew.

For the first time in his life, somebody knew who Daniel was ... and he was already tired of the insecurity that knowledge instilled in him. He was weary of the fear he now felt, as he walked through the sleeping ground of the dead.

At last he reached the grave for which he was searching.

He picked up the fallen vase and went over to the rusting faucet, filling the jar with clean water before arranging his flowers in it. He looked at the crinkled, crispy-edged leaves of the dead plants he had discarded, and could feel stinging tears on his cheeks as he remembered Melissa.

She had been beautiful, and he had loved her to the

point of killing her when she had threatened to leave him, hinted at sleeping with other men. He always returned here, because he loved her, and wanted to be with her again one day. He liked to visit her grave, took pleasure and solace from some of the warm memories it inspired, memories from before the dark time he was now living, and had been living for so long.

He was a bad man.

But then he remembered swimming naked with her in a lake, feeling her wet body against his, running his finger over every line of it. He remembered entering her under the water ... and the bad thing he had done that night.

He could not let people be close to him. They would reject him, hurt him. As his parents had ...

He had not meant to kill her, but he had gotten carried away by the thrill ... the ultimate rush as he suffocated in the monster's embrace ... and she had drowned in the lake.

He was a bad man.

'I love you,' he whispered softly to the tombstone, to Melissa, whom he knew would somehow hear him.

He placed the flowers in front of her plaque, a vibrant symbol of the life he wished she still possessed.

He wanted to be free of everything he had ever done. Too many people were becoming involved, and he was finding it hard to control himself. There had been no need to kill the man who had come to visit Peter Richards, but the anger had been inside, and he had pounced.

The monster was becoming all-powerful, ruling him, predatory talons ripping at his fragile sanity.

'What's wrong?' Angie asked, as she sat drinking fresh orange juice, wearing only a flimsy camisole top.

They had made love the previous night, when Dwight had returned from Ellen, and although it had been nice, something was missing. He had been distracted, as he was now. Last night he had just gone through the motions, done enough to please her and that was all. His heart had not been in the act of pleasure, and she felt the difference. Ever since he'd returned from his visit with Griffen she had never had his full attention – no matter what she said, no matter what she wore or did.

Something he had learned from Griffen was constantly nagging at the back of his mind.

'Nothing.'

It sounded fine, but it was only a single word, spoken without emotion. How could he expect her to believe what he was saying, when he obviously did not believe it himself?

'Tell me,' she demanded softly. 'Please.'

She genuinely cared for him. For as long as she could remember, she had been flirting, stealing men's hearts and using them, but when she had met Dwight that part of her had grown up. Matured. It sounded crazy, but when she found Dwight, she had found everything she ever wanted from a man.

She hated to see him like this.

'I feel like – I don't know.'

It was difficult for Dwight. A decision made – a promise of love broken – and he was in limbo. How long would it take before he knew if he had done the right thing?

'When I left Ellen, I left a part of myself back there – a part I can never go back and claim as my own. It's as if that part of me has died. I expected *her* to go through pain, but didn't think I would feel anything. I guess when I was with my wife, I didn't appreciate her.'

Dwight turned away so that Angie could not see his tears, but deep inside he knew that she had seen them last night.

'Look at me,' he joked unsteadily. 'You're turning me into a blubbering wreck with your questions.'

'I'm sorry,' she said, and took one of his hands in both of hers, clasped it tight. 'You're bound to hurt. You have just left a woman you once loved. You have finished a chapter of your life, and it's like you said – the page has turned and you can never have it back. But it is also the start of a new chapter – *our* chapter.'

As they kissed he smiled, almost believing that he had made the right decision. That he had no regrets about what he had done.

'So what happened when you saw Griffen?' she prompted gently, knowing that he would tell her soon enough in his own time, but she wanted to help him, and could only do that if he told her what had happened.

At first she thought he was trying to put her off by changing the subject with a question of his own.

'Did you notice that nobody was ever killed, or hurt, in any of the burnings?' Dwight asked, trying to find an easy way to tell her about the deal he'd made with Griffen ... trying to justify what he had done.

'I never really thought about it. I'm just grateful that nobody has ever been hurt. Why?' She wanted to know what he was driving at.

But he didn't want to tell her just like that, casually, as though it was a football score or something equally trivial. He wanted her to know and understand the moral dilemma in which he found himself. He knew that what he was doing was wrong – illegal. That, at the very least, he should have been on the phone to Hasky. But a part of him liked what he was doing. It was a risk, and thrills rarely came his way except, perhaps, for the first nights he had stolen away to be with Angie. Only this was bigger, more dangerous. The greed he felt, the greed Griffen had aroused in him, needed feeding.

'Who bought the Gleason place?' he asked.

'A doctor and his wife. Going to surprise her, he said. Real sweet – why? What are you trying to tell me?' Angie was fast becoming tired of his questions, no longer certain she wanted to know what was troubling him. With a sinking heart she remembered the trembling vodka glass from the previous night.

'Do they have any children?'

'No – and neither will you if you don't quit with the questions,' she snapped.

'OK, OK. I'm sorry, it's just ... well...' Dwight cleared his throat before continuing. 'The Gleason place is the next to be burned down. You have to trust me. Hasky was right, in everything he thought. Griffen cut me in on the deal. I – we – could get rich off this.'

'Oh Jesus, Dwight, what have you gotten involved in?'

He was silent.

'You could go to jail for something like this, and I mean somewhere big – not that Lego building in town. Do you know what you are doing?' Angie had started to panic.

'I'm getting ten per cent just for keeping my mouth shut. I told him, after this I don't even want to know which properties are going to get turned to ashes. But after each building goes down, we get a nice cheque in the mail,' Dwight explained, doing his best not to sound like a Mafia henchman.

Or a fool . . .

'Jesus! You have to promise me, Dwight, the most excellent promise you have ever given, that if I get involved in this, if I don't just call Hasky now, nobody gets hurt. Nobody gets . . . killed.'

'I can't give you that promise, Angie. You know I can't.'

'Then you better start praying.'

'So, Leigh,' Alice said as she poured gravy onto the home-baked meal, 'when are we going to see a woman steal your heart? When are we going to see some little baby firemen?'

'Hey . . .' Nichols began in his defence, as Alice sat

down at the table, 'I'm just waiting for the right woman to come along. Besides which, a lot of women *have* stolen my heart, you among them – remember?'

Leigh winked at Tom Hasky. Teasing Alice was one of their favourite pastimes. Huge grins spread wide across their faces, and Alice laughed as she remembered how they had competed over her years ago. She had been pretty in a homey sort of way. She was no cheerleader, and did not want to be. She was appreciated for who she was, and did not have to dress up and cover herself with make-up to look nice.

May the best man win ... she had declared with a smile when a friend had informed her that both young men were intending to ask her to the Prom. Never imagining then that she would be married to the same man twenty years later, and carrying his child inside her.

'As for your second question,' Leigh continued, and grinned. 'I think that was a cue. So you spoke with Doctor Cole?'

At this Tom's smile suddenly disappeared. She had not told him she was going to see the doctor, and he turned to face her, wondering what was wrong. She leaned over and kissed him, held his hand, but still his worry was not put to rest. He loved her more than any words could express, and did not want to see her hurt. They stared deep into each other's eyes, beyond their own reflections and into the darkness past that.

He swallowed.

'I'm pregnant, Tom.'

A dead silence came over the room, and Tom looked confusedly from Alice to Leigh, and then back to Alice.

'You're OK?'

'Tom,' she smiled. 'I'm pregnant. I've never felt better.'

'You mean . . . I'm gonna be a father?' he asked.

'Jesus, Tom! I always thought you were some kind of hotshot detective,' Leigh complained.

'I'm gonna be a dad!' Tom cried with great joy, even that not expressing how exhilarated he was inside. He looked across at Alice who was crying softly because she had never known how much this meant to him.

'OK – we eat out tomorrow!' Tom declared. 'The most expensive place in town.'

'But I've prepared—'

'Forget it,' Leigh advised her. 'The man's offering, so don't turn him down. Besides that, when Baby Hasky moves in, you'll not have so many opportunities to go out.'

Alice looked deep into Tom's eyes and kissed him on the lips. 'I'm glad you got rid of the moustache,' she told him, as they held each other's hands across the table.

For a second he wondered how much Leigh had paid her off to say that . . . but he let the thought go.

'I'm glad you're glad,' he whispered softly.

Voices.

. . . kill him, Jay. Kill him dead. Just shoot the fucker in the back. Take him down. Kill him.

Above the din of the radio, in the silence of his mind, he heard so many voices. Nameless and countless, all chanting the same mantra ... *kill him, kill him, kill him* ...

He was responsible to so many people now. Originally there was only the killer and himself, and his dead sister. But then came more voices, more people laying their burden on him, more begging and pleading, and now there was a whole chorus.

...kill him, kill him, kill him ...

Suddenly he was in the lake, not aware of how he came to be there, but he knew what had to be done. He swam deeper and deeper, kicking his legs hard in an attempt to save his sister. And all the time, crying out to him from the murky darkness of the lake surrounding him, were the voices.

...kill him, kill him, kill him ...

At last he came to Susan, standing upright on the bed of the lake, sand swirling about her feet, a fish nibbling one cheek. Her lips moved, and in his head, as clear as crystal, came one beautiful, perfect voice.

Kill him for me, Jay.

It was the only voice that mattered, the voice that kept him sane through all of this. Her lips moved, and by some miracle the water did not flood her lungs and she did not die. The voice was all he heard and all he knew.

'Crazy bastard!'

Jay woke suddenly. He was still at the wheel of the cheap rental car on his way to Chicago, only now the car was in the wrong lane and some farmer in his truck of stinking pigs had been forced to skid around him.

. . . for me . . . for me . . . for me . . .

For now he would consider himself damn lucky if he saw the killer again. And even if he did, at this rate he would be a wreck of a man when the final confrontation came. It seemed that he would never feel the heavy burden of the voices lift from his shoulders.

. . . kill him, kill him, kill him . . .

And then, suddenly, there was only Susan once more.

Kill him for all of us, Jay – and for all of those yet to come.

Chapter Twelve
Past Life

This is me...

I'm looking back now, down the halls of time, past all the deaths and the horror, back to a time of innocence and childhood joys.

I close my eyes and can see myself – a small boy with sandy blond hair which was cut short and combed tidily, as my mother insisted, and which would darken, as did my pitiful soul, as I got older. I wore shorts in the hot weather, and carried a bag on my shoulder which was packed with my school books. I ran quickly through the fields, eager to get home.

Randy Newman was my best friend, and he'd invited me to stay with him and his aunt in the city for the weekend.

Of course, I needed my parents' permission, and that was the reason for my tiring race home. The train would be leaving soon, so I had to move fast to get back to the station and meet Randy.

I'd had a guarded upbringing until then, shielded from the world, over-protected by my parents, who rarely let me go outside, I never really enjoyed the thrill of chasing a ball, or playing tag – none of the things that normal children do.

They nurtured me.

Insisted I stay inside and study . . .

Help them with their chores . . .

They used me!

The visit to the city was to be different – an adventure for both Randy and myself, an experience to savour and remember. I had never even been out of Leighton, my home town.

I was certain I could convince my parents to let me go.

Ritz, my handsome Golden Labrador, bounded across the field to meet me as I approached the large house, jumping and yapping wildly. Ritz was always loyal and obedient. The best dog ever. A friend, and my only true companion. He jumped up at me, his power knocking me to the ground. He licked my face, and drooled all over me.

'I'm going to the city, Ritz! I am, I am! In less than an hour. I love you, but I don't think dogs are allowed on the train. I really want you to come too, but I'm going, and that's the important thing.' I stroked Ritz, patted his head . . . and can still feel the soft texture of his fur on my fingers.

Ritz barked, the excitement of the moment easily capturing him.

'What was that? How noble! You don't mind being left alone for a couple of days. Great!'

Ritz had accepted the notion of me going to the city rather well. That just left my parents . . .

'Nelson!'

He stopped, his pen coming to an instant halt.

Nelson.

A name. An identity.

I am Nelson. I am a small boy, catapulted from the past and trapped in the mind of the killer I have become.

If I am strong enough I can stop all this . . .

I can end it.

And then the pen continued, as if it had a life of its own.

'You get off that grass before you stain your clothes!'

This was going to be tougher than I'd thought. I walked into the kitchen, a sullen look of guilt on my face.

'I'm sorry, Mother.'

'You should be. Your father works hard so that you can have nice clothes, and look how you treat them.'

My mother was in a bad mood, and I felt my hopes coming apart. At least my father wasn't home yet. Just one to convince.

There was silence, the room cold and forlorn. The timing was all wrong, but seconds were ticking by, turning to minutes ... I had to make my pitch.

'Mother, Randy Newman is staying in the city for the weekend. He has asked if I would like to accompany him on the journey.'

'I don't know, Nelson,' she mused.

'We will stay with his aunt, and—'

'No.'

'... and ...'

'I said no, Nelson, and I meant it. You have responsibilities here. Who will look after Ritz while you are gone? Did you consider that? Now, go take your dog for a walk before your father gets home.'

'But Mother—'

'I'll have no more talk about this foolish trip.'

I nodded slowly, not wanting to anger her.

The basement of our house was cold and damp, dusty. It was rife with spiders and other creatures the dark harbours. I had spent many hours down there alone, the door locked tight ... unjust punishment.

The basement was not on my agenda that day.

I left, and found my baseball bat and ball in the garage. 'Come on, Ritz!'

I walked with the dog at my side, occasionally hitting the gnawed ball ahead. Ritz would run after it, often catching the ball while it was still rolling,

*scooping it up in his mouth. He would then run back
to me, drop the ball and lift his head.*

I would stroke him gently...

The boy called Nelson, trapped in the body of the violent
adult he had become, looked at the words with misty
eyes.

He knew what was coming, but did not want to
remember...

*Fifteen minutes later we came out of a small patch of
woodland, and stood before a lake. It was shaped
like a crescent moon, and we were on the inside
curve.*

*I hit the ball ... and knew it was for the final
time.*

*I was confused as I watched Ritz run ahead,
chasing the ball, could not understand why I suddenly hated my dog so much.*

*I loved Ritz more than anything else in the
world, yet it was Ritz, and all the principles Ritz
now stood for, that prevented me from going to the
city.*

*The monster was coming ... the glory of death
burning in its eyes as it revelled in the capture of my
soul.*

*Ritz came bouncing back, the ball caught between
his teeth. It would soon come to his favourite part —
when the boy-master hurled the ball into the lake
and he swam out to it, paddling in the cool water,*

*disturbing and chasing the fish. He sat and dropped
the ball, waiting for the reward of love he deserved.*

*. . . its cloven hooves pounding hard . . . breathing
heavy and loud . . .*

'Good boy,' I whispered.

*I looked at my watch, a gift from my father – the
bastard. The train would be leaving now, pulling
out of the station without me.*

The monster was close.

*'Good boy,' I whispered again, and stroked Ritz's
golden fur.*

*I could taste its breath in my mouth, feel its
heartbeat join mine in unison, one heart, one mind.
The monster became me . . . swallowing my desperate soul, turning it dark.*

*I don't profess to understand my next actions, or
anything that has happened since that day.*

*But I do know that it is wrong, and I must do all I
can to end it.*

*Its vicious claws sharp and quick; ripping and
tearing ferociously.*

*I swung the bat quickly and savagely, and it hit
Ritz on the top of his head, making a satisfying
cracking sound. Ritz let out a yelp of surprise, and
then leapt forward, ripping with his teeth at the bat
and my hand . . .*

Nelson smiled and wiped the tears from his eyes. He
remembered the fear he had felt for a second, and
thought about Daniel killing the dogs.

THE EDGE

He remembers...

I hit Ritz again and he fell to the ground, mewling. It was a horrible, high-pitched whining that filled my ears and tortured my mind. I had to end that sound, so I swung the bat again and again.

... the monster smiling, fangs naked and rough, as it devoured me ...

Soon, the dog was silent and dead.

I let the bat fall clumsily to the ground and ran, frightened by what I had done.

I wept and cried for the loss of Ritz, whom I loved greatly.

When I reached home I told a story of how Ritz had run away chasing a rabbit – as he sometimes did – and never returned. I had searched and shouted, but all to no avail. My father called me irresponsible and beat me severely before sending me down to the cold, dark place ...

At dawn the next day a local man called Tom Keel, who had gone out to the lake for some fishing, came up our road with only the rising sun for company. In his tired arms he carried Ritz.

My mother wept as she touched the mass of fur, and then stroked Ritz's bashed-in head. Who would do such a thing to a poor, defenceless animal?

'I cleaned him up a little. He was not a pleasant sight, I can tell you. I found this by the body,' Keel told them, and produced my baseball bat, coated with dried blood and mud.

They brought me up out of the basement, and I sobbed, first at the sight of Ritz and later – kicking and screaming – when the men arrived whom my parents had summoned to take me away.

For the next three years I grew up in a special home, a place I came to think of as a prison. It had a system all of its own, and with the sadistic and brutal treatments meted out there, even though the staff thought that what they were doing was right, it was actually a breeding ground for psychopaths.

When I was nine I escaped, and on my tenth birthday I came home ... the monster leading my path and lighting my way.

I killed my father first. His screams woke my mother, and the monster delighted in her suffering, especially when it saw she was pregnant with their second child. My unborn brother or sister ...

With maniacal rage that I could not control, I left the knife buried deep in my mother's womb, deep in the foetal chest of the unborn baby.

I fled then, after taking all the money I could find. There was more than enough to live on ...

That had been the start of my new life. I felt fresh and clean from all the shit and dirt in the world, as only a newborn baby can ... corrupted from the second it is born.

That was the day—

... but the images were fading fast now, as was the

small boy called Nelson. The monster and Daniel were waking from a deep slumber.

They were both strong. Both his enemy.

The monster had decided they were going to Haddonfield, Illinois ... a town it had picked off the map.

Nelson did not know what they would find there, but he knew that the monster would kill. He wished he could end his private hell, but did not have the strength to take a knife and draw it across his own wrists or throat.

He thought about the man who was searching for Daniel.

This man wanted to kill him, destroy the monster ... and, given the opportunity, he would.

Nelson decided to lead the man to Haddonfield, leave him an unmistakable sign pointing him in the right direction.

In Haddonfield there would be a final conflict – and all the pain would be over.

Chapter Thirteen
Summer Heat

Chicago.

Jay walked into the small tavern across the road from the *Here & Now* editorial office. Several men sat at the bar. Cowboy hats and boots; denim jeans and shirts – all crunching nuts and drinking the strongest beers. Tough guys.

'What'll it be?' the bartender asked, a burly man who obviously drank more than he poured, as Jay sat on a stool next to three of his regulars.

'A Bud,' Jay responded, and then pulled a picture – a frame they had enhanced from Mason Adams's film of Susan's killer at the derelict store – from his jacket and handed it to the guy. 'You seen this man?'

'You a cop?'

Jay sensed muscles tense all round him. The regulars were obviously used to trouble, and used to handling it their way. The last thing he wanted was to take a beating from this bunch of rednecks. They were mostly overweight and drunk, so they would be slow and lethargic, if violence did erupt. But Jay was still hurting from his days in a Detroit jail cell, as well as being outnumbered, and knew he wouldn't stand a chance.

The bartender was aware of all the illegal activity that was conducted in his place on a daily basis; everything from prostitution to drug deals of varying quality and quantity. If it was illegal, it took place here . . . often behind the bar. He was damn proud. There had been no busts for a long while, and he was fast developing a good reputation among all kinds of creeps and losers looking to do a little business.

The men here now were his own entourage, his crew, and no way did he want some cop sticking his nose in where it was not wanted. He saw the guys brace themselves for action, but still waited for an answer before giving them the nod.

The bartender looked at the photograph, and remembered the man who had been in that day. He would never forget those eyes, glowing like magnificent pearls. At first he'd thought the man was trying to score some dope or crack. He had that kind of wired energy about him, like an addict on the brink of insanity because he cannot get a fix . . . willing to do anything to score and desperately trying to hold on. It was a face he had seen many times.

But the man had drunk some beer, and then made a pass at Katrina, a pretty, young hooker who had recently started to work the bar. Unlike the older, wearier women of the night, Katrina had yet to acquire that haggard air. She and the man in the picture had had some more to drink, and then they'd left together . . .

Katrina was lying facedown in her bathtub, in a growing puddle of her own blood; which contrasted sharply with the bright white of the tub. The monster had been in a frenzy, cutting her, torturing her, deliberately hurting her before the kill. The beast had bayed into the evening air, like a wolf howling at the low moon.

He looked at the body, repulsed by what he had let happen, and fought the natural urge to vomit. The monster was out of control and had to be stopped. This was the only way he knew how.

Nelson stooped and dipped his finger into a splash of gore, and then trailed it across the small mirror . . . writing a single word, a message for the man from his past.

'No,' Jay answered calmly.

He felt his body tighten in preparation for the battle that might easily come without warning. A bottle smashing, a wild punch thrown in his direction, it could be anything – and then again, it might never happen. His answer was flat, and they would either believe it or not.

The bartender could feel the tension, and gave his men a look to ward them off a little. He was not sure whether to tell this man about Katrina's client. He had heard all kinds of crazy shit – parents looking for their

kids, hiring PIs to find them and take them off the
streets.

Well, he had spent more than a few hours alone with
Katrina himself, and he didn't want that to happen to
her. She was a nice kid, and good at her job, too. He
would miss her if she was taken away, although this
man who claimed not to be a cop was looking for her
client, not her. He didn't even seem to know about
Katrina.

The bartender told the stranger all he knew.

Fearing that the girl might be in some kind of
danger, he gave Jay an address while his regulars –
who still had an air of wanting to take Jay out back
and break a few bones – looked on with subdued
attention.

'So long as he did not have a place, she would have
taken him there.'

Katrina had a roommate and mentor, called Solice.
Solice was only a few years older than her but those
years had all been spent in the business. She knew the
ropes.

They sometimes did doubles, and if the pay was right
– *high* – they were willing to perform light lesbian
action for the many depraved men and women in the
world. But mostly, they just split the rent and were
damn good friends. They both deserved better...

In another time and world, they would have been
sharing a picket fence, good neighbours.

Solice ran up the stairs at the sound of the phone.

'Jesus, Katty,' she moaned, 'would you, like, pick up the phone? *Please?*' Katrina had to be in because it was too early to be downtown at the bar, and they usually didn't work the streets alone because it was getting too dangerous. The city was full of fucking schizos.

She reached the top of the stairs and raced along the landing to their apartment, where she found the door ajar. Until that moment, her only concern had been for a steaming hot bath and some sleep, but now she stopped, as did the phone.

'Katty?' she asked, and pushed the door fully open.

Empty air. No answer.

Solice went in and put down her bag. Clothes were strewn everywhere – the place was a mess. She spotted Katty's shoulder bag, and quickly looked through it. Her friend's wallet was still inside, containing seventy bucks. So ... they had not been robbed, and her bag was evidence that she should be here.

'Katty?' she called again, a slight tremor in her voice ... and still there was no reply.

Maybe she had just run down to the store, gone for cigarettes or something. Left the door ajar by accident.

'Katty?' *Where the fuck are you?*

Solice shrugged, and looked around. She couldn't see or hear anybody in the apartment. The kid could look after herself, she thought uncertainly, and walked into the bathroom. She was about to pull the curtain aside, *clackety-clack* on the rail, when a man walked into the bathroom.

Solice spun round quickly.

She didn't know who he was, but figured him for one of her friend's clients. He was quite attractive and she wondered what he wanted with her. He looked like he would be a good screw, but she didn't care enough to ask at the moment. For the first time ever, it occurred to her that Katty might have a steady boyfriend.

'Don't you ever knock?' Solice asked, as nonchalantly as possible.

'Who are you?' the man asked bluntly.

He wore jeans, a T-shirt and jacket, and while he looked normal enough, he might still be a jerk. That remark of his was rich; you could fertilise the lawn with it. Fucking horse-shit ... *who am I – like I don't even live here!*

'Who am I? Well, who the fuck are *you?*' she asked ... *the door ajar, Katty missing ...*

She made to pull the curtain open, her hand gripping it tighter than she realised, needing its sane and familiar *clackety-clack*, when he reached across and grasped her arm.

'I wouldn't do that,' he warned.

He looked pale, slightly off-colour, as if he had just learned a friend had died, and suddenly, the whereabouts of Katty became a secondary concern to that of her own safety.

Solice looked down at his white-knuckle grip, and felt pain in her arm. She realised then how easy it would be for him to fly off the edge and hurt her real bad. She wished for the bag she had left in the other room, and the Mace it contained.

'Relax,' he told her, and relinquished his grip as he led her out of the room. 'My name is Jay Austin. I'm a cop.'

He could be anybody, having offered no proof of his identification, and she still wondered about Katty ... *the bathtub*, she almost gasped, but then managed to block out the horrible thought. Katty was OK ... she *had* to be.

'Is Katty all right?' she asked.

There was no point in lying to her, Jay decided. She would find out soon enough, but then it would be in the cold room, where an unfeeling stranger would ask her to identify the body of her friend. At least here she was in a familiar environment.

'She's dead,' Jay told her, compassion in his voice. '*He* killed her. I didn't get here in time. I found her in the—' He motioned toward the door.

Solice immediately made for the bathroom, but he intercepted her and grabbed her arm, softly this time.

'You don't want to see ...'

'But how—?' she began, already crying, even though she did not know who this man was, what he was doing here, or even if she could trust him. 'How do I know I can believe you?'

Jay eased the door open, and she saw the mirror. On it, in a dull red that at first she thought was lipstick, was a single word.

A name.

H a d d o n f i e l d

Blood had trickled down from each letter, dried now.

Solice gasped, then twisted away, lifting a hand to her mouth. She made for the couch and fell onto it, burying her head in a cushion as she sobbed.

Jay walked over and touched her gently. She was grateful for that; his touch was comforting.

'What does it mean?' she asked.

'It's a message the killer left for me. I've been chasing him for a few days now, ever since he murdered my sister.' Jay wondered about that. *Ever since he murdered my sister* ... and now so many others, and so many before. The killing had to be stopped. 'Listen, the police will be here soon, but I shall have to leave before they arrive. I have to go. He will be waiting for me.'

'But—' she began, fear still holding her hand, grief gripping her heart. 'But, I thought that you were a cop?'

'I used to be,' he whispered. 'A long time ago.'

His name was Greg Harris, and he was Haddonfield's resident arsonist.

That was not his full-time occupation. During the day he was a mechanic, the only mechanic, at Jim's Car Sale and Repair – *most of the cars he sold were in great need of repair*. To boost his meagre wages a little, he torched a few empty buildings on the side. For the Gleason place he was getting a respectable five thou'.

Even without a bribe, he would still burn things. But while he was getting paid for what was essentially his own dark hobby, it added a little thrill, an extra buzz. Greg felt he was achieving something, and not just satisfying his own primal needs and desires.

He liked to watch the dancing flames, feel the heat leap over his face. He couldn't remember a time when he hadn't burned things ... although, after burning nothing, not even striking a match, for three whole weeks when he was a boy, the great God had shown him His anger by reaching out to touch him. The flame had lashed out at his hand, and he had been scarred – a horrible burn that covered his fingers, palm and the back of his hand; a loving touch ... and after that day, he always appeased his God, whether in privacy, or with these fantastic pyrotechnic displays.

The flame was his own God – a mentor and an idol. Something to worship and look up to. Something he could respect. It was a strong force, one he did not understand, but must always follow. He couldn't imagine life without it ... the boredom that would fill him.

Without the flame, there would not be life.

The Gleason place was big, and it had gone up in a glorious blaze, but while he was drenching the high walls with gasoline, he could have sworn he could hear someone shuffling about inside. But the place was supposed to be empty, so Greg put the noise down to his imagination.

He stood at the edge of the overgrown garden for several minutes, watching as the flames, looking like giant tongues, reached up in the night to lick the sky. Was that the sound of screaming? No, how could it be?

And now, drunk with the ecstasy of the heat and entranced by the glow, he cried out into the night and reached towards the fire.

He heard the sirens as they came closer; knew that he should be slipping away into the shadows, but could not move. And then he realised why.

It was not the sirens he could hear, but his God, speaking to him, calling out an invitation. The flames beckoned him nearer, taking shapes and forms he had never seen before, creating new mystery, persuading him to join them. The crackling voice of his God reeled him in, like a fish caught on the hook of a line.

There was nothing he could do but accept his destiny.

Slowly, unsure of the people gathering and the huge fire-truck arriving, Greg Harris walked towards the flames as they reached out and pulled him into a white-hot embrace.

It was the most horrible thing Angie had ever witnessed.

The sight of the man, nothing more than a kid really, with long straggly hair and acne that showed up in the light from the fire, walking trance-like into the flaming building. Not rushing, like he was meaning to save somebody, but walking, as if he were out in the park, holding his girlfriend's hand.

The night was alive with flashing lights and loud sirens, and a fireman – Brad, she thought – had dashed after him, his heavy jacket and equipment slowing him down. He was still feet away when he tackle-dived, in a final, futile effort to prevent the man from getting inside.

But the man seemed completely unaware of the fireman's gloved hand brushing against his ankle ... *as with marvel and bright reflections in his eyes, he became one with the terrible glow that illuminated the night.*

Later, as Dwight did his best to comfort her, Angie realised that the man had done it deliberately, willingly. Minutes after entering he had crashed from a third-floor window, screaming, falling like a burning meteor, leaving a trail of thick smoke behind. He was dead before he hit the ground.

It took Leigh Nichols and his seven-man crew – usually eight, but Dale Midkiff was at the Medical Centre watching over his ill daughter, Ellie; she was going to be fine, but all the assurances in the world would not have kept him away from her pale side – just over an hour to bring the blaze under control. A short time after that, the site was nothing more than a dark scar on the green landscape. Smouldering ashes and a part of the thin frame of the building was all that was left.

And amongst the ashes, partially hidden in the dirty grey, were two black, charcoal-crisp bodies, thin smoke still trailing up from them as they cooled.

When they had gotten the call, Leigh and Tom had left in the librarian's car. With a light kiss on the cheek, Alice had told them both to be careful. These days, with all the fires, they were beginning to look more and more like Paul Newman and Steve McQueen than a librarian and a small-town sheriff getting ready to retire. And these were the kind of worrying heroics she could happily do without, especially with, as he was affectionately becoming known, 'Baby Hasky' on the way.

So she watched as the car raced away from her home, and stood still for a moment, thinking what life would be like if she should lose Tom, if he sped off to this fire like he was in a big-budget disaster movie and never came back . . . but only for a moment, and never again, so frightening was the thought.

Tom would be all right. Tom and Leigh both. They would always be at her side . . . the two men in her life.

They arrived shortly after the truck, and were greeted by dramatic descriptions of a man who had walked into the building like it was his own personal funeral pyre – despite Brad's efforts to keep him out – and then plummeted from a window.

While he listened to these reports, Leigh quickly geared up, putting on a thick protective jacket that would keep the flames at bay, and cumbersome breathing apparatus.

Brad, with Holly – the only female on the team – had already entered the inferno, while Jules and Yeager operated the cannon outside.

'Johnson!' Leigh shouted as he quickly ran a test on his equipment. He wanted to get inside as soon as possible. Not only would Brad and Holly need help, they might also need a break. 'Johnson . . . you're up.'

'But I've never—' Johnson began to protest. At

twenty, he was the youngest and newest recruit on the crew.

'You're all there is,' Leigh told him bluntly. 'The time is now, so gear up. Jules, Chuck – get on the smaller jets! This wind's a bitch ... the flames are spreading. Set up some kind of perimeters. Hasky! Move that crowd back!'

Hasky was already on it, had been from the second the car stopped. Leigh's efficiency, however angry it was, did not bother Tom. This was Leigh's territory, and he was quite happy to let him run the show. Hasky knew he was just another pair of hands.

'You ready?' Leigh asked.

'Sure,' Johnson said without enthusiasm as he pulled the mask and visor down over his face, and tried to forget how crazy this was. He had never been inside a burning building before, and was not even sure how to fight the fire from within.

'You'll do good,' Leigh said, and then they were running into the hot blaze, a thick hose trailing behind them.

The fire had been a challenge ... but everybody had risen to it.

Brad and Holly came out first. The fire was under control by then; it was just a matter of time before the defeated flames were extinguished, so they went off to help direct the main cannon.

Ten minutes later Nichols emerged carrying Johnson.

The kid had spotted a beam about to crash down and had flung himself at Nichols, knocking him clear. The hose had jerked out of Nichols's hand, spinning and whipping around, spraying water in every direction, and the beam had landed on Johnson's leg.

He was rushed to the Haddonfield Medical Centre, where the night staff took X-rays showing that his leg was broken in two places. He would be OK – contrary to the worries that raced through Nichols and his crew as he carried him out.

Now, cleaned up a little, Leigh stood over the two corpses, studying them. One of the bodies was obviously less burned and charred than the other; it must be the man who had fallen from the window. Had he still been alive, however badly injured, Hasky would have set fire to his ass again for even going near the building.

'Who are they, coach?' Brad asked, as he finished closing down the main cannon.

'I don't know,' Leigh said, and pointed to Harris's body. 'From what I hear, and the way I figure it, this guy is our arsonist. I don't know about the other one – perhaps Cedar Court can help us out. Maybe it was a vagrant who had found his way into the building. As for identification, I guess we will just have to wait for the ME's report.'

'Is Johnson going to make it?' Brad asked.

They were all concerned about Johnson, but especially Nichols, who had sent him into the building, and Brad. He and the much-younger man were business partners, and it was Brad who had persuaded him to join the department.

'I think so, but he's going to be out of it for a little

while,' Leigh said, regretting the decision he had made. Johnson could have been killed. 'It was a bad call, a big mistake. I should never have sent him into the building.'

'Don't be so hard on yourself,' Brad told him. 'You did the best you could, with the resources at your disposal. You did good ... we all did.'

'Yeah – he saved my life big style in there. I'm going to speak with the Mayor about some kind of award. Will you back me up?'

Brad's guilt was almost as great as Leigh's.

'Sure thing,' he said. 'Hey, don't worry about it. Johnson's fine.' And then he kicked at the ashes. 'I just don't get it, Chief. No fires for years, and now all these. And this time, we got fatalities. What do you think this is all about?'

'I don't know,' Leigh replied. 'And I'm not sure I want to.'

That was the night Daniel arrived in Haddonfield; and as he walked down its streets he picked up on a low-energy buzz that filled the air. Something had gone down here recently, something bad. People pushed by him without excuse, hurrying towards an unknown destination. Somebody pulled open a door and shouted something, and a stream of bodies raced through it.

...again ... the Gleason building ... another property ... somebody died ... two ...

He heard snippets of conversation as he patiently waited for them all to pass him. Cars drove by fast. This

Gleason place acted like a magnet – a Pied Piper for the local people – one without music, except for the soliloquy of the dead.

He walked into a nearby bar; it seemed pleasant enough, if deserted. Half-finished drinks were left everywhere, and only two customers remained – a drunk, unconscious, his face in the pretzel bowl, and a woman sitting at the bar, sipping what looked like a straight vodka.

Behind the bar was a small, squat man performing various cleaning tasks as he prepared for the predictable rush back from the Gleason place. The people of Haddonfield would need somewhere to talk and gossip.

Ignoring the drunk, Daniel seated himself beside the woman, who turned to see who was there. She was about thirty, and had a childlike look of wonder on her face. He could tell that she'd had far more to drink than she was normally accustomed to.

'Are you not going to the Gleason place?' he asked them both, but particularly the woman.

'Not me,' the bartender said, and then went on to explain his reply, even though Daniel did not care. 'I have to get ready. I saw it the last time, so I'm not taking any chances now. This place is the first stop after a fire ... everybody can use a cold beer. I like to think it's my good ale, but I doubt it.'

'Dwight will be there,' the woman whispered softly.

Ellen had awoken that morning, alone and feeling disoriented. It felt strange, not to have somebody to hold you, somebody for you to depend on. She had rolled over, and found herself on the other side of the bed ... *his side* ... an unfamiliar territory. It brought instant feelings of rejection and loneliness, of fear. But it brought freedom, too, she realised – a freedom she hadn't experienced in far too long.

She did not have to get up. There was no breakfast to prepare, no errands or chores. She could do whatever she wanted to do. She had her own life now, yet all she wanted to do was go back to sleep and forget everything.

The rejection, her sense of loss, self-doubt and fear of what the future held ... she wanted to tie it all in a bundle and throw it away, never to be seen again!

But as she woke properly, rubbing the sleep from her eyes, she knew that was impossible. The memories came back, quick and ruthless, bringing with them all the pain, and they were so strong that she could not fight them.

Hours passed, and come evening she still lay in the bed, her face streaked by painful tears of remembrance, her eyes sullen and red. She wished he was back, longed for Dwight to be at her side again. The next minute, she wanted him out of her mind, as he was out of her life.

She had to get up, get out of the house. She needed somebody to speak to so that she could chase the memories away and vanquish them. And so she had found herself at the bar, a bottle for company.

'Who is Dwight?' Daniel asked, not concerned with her personal problems. It was just a hook, an easy way to get to know her, before the monster's feeding-time.

She looked at the man, and hated him for his question. Who was he to ask about her private life? She did not even know him. She stared into his piercing blue eyes which were like oceans, easy to drown in, and realised the question was honest and sincere. He wasn't prying, or simply pretending to care – he was just a harmless stranger in town, trying to make a friend.

You wanted somebody to talk to, so talk.

'Dwight is my husband. He left me last night ... after ten years together.'

He had really left her months ago, the first time he had made love to Angie. Ellen found the words easier to say than she had anticipated. She'd thought it would be difficult to find the right words, that she'd be sobbing when she said them, and before this conversation ended, she knew she would be.

'Crazy guy,' Daniel observed.

She smiled, doing her best to hold back the tears. The stranger was sweet, but she knew he had only said it in a vain attempt to cheer her up.

It wasn't true. Dwight wasn't crazy. He had done the best thing for himself, and there was nothing crazy, or wrong, about that. It was a selfish world.

She would have hurt herself before she hurt Dwight.

She laughed pathetically, shaking her head. She couldn't believe she was actually defending him.

'No. He did the right thing for him,' she whispered.

'Hey, I'm not looking for an argument. I don't even know the guy. It's just that, well – you're quite attractive. Lose a few of those extra pounds, and dress up a little, and I would use the word "gorgeous" in the same sentence as your name.'

As she finally let the tears go, Daniel knew she was his. He could mould this situation however he wanted. He could manipulate and control this bitch. He had absolute power.

He reached across, gently wiping the tears from her cheeks. The monster was going to kill this woman, but he wanted her to experience hope, to feel good about herself before he cut her down.

The monster was going to kill this woman ... and then he would declare open season on the people of Haddonfield. And when that dirty fucker from Detroit finally arrived, he would make it open season on *him*. He would hurt him so bad, the man would beg Daniel to kill him and end the pain.

And then he would move on. Free, safe once more.

As Ellen looked at his thin smile, with perfect teeth he should learn to show off more often, as she stared into the stranger's cold yet compassionate eyes, she realised what they were saying. He was ready to walk out of the bar now and go back to her empty home, and make love, where his gentle touch would become a soft caress.

But it would not be love. Nor would it be gentle.

It would be sex, angry and hard – and she did not know whether she was ready to do that, not so soon. She still hurt, and had not yet comprehended that the pain was all in her mind, and that life would always go on.

She wanted to lick her wounds clean; needed time to heal by herself.

But ... to spite Dwight. As an act of pure malice against him. He'd sure had a good time while she was being faithful and true, so why shouldn't she? Why should she sit and worry and grow old while the world passed her by? No morals were involved. No strings attached. No questions asked. And no guilt. The man before her was the original Sure Thing. A 100 per cent safe bet that she would wake up feeling happy in the morning.

It was her turn to have some fun.

She smiled coyly, sexily. She had never lost it, and never would. 'You mean ... ?'

'No words,' he whispered. He stood, and took her hand as he led her out of the bar.

Soon the killing would begin again, a maelstrom of death he could not control.

His destiny.

A preordained fate he could never escape.

Angie jolted awake in the middle of the night.

Full of fear, all she could smell was the repugnant stench from earlier that night. All she could feel was the sickening nausea she had experienced as she watched the body burn. All she could hear was the crackling of flames, as the Gleason place was consumed by fire.

There had been no screams of pain. The man had wanted it, she understood that now. All she could see – behind her eyes, in the darkness of her mind – was him walking head up, triumphant, into the building which was nothing more than a huge mountain of fire lighting up the night and warming the stars.

Angie was in a feverish state. Hot and cold, sweating and then suddenly chilled. But then sleep came once more and, except for her dreams, she managed to forget for a short while.

Jay was tired.

Through aching eyes he saw the rental car wandering into the wrong lane, and he pulled at the wheel, nearly sending it into a skid.

But he could not sleep.

He could not stop.

Haddonfield. The name was like a beacon, beckoning him on.

The sonofabitch was in Haddonfield ... waiting.

He had not wanted to leave Solice alone in her apartment, and she had begged him to stay with her, but he knew now that even a delay of seconds might mean the difference between a life lost and a life saved. Billy Rogers was proof of that.

After leaving Kamski he had purchased a map of the area around Chicago. It took him a while to find the small town, and as he roughly calculated the distance he figured that the killer was already well on his way there.

Already there!

So he must not stop.

He would drive slower, though, for however much he

wanted to speed up and send the car racing through the night, he would be of no use to anybody dead, or bleeding in a car wreck. He set a steady pace and figured on arriving in Haddonfield early the next morning, along with the rising sun.

Again the car wandered, and again he pulled it back.

His eyelids drooped and felt heavy. Sleep was creeping up on him, but if he stopped the car and lay down for a few minutes, it would beat a retreat and never arrive.

He was too close to the edge.

He was ragged and tired, but at the same time his heart beat fast at the thought of catching up with the killer, avenging Susan and Billy, and all the others, and bringing his reign of terror to an end.

Chapter Fourteen
First Kill

It was morning, and Daniel watched her as she cut through the bread, making smooth, thin slices, holding the knife delicately in her hand. He studied the light grip she used on the handle, so different from the strong hold he would use when the time came . . . but mostly, he was transfixed by the light glinting and bouncing off the blade itself.

He moved forward and wrapped his arms about her waist.

'Let's make love,' he whispered in her ear.

Fool her . . . let her think that you want her bad. Put her on top of the world, and then cut her down.

'But I've started breakfast,' she argued weakly.

Ellen was not even sure she wanted to sleep with the man again – not yet, anyway. Not so soon after the first time. She needed to think, figure out what he meant to her. She did not want to jump into anything she might regret later.

He held her wrist, at first gently and she thought he was going to massage it ... *a fooling lullaby* ... an attempt to make her feel good and positive about his advances. Her wrist was a starting point; from there he would move up to her shoulder – a kind, soft, slow movement. He would reach under her satin nightgown, and then he would venture deeper, and he would *touch her*. And she would want him to be inside her, so she would let him take—

Suddenly his grip on her wrist was tight, and he continued to apply more and more pressure, his rough hand enclosing her slender arm. He was hurting her and she wanted to pull away, but knew that if she struggled ... or screamed ... it might only excite him further.

She knew now that it had been a mistake to let this stranger into her home. She did not need him, and never had. If he wanted to ... *she could feel his other hand snaking up her leg, beneath her nightgown and across her thigh, up and ...* rape her, there was nothing she could do, nothing she could use to stop him.

Nothing – except for the knife.

But she could see it waver in her hand as he gripped tighter. She valiantly tried to keep hold of it, but was convinced that within seconds her wrist would be crushed. Her fingers slowly unfolded from the knife. There was nothing she could do to stop herself from dropping the ... *weapon*.

Her only defence gone ... *as his fingers reached inside her* ... the knife clattered on the worktop, and all she

290

could think was ... *please don't rape me, please don't rape me, don't rape me, don'trapemedon't* ... the words rushing together, ringing in her mind like silent alarm bells.

Suddenly, he let go of her wrist and she looked down at the deep red mark he'd made. He grabbed her around the waist and dragged her towards the bedroom. When he had been watching her with the knife, Daniel's mind had been going crazy. The monster wanted to take that knife and cut her across the face with it, wanted to see the bitch's blood run freely.

Angie could not think straight.

She was haunted by the fact that there must have been something she could have done to save the men. Nobody deserved to die in such a horrible manner.

Except, perhaps, for one man ... She was actually smiling at the thought now, and it was clear what had to be done.

Two people were dead as a result of her acceptance of Dwight's criminal behaviour. She looked at him, watched the steady rise and fall of his stomach, and noticed, even when asleep, how smug he looked, how pleased with himself. People had died thanks to Griffen's scam, and all Dwight cared about was his cut, his percentage.

The deaths were partly her responsibility as well. She had known the Gleason place was going up, and could have done something about it, but hadn't. She should have called the doctor. She was on Dwight's level now, just as negligent, and she didn't like being there.

Angie stared at the man in her bed, and wondered how much she genuinely loved him. She leaned over and ran a finger across his stubbled jawline. Doubt and confusion were creeping into her mind again. Sure, she had been negligent, but Dwight's behaviour had been worse. He might just as well have set fire to the building himself, or put a gun to the victims' head and pulled the trigger.

She eased off the bed, slowly, so as not to wake him. For the first time ever while Dwight was in her home, she dressed; really put clothes on, not just some sexy underwear and make-up. She wasn't sure she wanted him near her any longer, and she definitely didn't want him touching her.

She went to the phone in the kitchen – not even thinking about what she was going to do, because if she did, she knew she would never go through with it – and quickly dialled the number of Griffen's office in the city.

'I'd like to make an appointment to see Mr Griffen,' she said quietly, so that Dwight would not be able to hear her if he was awake.

But Dwight was already out of bed, and listening at the door as Angie made the call; he knew immediately what she was trying to do. She was going to talk to Griffen, try to undermine the position he – Dwight Little – had so recently dug out for himself. She was going to make some stupid demands and ruin all that he had achieved.

Dwight would not allow that. He would not let her destroy his dream.

'Thank you,' she whispered, and hung up.

Dwight pushed open the door as she replaced the receiver. She turned, no doubt intending to check that he was still sleeping, and nearly hit the ceiling when she saw him.

'I didn't mean to startle you,' Dwight lied. 'Who was that?'

She hesitated, not knowing how long he had been in the room ... *listening – had the bastard been listening at the door all along? ...* not knowing how much he'd overheard.

'Wrong number,' she said and went to move past him, but Dwight grabbed her arm roughly.

'Don't fuck this up for me!' he whispered harshly, and held her still.

Dwight had her scared, and Angie wished she had called Hasky the second he had told her about the deal. This whole thing had twisted him and bent him out of shape. It had destroyed his character, and turned him into a different person.

He was hurting her arm now, squeezing tighter, and she could feel his fingers digging deeper and deeper into her flesh. Looking into his eyes, she wondered if he was actually enjoying it, if this power trip was giving him some kind of hard on. But she knew it was more than that, and almost sympathised with him. Her lover was blinded by greed and confusion.

'Dwight, you're all screwed up,' she told him.

She was pulling away again when he pushed her back – hard. This was no power trip, he had really meant to hurt her then. She felt the corner of a cupboard dig sharply into the small of her back, and almost keeled over with the pain, but refused to lower herself before him. She could feel the tears run quickly to the front of her eyes, but would not set them free; she would not give him that pleasure.

She would not let him know how much she was hurting.

'Don't speak to me that way, bitch!' he snapped.

Angie was at a loss. Except for his bullshit suspicion, she did not even know why he was so angry at her, but she'd be damned if she'd let him believe he could kick the crap out of her for no reason.

Overnight, their love had turned sour and rotten.

'I'm surprised Ellen didn't leave you first!' she shouted, hitting him where she knew it still hurt.

He screamed in rage and lashed out at her, but he was angry and predictable, so it was easy for her to duck beneath his arm and make a run for the door. She didn't care about packing or grabbing any clothes ... *she was going to the city and she was torching that cruel bastard, Griffen* ...

It was the only way justice could be served.

'Come back here!' he commanded.

Angie slammed the door and left him.

Who did she think she was? Setting out for the city to steal his thunder, to claim his prize. She had deceitful intentions. Dwight wondered now if this had been her plan from the first day they had slept together. She had wanted to use him, take advantage of him ...

294

He slammed his fist onto the counter, wondering what had become of his life. He had walked out of his marriage because of Angie, and now, thanks to that fat fuck Griffen, he had also lost his mistress.

Dwight was crying now, his anger suddenly forgotten. This whole fucking arson business had turned him inside out.

He was so confused.

He could feel his thoughts ripping his mind in every direction.

He had lost Ellen, and wanted her back so badly.

She was the only person who had ever counted in his life, the only person who had ever truly loved him, and he needed her ... but what if it was too late?

It was burning daylight when Jay arrived in Haddonfield.

As he steered the car around rolling fields and beautiful trees, following the road that cut straight through them, he pondered sombrely on how, else-where, Man was destroying nature. *Had destroyed it.* Had turned tranquil landscapes into dark, slum cities, into sprawling metropolises that simply grew and grew, out of control.

And now that Man had finished with nature, he was turning on himself.

WELCOME TO HADDONFIELD pop. 10,069

Ten thousand and sixty-nine – and every one of them,

from the youngest child to the oldest resident, a potential victim.

As he drove around a curve, the road following a fast-flowing river, the town came into view. Compared to New York, where Jay had lived for most of his life, it seemed minuscule, and looking at the tiny – almost model-sized – buildings in the valley, he found it difficult to believe that the town was home to nearly 11,000 souls. Absently, he wondered how long it would be before this town ate up the surrounding greenery to become something bigger.

An old wooden bridge allowed him passage across the river. Then, almost too suddenly he thought, as though it might be easy for the river to just drop off the hill, he found himself descending towards Haddonfield, which was beginning to look a lot bigger now he was closer to it.

The town swallowed him...

Because school was out, Kirby McCaul could do his paper round whenever he wanted. He no longer had to get up at six in the morning just so that people he did not even know could read about all the badness in the world. This was his holiday, so they could wait for their papers; and if they should complain he would remind them of the efficient service he provided all year round ... and let them try and argue with that.

He let another paper fly and ... *seven for seven* ... another one right on the doorstep. Just let them complain! He would show them ... papers would be landing at the ends of yards and gardens, sitting there in the pouring rain until somebody came out and lifted up the soaked pages which would be sticking on the ground, soggy and moist.

Another flyer ... *eight for eight* ...

He was coming up on the north end of town now – the least favourite part of his round. He liked to get it out of the way early. About ninety per cent of the town was successful and prosperous, but the north end was the *rich* part of town, the exclusive suburb ... and some of the driveways were so fucking long, he had to go halfway up them before he could get close to hitting the door – and that was with his good arm.

He lazily let one go with his left, and scored another hit.

Most of the streets were wide, and in various places they were lined by huge trees, their thick branches draping over the road. But as Jay came into Haddonfield, searching for the Sheriff's department, constantly watching for a face so familiar it could be his own, the roads began to narrow and the expensive houses gave way to cheaper – although not cheap – dwellings.

He swerved as a crazy kid raced by him on a bicycle, travelling in the opposite direction, launching papers from both his left and right hand. A faint smile, more like a grimace, played across Jay's face. It was the best he could manage. Smiling had become difficult these past few days.

Talented sonofabitch, he thought.

Jay remembered when he'd had his own round, years ago, but he'd never been that good, not with both hands. He looked in the rearview mirror and watched the kid – *no-handed* as he took a corner and went out of sight, one hand reaching into the plastic basket on the handlebars for a folded and banded paper, the other letting one fly.

Jay watched it hit the wall of a house, and could easily imagine the unconcerned dismay the kid was feeling because he had missed the door, and wished that he himself was still on his bicycle ... when the world did not matter and there was no responsibility, no laws. When you are young and innocent, nothing can touch you.

Back when they were alive, *all of them* ...

He turned onto Main Street, and cruised slowly, watching the stores pass by. Then he spotted the bar. He drew up and parked in front of it. This was where the countdown began. The beginning of the end.

He walked into the tavern and approached the bar. The man behind it was polishing glasses, occasionally holding one up to the light so that he could see the gleam he had produced. He seemed taller than he actually was because the wooden floor behind the counter had been slightly raised, so that he could look down on most, if not all, of his patrons. In such a small town that must give a guy a satisfying feeling of power.

The bartender watched through the bottom of a glass as the man walked towards him. His face was bruised, but he looked like he could handle himself in a fight. He replaced the glass on the counter.

'What can I get you?'

'Where is the Sheriff's department?' Jay asked.

'Why?'

'I'm looking for this man,' Jay explained, less tense than he had been in the tavern in Chicago, and again produced the picture that had been lifted off the dead cameraman's film.

The bartender looked at the photograph and nodded his head slowly, raising an eyebrow. It had not escaped his notice that two strangers had arrived in Haddonfield within twelve hours. Haddonfield was a small town – you needed a map to find it, and you wouldn't just stumble upon it while following the main routes across state. He wondered who these men were.

'I know him. Who is he?'

'When did you last see him?' Jay asked, ignoring the question.

'Last night – he came in here then left with Ellen Little. Why are you looking for him?' the bartender persisted.

'Where does Ellen Little live?'

'Why?'

'Jesus . . .' Jay sighed under his breath. 'I'm a cop. This man is a killer.'

The bartender paused for a second, taking this information in.

'The address?' Jay demanded.

'It's at the north end of town. Twelve, Riverside Road – I think. Bunch of snob houses.'

'I came into town that way,' Jay whispered, and

jogged to the door. He looked back, afraid that his fear might be visible. 'Call the local force and tell them to get over there – now. Then call her place, and tell her to get out of the house, as quickly as possible. Tell her to hide somewhere she knows is safe.'

Jay ran to the car and climbed in. He started the engine, and only then did he realise how tight a grip he had on the wheel, to prevent his hands from shaking.

'Please,' Ellen cried as the man threw her onto the bed. 'Don't do this.'

She looked up and saw him slowly unbuttoning his shirt. Her nightgown had rucked up and she desperately wanted to cover herself so that he could not see her. Cold tears were rolling down her face, but she did not try to stop them. She sobbed and pulled at the nightgown.

'Please,' she begged again.

She had to get out of the house. There was nobody here to protect her. Dwight was gone. There was only herself, and ... *the rapist*. Just thinking that word terrified her.

She looked at the window.

It was open, just an inch. She would have to pull it up to fit through. That would cost her valuable seconds, but once down the driveway she would be able to stop a car on the road, or rush to a neighbour's house. Once on the street she would be safe.

She sat up, noticing with a shock that her attacker

was no longer in the room. She looked around, and saw his clothes on the floor at the foot of the bed. She was torn between going for the window, or searching for his wallet so that she could give Sheriff Hasky some kind of identification. Then she looked to the phone, and saw herself quickly punching in a number, calling for help...

It was all this crazy hesitation that cost her ... everything...

He returned, and looked at her pleading face, panicked and sad. The face was so familiar, one he had seen so many times before, except for one slight, subtle difference. Her face was tear-streaked and she was whispering incoherently, but this woman had scheming eyes. Here was one victim who had not given in. Her eyes burned with hatred as she tried to figure a way of escape.

Perhaps he should start with the eyes...

'You have to understand. I must do this,' he explained softly, and then she saw the knife in his hand – the one she had been using to cut bread only short minutes ago. He touched her cheek with the tip of it.

She screamed as he came down on her.

'I must,' he whispered again, and neither of them heard Dwight walking up the driveway, his face also streaked by tears. Then he began running because he needed to see Ellen so badly, needed to salvage what he could of his marriage.

Kirby only had to deliver to four of the houses on

Riverside, so he quickly pedalled to the top of the road and skidded the back wheel to a halt, before the road ascended towards the river. Going this way, he could throw the first two papers from the street, but would have to go up the driveways of the others.

From the bottom of Riverside, he would cut onto Thompson Avenue.

He reached the first of the driveways and stopped halfway up number 12, about to launch the paper when he saw a woman run past one of the bottom windows. *Breasts, she had breasts* ... at least, the top half of her body, the part he could see, was naked.

Well, don't stop now, he urged himself. *Go on up and get yourself an eyeful.*

He pedalled fast up to the front door, lowered the bicycle to the ground, carefully making sure the remaining papers did not fall from the basket, and then crept silently along the front wall until he reached the window.

He looked in and saw the woman crouched in a corner. She still had a nightgown on, but it was hanging useless at her waist, only hiding her thighs and legs.

Although she was old enough to be his mom, the woman was gorgeous...

Then Kirby saw that she was sobbing, could see her tears. He felt bad about staring at her, invading her privacy. He was no pervert, just a curious kid. But he still felt guilty.

That was when the man passed by the window.

Shocked out of his dreamworld – in which the woman

was taking him, showing him, teaching him – Kirby ducked down quick. If the window had been open any wider, he could have reached out and touched the man ... reached out and touched the ... *knife in his hand!*

When the man had passed the window, Kirby peeped in again and saw him advancing towards the woman, the knife glinting.

What am I doing here?

He looked at the woman, her sullen red eyes begging and pleading with her attacker. And then she saw him. Her eyes widened, and now she was begging Kirby, silently begging for him to do something – to save her life.

The naked man reached down. The woman pushed herself back against the wall, as if it might give way under her feeble pressure, as if it might collapse due to her fear. But there was nowhere to run. Nowhere to hide. The knife came down slowly and Kirby saw it dance across her breasts, marking them for ever as blood trickled forth.

Do something...

Do something now!

But Kirby was frozen, mesmerised, as if watching some kind of macabre play. He half-expected the couple to stop at any second and take a bow at the window, because there was no way any of this could be real.

The woman screamed.

Kirby quickly scanned the room for something he could use, anything that might distract the man and his lethal blade. That was when he saw the body, and the blood. It had no face, only the figure and shape of a person, a human mass, pale and red.

Kirby could feel his breakfast rising, could taste the bitter bile in his mouth. He took one hesitant step back, and then stopped because the world seemed to spin about his head. The body was there, wherever he looked ... dead in front of his eyes.

Don't faint!

He was dizzy, being swallowed by darkness. Kirby felt his legs buckle, but managed to remain standing ... and as suddenly as the world had begun to spin, it stopped, so still it could have been a photograph.

He looked in the window ... *not the body, don't look at the body* ... and saw the woman. She was bleeding quite badly now – although it looked strangely superficial, like bad make-up in a horror movie. The man still stood above her. All-powerful and dominating.

And he still had not seen Kirby at the window, so even though he was more powerful, angrier, bigger and stronger, Kirby had the element of surprise, and that surely gave him an edge.

He would save the woman, and together they would ride into the setting sun, and she would—

Her scream cut savagely through his thoughts and, without thinking, not caring about the repercussions, Kirby picked up his bicycle, papers tumbling everywhere, and hurled it at the window with all his strength.

Daniel stood above the woman and listened to her

scream, savoured it and stored it alongside the ranks of so many others.

Then the window smashed in with a loud clatter. The monster, poised, ready to push the point of the knife into her mouth and ram the whole fucking thing down her throat, turned, surprised, and saw a bicycle – half of it inside the room, the rest dangling out of the window. He stepped over and grabbed the back wheel of the bicycle, pulled it all the way into the room, knocking shards of glass away, and threw it onto the bed.

He looked out, the monster inside him snarling at this interruption.

It took Ellen a few seconds of black terror before she was even aware that the man was no longer before her. She looked around and saw Dwight's body – a scream rose to her throat ... *don't look* ... and a bicycle on the bed.

A bicycle! Perhaps she had been tipped over the edge into madness. Or was it that somebody, or something, had diverted Daniel's attention? Ellen wasted no time. Bleeding heavily, one hand clutching at her trailing nightgown, her whole body shaking, she made a run for the door.

Daniel did not try to stop her ... *Thank God, Thank God* ... but she froze when she heard a child screaming, and looked back from the door.

The man had a greater prize – also one Ellen could not ignore. She recognised the boy, and she could not run while he held the fragile body of Kirby McCaul, kicking and screaming in his hands ...

* * *

Jesus fucking Christ on His throne!

Kirby had not known what would happen, what to expect due to his impulsive action, but he guessed now, as he crouched low under the window, up against the stone wall, that the man's response was perfectly logical.

Kirby could sense him above, looking out. He had felt it as tiny shards of glass fell on him as the bicycle was tugged through the window. Kirby held his breath. The man continued to look out, until—

A hand gripped his hair, and the ground fell away as he was pulled up and lifted inside, dragged roughly across the sharp glass.

Kirby heard his clothes rip, felt the pain as the glass cut through the skin on his back.

He could do nothing to stop the screams escaping his lips.

She ran from the room, leaving the boy trapped in the man's iron-tight grip. It was fear that drove her away, and before she knew where she was – all the blood and pain forgotten, the unspeakable *thing* that was her dead husband – she had burst out of the front door in a frenzied panic, and was running down the driveway.

She did not care that she was naked, except for the bloodied nightgown which hung about her legs. All she wanted to do was get away from the house, and the horror that was there.

Then, as partial control came back and she slowed

near the bottom of the driveway, she realised what she had done. A young boy was in the hands of a madman, who had killed her husband ... *but she dared not think about what had happened ...*

She had left Kirby McCaul back there to die, so that she could save herself and live. A small boy who had risked everything in his precious world, just so that she might have a chance – and now she was turning her back on him, leaving him in mortal danger.

She stopped and looked back at the house, and her own fear stared back at her. The boy continued to scream. She raised her hands to her ears and wept, wishing she could block out his misery.

A car screeched to a halt at the bottom of the driveway, and she turned to see who it was – not really caring, because the only important thing was that someone had come to rescue them; she and the boy were saved.

A man climbed from the car, a gun already in his hand. She had never seen him before. But he was here now ... to protect her, and save the boy.

She ran to him.

Chapter Fifteen
Nightmare Realities

Jay held the woman for a second, his arms wrapped around her, his grip tight and comforting. Then he eased away and checked her over. She looked like she had been through Hell, and Jay knew the man who had given her the guided tour.

But she had survived.

'Are you going to be OK?' he asked, pulling his sweatshirt over his head, and handing it to her. She was bloody, but the cuts did not look too deep.

'I . . . I think so,' she replied, stammering in her haste. 'But he . . . has a boy inside.'

'OK, listen,' Jay told her, trying not to sound nervous, *frightened*. 'I want you to go get in the car. The police should be here soon. If anybody other than myself or the kid comes out of the house, you drive away.'

'But—'

'Do it! You drive out of here fast. Understand?'

She hesitated, then nodded. She looked at him. He

was thin, but had a muscular build, and he was sweating, sunlight glinting on beads of salty liquid. There were bruises on his naked chest, and his face also wore light shades of pain. He carried a gun, and looked like he knew how to use it ... but even so, he did not add up to much against the lunatic inside her apartment. She wanted to tell him not to go inside, but the boy was still in there, and somebody had to save him ...

The man before her stood, waiting for her to get into the car before he headed for the house ... perhaps waiting for an excuse not to go, a reason not to die.

'Look – you don't have to go,' she whispered. 'The police will be here soon.'

'I have to,' he stated, and she knew from the tone of his voice and the grim determination that marked his face, from the way he brandished the gun ... from everything about him, including the fact that he had arrived just when he was needed, that he had been waiting a long time for this moment.

That this was one traumatic scene in her life, but also a small part of something much bigger which she could never imagine ...

And never wanted to.

Louise, the day-time phone operator, receptionist, and radio call-out at the Sheriff's department, and part-time waitress down at the coffee shop, looked up from her nails when the phone rang. Before the first ring had completed she had it in her hand because this could be the one she'd been waiting for ... this could be a *real* emergency.

She had been with the department for nearly a year now. The work was easy, if somewhat boring and routine at times, and Sheriff Hasky made sure she was paid well for her meagre duties. She had no intention of staying there all her life, as she had no intention of staying in Haddonfield. She had seen too many of her young friends get pregnant and get stuck here with Neanderthal boyfriends whom they did not really love. The job made for good savings, and she liked the attention the younger deputies paid her. Especially Conrad, with his cute ass. She would fix to go out with him soon.

She knew she had a good body and figure, and at least half a brain, not having wasted her school years fucking in the locker room. Conrad made her laugh, and she wouldn't mind starting something regular with him. He was also looking for a way out of Haddonfield, and they could make it together – but she did not want to go over the top with him, move too fast and scare him away.

Anyway, it had been nearly a year now, and every time she answered the phone, she heard the same old thing ... *my cat is stuck in a tree ... my little boy is late from school ... would the Sheriff like some home-baked cookies ...?* and on, and on.

Home-baked cookies – there was a thing. She could use some of them. She wondered about her skinny figure. She was nearly twenty and attractive enough, but with a little more weight ... fill out her figure a little, give Conrad something to hold onto, and—

'Goddamn it! I said, is Hasky there?'

The voice sounded urgent enough, and she nearly fell off her chair as it cut through her daydreaming like a loud car horn. There was an actual emergency, other than the fires, taking place in Haddonfield.

Procedure ... and she took a second to compose herself. Remember what they taught you a year ago? Well, remember it and use it!

And Louise – stay calm, honey.

'Sheriff's department,' she said as cool as ice. 'What's the problem?'

'I got an emergency, lady! Is Hasky there or not?'

'What name is it?' she asked.

Yes, do tell. Who are you, with your goddamn impatience? Didn't he know they all had their jobs to do? If she screwed up here, it could cause Hasky trouble further down the line.

'Stevie, from the bar. Listen lady, I'm sorry for how I spoke, but hurry the fuck up!'

Oh, she wanted to cut him and his attitude off so badly, but if this was a genuine crisis – and she had to admit, this didn't sound like kids fooling around – she knew that would achieve nothing.

'Please hold,' she told him briskly.

'For—!'

But she pushed the button and smiled to herself.

'Eat muzak, shithead,' she laughed, and then pushed another button which put her through to Sheriff Hasky.

'I have a Stevie, from the bar, on the line. Sounds pretty urgent.'

'Put him on,' Hasky's voice came back immediately.

She hit the button.

'Jesus fucking—!'

'This is Hasky,' he interrupted calmly. 'What's the big emergency?'

'Well, about fucking time! This doesn't exactly restore my faith in our policing system,' Stevie began.

'You called to insult me? Well, I guess that is pretty important. Now, why don't you just tell me the problem, and then we can all get on with our jobs,' Hasky told him.

There was a long pause, and Hasky could hear the anger in the silence as the man tried to calm down.

'Last night some guy turned up in town and left my place with Ellen Little. Today, another guy came in, said he was looking for the first guy and that Ellen was in danger. He went straight on over to her place and told me to call ahead, and then give you a ring.'

'Ellen Little? Dwight's wife?' Hasky asked, already knowing the answer.

'Yeah. But I hear he's got some poontang on the side, if you know what I mean, and I think you do.'

Yeah, sure . . . and for a second Hasky thought about Alice. He would never be unfaithful to her.

His town was already going down the toilet with this arson business, and now this. He hoped it was Stevie's mistake. He looked at the gun on the table, and felt certain he was going to have to use it soon.

'I know what you mean. What did she say when you called?'

'That's just it, man. I tried twice, but both times there was no answer. I let it ring and ring, but nobody picked it up.'

Dwight Little . . .

Hasky was in half a mind to just let the call go by, but it wasn't Ellen's fault she had married an asshole. Besides, it was not in his character to ignore such a call. If somebody needed his help, he would gladly give it. He was responsible for the safety of Haddonfield's people, and that included all the jerks and cheating husbands.

'OK. Thanks, Stevie. Somebody will call by the bar later for a statement.'

Hasky pushed a button and then, as his hand went instinctively to his mouth, he wished he still had his moustache. It comforted him to run his fingers across it when he was thinking; it kept his mind on track.

'Louise,' he said, 'get an address on Ellen Little. The property might be in her husband Dwight's name, I don't know. Find out where El Paco is, and tell him to go check it out. I don't know what he will find, if anything. Just tell him to go knock on the door, and see what happens. Oh – and warn him to use caution.'

'I'm on it,' Louise said, and he could hear her fingers tapping on the keypad of the computer.

Hasky could sense a very bad feeling welling in the pit of his stomach. He picked up the phone and called the library.

'Leigh, that you?' he asked.

'Yeah, Tom. How's it going?'

'I may have an emergency. A real bad one. Can you get out of there?'

'Sure, Jodie's here. She can hold the fort,' Nichols said. 'What's happening?'

'I'm not sure. I just want to know that I've got all the bases covered. In a minute, give Louise a call and she'll give you an address. On your way out there, you can pick up Doc Savage,' Hasky told him.

'No problem. See you soon.'

'You will,' Hasky told him, and put the phone down. He fastened the holster and checked the load in the gun ... *I don't need this, not now* ...

He left his office and waited for Louise to finish telling Paco what to do.

'I'm going to take a look out there myself,' he announced. 'Keep an eye on things.'

'All right. That address is twelve, Riverside Road,' she said, and then looked into his eyes, and remembered all that he had told her this morning ... the baby, and how much it meant to him. 'Be careful.'

'I will,' he whispered.

Kirby watched, his eyes hypnotised by the knife, following its every move. The man waved it slowly in front of his face, occasionally placing it lightly on it. Kirby felt the cold steel ... and was too afraid to move, breathe even.

Kirby wished he was back at school, that the blitz was about to happen ... and this time he would let them get him, let them kick his ass real good. Break a few bones, even – and then he would not be doing his paper round this summer, and he would not be here.

It was a pleasing fantasy, yet in reality, he was about to die ... At least the woman had escaped. He had saved her, just like the hero in the movies. Only in the movies, the hero always lived to tell the tale and get the girl.

A little boy, so little and so young, straight into his grave.

Kirby screamed, but the sound was muffled, coming through the tears and sobs he was choking on.

The man glanced out of the window to see if the woman had found the courage to return yet. He looked down the driveway, and could not believe what he saw.

Perfect.

He was here ...

He watched as the man embraced the woman for a couple of seconds, and then began to run up the driveway like John Wayne on a fucking horse.

'This is your lucky day,' he whispered to the kid, but Kirby did not feel very lucky. He felt terrified.

Kirby could feel blood trickling down his face, could taste it on his lips. He trembled fearfully as the man dragged him across the room to where the body lay, looking frantically about for anything else he could use to protect himself. There had to be something, anything – but then time ran out.

Daniel punched the kid in the face, and he fell

unconscious onto the warm, stinking mass that was Dwight Little.

Daniel wanted to kill the little shit now. The monster was angry, cheated of its knife-games. The brat should bleed. But something was holding him back . . .

It was Nelson, fighting on the inside to save the woman and the boy. But he was exhausted, and knew he was nearing the end. To write a few notes in the journal was one thing, but to actively fight Daniel and the monster was impossible.

Jay was running up the long, winding path when the Toyota four by four came hurtling down the sloping concrete driveway from the back of the house at an insane, murderous speed. He stopped and lifted his gun, but did not even have a chance to aim, let alone get a shot off. The best he could do was to dive out of the way of the oncoming vehicle. The huge metal grille on its front hit his body and sent him spinning in mid-air, leaving him disorientated and rolling when he hit the ground.

Jay looked back towards the road, ignoring the pain as he pulled himself upright. He could see the woman still sitting in the driver's seat. Why didn't she get moving?

Ellen looked up just in time to see a monster pick-up driving straight at her. It was all black and chrome, gleaming in the sunlight. Suddenly, she remembered the keys, sitting useless on the plastic dashboard, and scooped them up, fumbling through them until she'd located the ignition key.

The Toyota was approaching fast now, and their saviour stood in the middle of the driveway, aiming his gun, surely leaving it too late before he dived out of the way.

She waited until she saw him safely stand up again after being hit, and then she returned to the key. Ellen missed the ignition slot twice, the key slipping, seeming too large for the hole. But on the third try she managed to steady her hand and it fit the lock perfectly. She looked across and now the pick-up was massive, eclipsing the sun behind it.

When Daniel spotted the woman in the car he laughed out loud and pushed his foot down harder. The pick-up would make mincemeat out of the rental car, and the stupid bitch inside it.

Get it going . . .

And at the last possible moment, as Jay half-hobbled and half-ran down the driveway – firing the gun and shattering the back window of the four by four – the rental car reversed safely out of the way and the Toyota hit the road and skidded to the right.

Ellen's mind measured the inches between the car and the truck as it passed onto the road. She saw Daniel inside, but there was no sign of the boy. That meant he had probably killed him inside.

And her cowardice was to blame.

The Toyota was pulling away fast, and she would be damned if she was letting the bastard escape this easily. Ellen threw the car into gear and as it jerked forward somebody slammed into the door. She screamed with shock and tugged the parking brake on with shaking hands, then dove away from the wheel to the other side of the car.

The door pulled open, and the man climbed inside.

'I'll drive,' he said, and had his foot on the gas even before he'd slammed the door shut.

Ellen winced as he swung the car into action. He had already halved the distance between the Toyota and themselves, when he raced into an intersection without slowing and another car cut across their path.

He hit the brakes and threw the wheel around. The car skidded to a halt and they were both thrown forward. The wheel stopped Jay from going too far forward, although he got a nasty knock, but Ellen was not quick enough to duck and stop herself from hitting the windshield. She fell back dazed, and he looked to check if she was all right.

He wanted the woman out of the car. She was already wounded, and he did not wish to see her hurt further. But when she did not move, he did his best to smile.

'Maybe you should fasten your seatbelt.'

'Yeah, I think so,' she said, and pulled the belt across. As he continued the pursuit once more, she reached across and did the same for him.

From the grim concentration in his face, Ellen knew that this pursuit meant more to him than anything else in the world. He would not make another mistake, she could see that – but then he was forced to bounce the car right up onto the sidewalk for a couple of minutes to avoid a jam, and she wondered if she had done right to stay in the car. The horrified expressions of pedestrians began to fill her vision as people dived out of their way. His hand was stuck on the horn, warning people to stay clear as they came out of doorways. And then they had bounced back on the road again.

It was a miracle that nobody was hit.

And there, at least fifty metres ahead, was the Toyota.

'Go right!' she shouted.

She knew the streets of Haddonfield so well, and if the Toyota was heading where she thought it was, they should take the short cut. If Kirby McCaul was dead, it was her fault and she would never be able to live with herself, unless she did everything in her power to avenge that death. Her thoughts dwelt for a second on the body of her dead, unfaithful husband – but then fled, full of horror.

'Short cut!' she screamed, and grabbed the wheel at the final intersection before the road curved out of town, pulling hard to the right. For a second there was a car heading straight for them, and neither of them had a chance to do anything about it. But the other driver was quick-witted enough to react, and then the street ahead was clear.

Jay locked crazy eyes with her then gathered speed and momentum again. Shock made him grin sheepishly. For a little while back there they had been out of control – but good luck and instinct had pulled them through.

She smiled back, her teeth stained with blood. Her

face was almost untouched, but there was a slight swelling under her left eye and a bruise already forming there, and a small cut from which a thin rivulet of blood trickled down her chin.

She looked beautiful.

He saw all that in a split second.

'Left!' she shouted, and the tyres screeched obediently, leaving rubber on the road.

She had never been in a situation like this before, yet here she was navigating and telling the stranger what to do. And the man was listening to her, trusting her directions.

She felt in control.

Morbidly, Ellen found herself enjoying the chase – the thrill, the rush of adrenaline, and the man beside her, who managed to find humour in this situation just to keep her from falling into shock.

'He's heading out of town,' she explained. 'This way, we might cut him off at the bridge.'

Considering all she had been through, Jay was impressed by this woman's confidence. She had just reached across, grabbed the wheel, and put herself in charge. She was the boss – one slip from her, one wrong turn, and it would all be for nothing.

She had not collapsed and folded inwards like a house of cards; her walls had not come tumbling down. She had risen above the turmoil and trauma.

Jay found it easy to trust her instincts, and listened to everything she had to say.

Now they were racing down something that was little

more than a dirt track. It ran alongside the river ... *the river*; charging fast and bubbling, pushed on by the winds above and the currents below. Deep and admonishing – a Nemesis of which he was wary.

The river ... *the car was running a little too close to the river* ...

But that could not be helped. She could never have known of his phobia and, as seemed to be the case, if this road brought them closer to his sister's killer, this ordeal would have been worth it. Up at the top of the hill lay the main road, its surface smooth and hard.

Here they were so close to the edge.

Jay could feel sweat breaking out on his face. He knew that if he let go of the wheel, his hands would be visibly shaking ... then the track began to incline and he sighed with relief as the river fell away to the right.

At an almost perfect ninety-degree angle, they could see the black Toyota riding on the horizon from the left.

The woman had been right.

As they screamed up to the top, the Toyota was only feet away, still not past the point of intersection. Jay saw its chrome gleam, silver and black and mean – a beast within a beast.

It was going to be close.

The rental car ricocheted off the dirt track, jumping off the ground for a second as it bumped onto the real road. Jay pulled the wheel hard to the right, barely touching the brakes, and the side of it hit the side of the much bigger vehicle.

Jay pulled away and let his car fall slightly back,

before speeding up and guiding it into a position alongside the four by four.

And then they were on the bridge, the river racing by below, and Jay did his best not to think about that.

'*Steer!*' he shouted, and let go of the wheel, trusting her instincts one final time.

The car wavered slightly to the right ... *closer to the edge and the running waters down below* ... as Jay unclipped his seatbelt and Ellen, panic briefly flooding through her, reached over for the wheel and brought the automobile under control.

Jay climbed halfway out of the open window, and sat on its frame. He could feel the wind rushing against his back, through his hair, and was afraid to let go of the car ... his fingers froze for a second, but then he pulled the Beretta free from his jeans with one hand, held onto the car so that he could steady his aim, and—

Daniel had a revolver aimed, held across his body and out of the window ... *but at the front tyres of the car* ... And that was Nelson, still fighting, even as Daniel and the monster ravaged the small part of the mind that was his ... *to protect the man and the woman* ...

—fired three shots quickly. They all damaged the exterior of the Toyota – one blowing the sideview mirror apart. They all missed Daniel.

As Jay was squeezing the trigger a fourth time, Daniel fired, and there was a huge explosion of sound as the left tyre of the rental car blew out. It swerved sharply to the right, and Jay's last shot flew harmlessly into the sky as the woman screamed.

The front of the car hit the wooden side barrier with a powerful impact and crashed straight through it.

As the car dropped, it tumbled over and Jay fell free from the window.

The car's roof hit the river, leaving Ellen trapped inside, upside down, still fastened by her seatbelt and disorientated as the water quickly flooded in.

As Ellen struggled to release the belt, the car tipped back and she panicked, screaming as it began to sink. Water rushed over the windshield, and into the car ... deadly water as the belt still restrained her. She closed her eyes as the water level rose above her head and the car sank vertically. She reached blindly for the release catch but could not locate it, and sensed daylight, with its warmth and air, drifting away ...

Jay hit the water like a missile and sank; kicking wildly, he made for the surface, his only concern to reach the daylight he could see shining above. He had swallowed a lot of water, and when he broke through the shimmering surface he was gasping for air and coughing violently.

By the time he had recovered, all that was left of the car was the front of the hood, peeking out into the world. He swam quickly to it as he realised the woman had not made it out, and grabbed the front bumper, as it too disappeared, attempting the impossible – to hold the car up, keep it from going under. It was foolish and pathetic, and as his face went under the water he could see the shadow images through the cracked windshield. The woman was still struggling with the belt. She could not get free.

He kicked away from the car as the river swallowed it, and for a second felt the drag as it tried to pull him under in its wake. And at that moment, as he fought the natural momentum and broke through the surface once more, he felt the woman's life slip from his grasp.

He looked down at the water, surrounding him, all around. He felt cold. He had been here before, a long time ago ... and more recently in his dreams, which was all he could see now in the crazy ripples of the river's flow. He was so afraid, paralysed with the fear of seeing her struggle to get free and having to watch her die, the fear of seeing her tauntingly just out of reach, forever gone, just like his sister was ... Tears poured down his face.

... don't think like that! You saved her back then, and you know it. You saved her ... save her ...

But he trod water, and could not move.

His fear was too great.

Because of it, the woman would die.

Nobody knew why Patrick Constantine was called El Paco. An old girlfriend had given him the name years ago, and the guys had gotten hold of it and never let it go; but nobody, not even Paco himself, knew what the name meant, or why she had christened him thus.

He had pale clean skin, and a bush of curly black hair on top of his head, which never appeared to be combed. It just grew in whatever direction it wanted to, and Paco liked it that way. His uniform was smart and pressed.

'OK,' he said into the radio, speaking to Louise but for the benefit of Hasky, whom he knew would be monitoring the channel. 'I'm going up the driveway now, and everything looks fine. There are no signs of – oh, wait a second. I got to check this out.'

Paco had spotted the broken window. He stopped the car and climbed out, unclipping his holster as he walked towards the house, one hand falling to the gun on his hip.

The first thing he noticed was the blood on the window ... then he peered inside and saw an unconscious kid, sprawled on top of a—

Jesus!

Paco backed away at the sight, running to the car. He swallowed down the nausea he could feel rising in his throat before grabbing the radio.

'This is Paco,' he choked out, doing his best to stay calm, not even certain whether the killer had left yet, not even sure if the boy was alive.

'I got a ... a ... man down. Possibly a kid as well. I'm going inside.'

'Paco,' Hasky said. 'Give us half a minute before you go in. I'm just down the road, and I want somebody watching your back.'

'No problem,' Paco said, grateful that he would not be alone when the time came to go into the house.

But the boy might need urgent help...

Paco tried the front door. It was locked, so he jogged

round to the back. There were tyre marks visible, left by the speeding Toyota. He bent down on one knee and touched the melted rubber with one finger.

It was still warm.

The killer had left, but he was not far away.

As he swam deeper into the murky darkness, Jay's eyes stung. He strained to keep them open. If he were to close them, the woman would surely drown. Deeper he swam, straight down, praying that the currents were not powerful enough to pull the car far ... the water chilling his very soul.

And then, as the water battled to get inside his lungs, the pressure threatening to crush his throat, he saw the car, coming out of the shadows and darkness, suddenly close.

A metal shell. A coffin.

He reached for the driver's door and pulled it open. It came easily, the car full of water making the pressures on both sides equal – and inside, still struggling with the seatbelt with her eyes closed tight, her face bloated, her throat bulging with the last strains of air, was the woman.

Jay pulled himself across the seat, past the wheel and over the leather interior which would be rotting already. He pushed the release mechanism, and the belt drifted away.

The woman turned at the unexpected, new-found freedom, opened her eyes and saw the man briefly before she closed them again. The water hurt. It was trapped beneath her eyelids, and felt like acid as she struggled blindly across the seats. Her whole body felt as if it was going to collapse inwards, and ... *water* ... she could feel the water leaking slowly between her lips.

Ellen felt Jay's hand grasp her arm tightly, and it was the most comforting, reassuring thing she had ever felt. He guided her through the darkness out of the car, like a dog guiding a blind person. It was so easy with him here.

As he pulled her out of the car, she was not struggling or fighting, and the only thing that told him she might not be dead was the fact that her mouth was not open, like floodgates letting the water pour in ...

... and he should have known the water, the lack of air, his own haunting visions and unrealities had made him delirious. Made him believe she was alive, when she was already dead ...

But still he kicked frantically, dragging her up towards the faraway surface, higher and higher, a dead weight in his arms.

... she was gone ...

The light now, breaking through to the depths from the sunshine above, showing him the way.

... she is dead ... I am dead ... we are dead ...

It was the Pearly Gates of Heaven they were approaching. Nothing made sense in this delirium, in this strange gap between this life, and the Hereafter. The next world ...

They were both dead ...

And the hallowed light towards which they floated was their final dream, one which they shared.

* * *

'What have we got?' Hasky asked as he climbed from the car, and spotted Paco emerging from the entrance to the house, a small child in his arms.

The boy was unconscious and bloody.

At first Paco did not reply – he couldn't. He was still getting over what he had seen in the bedroom. God only knew what the boy was doing in there.

'In the bedroom?' he said, and motioned towards the broken window. 'There's a dead ... man, I think. I found the kid in there, on top of the body. He's cut up some, but I think he's gonna make it. Seems like a tough little guy.'

At this, Kirby lifted his head off Paco's shoulder and looked about him dreamily; he could see the flashing lights on Hasky's car and wondered if the nightmare he'd been having had come to life. Paco gently stroked the boy's ruffled hair, and he slowly lowered his head again and closed his eyes.

Kirby was excited by what was going on about him, but was too tired and afraid to explore his curiosity. Besides, as he fell into a deep slumber the pain went away, and that was good.

'OK. Leigh's on his way over with Doc Savage right now. Put the kid on the back seat of your car and keep an eye on him,' Hasky instructed. 'Are you sure the other person is dead?'

'This guy needed a lot more than a Band Aid,' Paco assured him, thinking of the skinned corpse. The town had never had to deal with anything this big before, and certainly nothing as grotesque. The killing did not appear to have a motive ... but it would be a while before the body was identified. 'Take a look for yourself,' he told Hasky with a shudder.

Hasky walked over to the window and looked in ...

Jesus Christ ... the Devil had come to Haddonfield.

Who could do such a thing? Or would want to?

He was grateful for the distraction as Nichols drove up, and Doc Savage – a rather elderly man with no hair, but one who could still hold a scalpel steady enough to operate – climbed out of the passenger seat.

'What's the problem, Tom?' Doc asked.

'Over here!' Paco shouted.

Doc Savage hurried over to where Paco was standing, holding open the rear door of his car. The back seat was bloodied, and Paco gently lifted the boy's shirt. It stuck slightly to the cuts on his back as they slowly began to clot.

'Good Lord!' Doc Savage exclaimed when he saw the deep lacerations. 'What happened to this child?' He gently moved the boy into the bright daylight where he could work better.

'Is the kid going to make it?' Hasky asked, nervously twisting the coiled wire of his radio transmitter in his hand. Over the past few months the town had been going to shit, and this last episode was just too much. It was outrageous that something like this could happen in a small, peaceful town like Haddonfield. He almost didn't believe it, but then he heard Leigh vomiting over by the front wall of the house.

Hasky had warned him not to go look in the bedroom window, but his old friend's curiosity had been aroused. Nichols had seen some bad shit as a fireman, and believed he could cope with whatever lay in that room.

Nichols was wrong.

'The boy is going to hurt a while,' Doc Savage explained. 'There can be no doubting that. I'd like him to stay over at the Medical Centre for a few days. I want to know who did this to him. These injuries are one of the most blatant acts of cruelty I've ever seen.'

You should take a look in the window, Hasky thought.

'So do I,' he said aloud, and then clicked the radio transmitter as the Doc went about his work, and Paco acted as nurse-aid.

'Louise, Hasky here. I want my people out of bed right now.'

'But, Sheriff—'

'Not now, honey. I know Marty and Roger were on the nightshift – I'll work something out with them. This is urgent. Tell them to get a search of the town co-ordinated – them and Conrad. They're looking for Ellen Little. She will probably be with one of two men – Stevie, from the bar, has their description. I'll send Leigh down to the office to help out. I want his men on this as well. Get Branigan and Hober down here as quick as they can make it.'

'You sent Branigan on that forensics course,' Louise reminded him.

He'd forgotten about that.

'OK. Tell Hober he's working prints alone, and he's

got a lot of work to do. Make contact with the rest of them and – oh, get Lulu in. You help Leigh with what he needs while she stays by the radio.'

'You got it, boss,' Louise said importantly. Action at last! 'What's happened?'

'Tell you later – but you don't want to know.'

Jay erupted through the surface of the river, coughing and spluttering water from his lungs. As he gulped down air, he pulled the woman up and held her head on one of his arms. She was still unconscious, and Jay clamped his other hand over her mouth and nose to feel her breathing.

Nothing.

He swam one-handed backstroke to the bank, towing the woman at his side, keeping her head above the water. She couldn't be dead, not after he had dared to go back in the water, not after he had vanquished his inner demons so that he might save her.

He was nearing the bank, nearly twenty feet down-river from the bridge . . . a small patch of sand, and then bushy greenery before the forest began. He staggered up onto the sand, carrying her in his arms, then gently laid her down.

Ellen coughed. It was quiet and weak. Water trickled out of her mouth.

Jay fell to his knees at her side. He felt for a pulse, but found no sign of life. The cough had probably been a reflex action as nerves and muscles relaxed and settled into the new experience that was Death.

But she must not die ... not now ...

He pushed several times on her stomach, and then pinched her nose shut and opened her mouth. He blew air into her lungs, and then pulled away, pumping her stomach with his hands once more. He bent to her face again, and placed his mouth over hers. After a couple of minutes, he lifted away and felt for a pulse.

Still nothing.

'Come on! You can beat this,' he told her. 'You can do better than this.' He hoped his words would encourage her, help bring her back. They had to.

He worked on her again, pumping more water up, out of her lungs. Mouth-to-mouth breathing. Searching for a heartbeat.

'Come on!' he yelled.

The killing had gone on for far too long. It was time for a break, for luck to change.

'*Come on!*' And this time his voice was a sob, and he was weeping.

He still pumped with his hands but the movements were mechanical now. Eventually he sat upright, his hands shaking with fatigue as he lifted them away. He held one above her mouth, but still no air passed between her lips. He sat back and cried. Having given up on hope, all that was left was rage – and he looked up to the sky and screamed at whatever Gods there were.

Screamed and bellowed, until his head flopped down and he was looking at the ... *dead* ... woman again. He brought his hands down on her for a last, desperate attempt.

Pumping and pumping.
Searching for a pulse.
Blowing air into her lungs.
Hope dying.

Chapter Sixteen
Waiting

Jay looked at the disbelieving Sheriff and shook his head – he had faced the same situation in Detroit, and he liked it even less this time around. He winced as the nurse stitched the gash in his arm, pulling ripped skin together.

'He was just a stranger, passing through. Admittedly, a pretty bad guy. But he was passing through, that's all,' Hasky told Jay. 'You said yourself that he ran you and Ellen off the road at the old wooden bridge. He was heading out of town.'

He had revived her . . .

They had picked him up, carrying Ellen back into town.

She was alive.

Jesus, couldn't this guy Hasky wake up and smell what he was shovelling, Jay thought exasperatedly. He was a small-time cop, used to small-time work in a real small community. He was good enough for Haddonfield,

with its *pop. 10,069*, but this was way out of his
league.

'That may be so,' Jay continued to argue, and bit back
a cry as the nurse moved his arm. 'But he's no stranger
to me. I know him. He's not on some kind of lunar cycle –
he's not your average serial killer. He *likes* it, enjoys
what he does – and he has decided to make Haddonfield
his playground.'

There was silence, and Jay remembered the conversation he'd had recently with Kamski on the phone.

The Captain's man – Detective Cohn – had managed
to track down the kid from the cellar after checking
records at the Home. The kid, Gary Lockwood, was now
a lawyer working in the depressed farm belt – helping
farmers there to fight against the banks and fore-
closures.

'Cohn said he's something of a celebrity in those parts,
a radical activist,' Kamski explained. 'He spoke with
him on the phone, and Lockwood swore he never killed
those dogs.'

'Did he check out?' Jay had asked, disappointed.

'Yeah. The guy's got alibis right up his ass. There is
one thing, though. He said he'd had a fight with
another kid a couple of days before ... one Nelson
Miller. Apparently, this kid was a real looney tune,
and he was the one who killed the dogs and set Gary
up for it. Put blood on his shoes, and then snitched to
the guardians.'

Jay had thought about the name Nelson Miller, and
was grateful that he could not put a face to it.

He shivered now, and looked at the doubt in Hasky's face.

'I've seen him pull this kind of trick before,' Jay explained, 'I know his work. I'm beginning to get a good idea of how this bastard thinks.'

'Yeah?' Hasky said, not all that impressed. There was no way this Big City reject was going to come here and dictate the way its Sheriff's department should be run. 'Well, that being the case, why haven't you caught him yet?'

'You sonofabitch!' Jay shouted and jumped off the table, causing the needle to rake across his arm, and the nurse to flinch away, letting it go.

Nichols, who had been stood at the door watching and listening, moved swiftly across the room to block Jay. He was beginning to feel like a regular bodyguard to Hasky. He held Jay for a second, and threw Hasky a glance. There was no point in pissing this guy off, just because somebody decided to take a dump on Haddonfield.

'Cool off,' Nichols warned.

Jay stood poised for the fight a second longer, and then let his arms drop to his sides – even though his fists were still clenched tight. Then he went back and sat on the table, allowing the nurse to retrieve the needle which was dangling from the thread in his arm and finish her work.

Anger burned hot and bright within Jay. It was visible on his face, in his eyes.

'I'm sorry,' Hasky apologised. 'That was way out of

line. But the guy *has* gone. Will you at least accept that?'

'When will you accept *this*?' Jay asked bitterly. 'I saw him kill a man, and shout that the same thing was going to happen to me. I was told that he had left Detroit — then the next night he wiped out a whole fucking police contingent! They had a witness, and set a trap for him. He didn't have to kill all those people: he did it because he wanted to. He enjoyed it.'

Jay paused, thinking about his childhood, and wondered if, somehow, he himself might have turned out that way. The anger began to dissipate, and tears welled in his eyes. It was easy to let them go, easy to remember Susan and her cascading hair.

'He left me a deliberate trail to this town,' Jay whispered, seeing again the name written in blood on the mirror. 'Don't you people understand? He has to be stopped before he turns this place into a ghost town. He will kill everybody here! Turn Haddonfield into a fucking graveyard! I have to find him and kill him ... or we're all gonna die.'

'Why you?' Nichols asked.

'I don't know,' Jay answered truthfully, but then decided to talk anyway, clear his head a little. 'He knows I'm chasing him, although he probably doesn't know why. And he seems to realise that unless he kills me, he will never be free. He will always be looking over his shoulder to see if I'm still there ... and that scares him. So he has become obsessed, and fixated on me, as I have on him.'

Jay began to unwind as all this came out, as he finally put his feelings into words.

'On the flip side of the coin, he might see my killing him as a release from any pain he is experiencing. Psychological pain, that is. I don't think anybody has ever seriously hurt him physically ... he may even believe he is invulnerable, cannot be hurt that way. I think he *wants* me to kill him, which is why he leads me to him, instead of just disappearing.'

'He likes the game...' Hasky whispered.

'In that case,' Nichols asked, frightened for the people of Haddonfield. For Hasky, Alice, and their unborn child ... for himself, too: 'Why doesn't he just kill himself?'

'I don't know. He has killed so often, more than any of us will ever know, that I don't think death itself scares him. Perhaps he's afraid of himself. He is a dark man, with dark ways ... maybe he is frightened of what waits for him beyond death.'

'OK,' Hasky said. 'Bottom line, all that was a pile of psycho-bullshit, but I'm not entirely convinced now that this guy has gone for good. What do you suggest we do?'

'Protect your people. Look for him.'

'Where?' Nichols asked. 'Where will he hide?'

'I don't know, it's your town,' Jay said. 'I'll help with the search.'

'No way,' Hasky said, shaking his head. 'You're staying right here at the Medical Centre, at least for tonight – if not for a couple of days. You're in no

339

condition to be running around town, playing cops and robbers.'

'It's only a few stitches,' Jay complained.

'Take a look in the mirror. You look like shit,' Hasky grinned.

'Worse,' Nichols added.

'Doctor Mayberry wants to keep you here for observation. Your heart almost stopped back there, after the auto accident, and he's afraid you might relapse. That fear is stronger still in Ellen's case. After tonight, I'll pull rank if I have to, and then you can help out. For now, get some rest,' Hasky ordered. 'Besides, you will be closer to Ellen and young Kirby in here.'

Hasky and Nichols left then, leaving Jay with the nurse and the needle. After a minute she was finished.

'All done,' she said, and let him jump off the table. 'You really think this guy will come back?'

'Yes,' Jay said solemnly. And he would be waiting for him.

This will be my final entry.

I am a boy living a nightmare, living in terror. I am innocent, but how can I prove that? I saved the child, looked into his eyes and saw my own fear ... and the woman, I helped her. But mostly, I could not let the boy die.

I doubt I will ever find salvation, or peace.

I am weak.

I will be dead soon, gone for ever.

I can feel Daniel and the monster haunting the

*corridors of my mind, devouring all that I have left. I
cower in fear, but there is no place to hide.*

I hope that it will be over soon.

*And that one day, somebody will find this journal
and understand.*

'It's Doc Savage,' Louise said.

It was turning into a very long day, Hasky sighed.

Lulu had just gone out for coffee and sandwiches, and
the sun was beginning to set, its beautiful colours full of
lamentation, mature and mysterious . . .

A very long day – he sensed that it was far from over.

Hasky nodded as he spoke into the intercom. 'Let him
in.'

About an hour ago he had spoken to a cop named
Caldwell, who had asked for Jay to be sent back to
Manhattan. And if it was possible – in order to ensure
that he did not go shooting up another town or city –
could he be accompanied for the whole of the journey.
He's a loose cannon . . .

Like Hasky did not have more than enough on his
hands right now.

*Yeah . . . I'll bring him home myself in a few days. He's
cut up pretty bad, and might have to slow down for a
couple of months, but—*

He's OK?

He's gonna live. But all the same . . .

Hasky had not learned a whole lot more from the
conversation. Some bad shit had gone down in Detroit,
and the reason Jay wanted the killer so badly was

because he had murdered his sister ... Small talk and pleasantries had been exchanged, and that had been that.

He looked up as Doc Savage entered the office. 'Doc, please tell me something nice.'

Doc Savage dropped the report he had written on Hasky's desk. He was a man who perhaps drank a little more than he should in his old age ... and on occasion, a lot more.

'You've been drinking?' Hasky asked, smelling the whisky on his breath as it scented the air.

'After that autopsy, I needed a drink. And so will you, when you've read my report,' Doc warned him, as he sat opposite Hasky.

Doc Savage, Man of Bronze ... that was the name of the comic-book super hero, and it had been a good joke before it had worn out its welcome. Then they had left it at Doc Savage, and even this still aroused a wry smile sometimes. But he was old now and, especially after seeing this, he no longer considered life to be a joke. He did not have long left, and just wished, for once before he died, that somebody would call him by his given Christian name.

His wish was granted sooner than he expected when Hasky looked up from the report.

'Jesus! Are you serious about this, Harold?'

'Every last word. He cut out Dwight Little's tongue and tortured the poor bastard, hurt him bad before it was over. I think he was actually torturing Ellen, by making her watch ... although she may have been unconscious for some of that time, so that she could see what he was going to do to her. If it wasn't for the boy, and Superman down at the Centre, I think she would be in a much worse state than her husband. He virtually skinned him alive, Tom.'

Dwight Little, you poor sonofabitch...

'What about the boy?' Hasky asked.

'He's going to be OK. He seemed to like Ellen and Jay so I'm letting them share the same room down at the Centre. Poor kid's had enough pain to last him a lifetime. He was in a state of shock when Paco found him, and I fear he's going to suffer psychologically from this...'

Hasky sighed as the Doc continued. He was the Sheriff – how could he have let this happen in his town?

'His parents seemed a little too eager to take him home,' the Doc said reflectively, 'and not out of love, either. I checked the McCauls out. Drunks, violent alcoholics – both of them.'

'I should put you on the payroll,' Hasky said, trying for some humour, but it fell flat.

'I persuaded them to let Kirby stay at the Centre tonight, but they will be knocking on the door early in the morning, probably to beat the shit out of the poor little guy for getting involved.'

'I'll see it doesn't happen,' Hasky promised as he looked into his drink, not even aware he had poured it.

He swallowed the whisky in one long gulp and then poured out another. He considered the Doc a great

343

personal friend, and now he looked at him with sad, hurt eyes.

'Who would do such a thing, Harold?'

'Perhaps we're asking the wrong question. *What* would do such a thing?' Savage said, not meaning anything fantastical or monstrous, no alien creatures to chew faces off ... but what kind of mind?

Hasky did not want to think about that. He swallowed the second drink quickly, and found himself pouring a third.

Evening fell slowly over Haddonfield, coating the town in a dull, grey night. Despite the earlier heat, the air had grown cold and dark clouds were gathering in the sky.

Jay looked at his watch. Seven fifteen.

It was the waiting that put him on edge the most. He knew that the killer would not fail to arrive some time tonight. Just knew it ... He might even be stalking the corridors now, which was why Jay didn't like Ellen being away in the television room, with only Leigh to watch over her.

When he came, Jay intended to be ready.

But the waiting...

He looked across the room to where the boy ... *Billy Rogers* ... was sleeping, and then to the bed next to his, where Ellen had been dozing an hour earlier. And now she was alone with Leigh, who was a librarian. What kind of a police force did Hasky run out here, anyway?

He reached over to the bedside table and quietly

pulled open a drawer, the wood whispering softly in the grooves. Inside lay Jay's Beretta, loaded and ready to kill. He picked it up, the cold metal comforting.

It felt good, truthful...

He turned the gun over and flipped the magazine out, catching it in his other hand. Then, one by one, he emptied the bullets out, holding them in turn, closing his fist about each one ... and then letting it fall to the sheets.

Counting.

One ... two...

The boy rolled over, and Jay looked up to make sure he was still asleep. Prayed that – unlike Billy Rogers, whose throat had been cut in the dead of night by the man he sought – he would be given the chance to wake.

... seven ... eight...

Earlier, he had left the gun on the table and the boy – Kirby, his name was Kirby – had soon taken an interest in it. Jay had let him hold it, and aim it at different objects, let him squeeze the trigger ... all of this without the magazine loaded, of course. He had taken a certain pride in the handgun as he spoke of it, explaining various details ... the difference between the hollow point bullets he used and normal ones – *these suckers, especially weighted for the gun I use, make a real mess* – the safety, everything and anything he could think of – and anything Kirby could think to ask.

And then Leigh had come into the room, without knocking, and Kirby just happened to have the gun aimed at the door.

Kirby squeezed the trigger, squinting, doing his best not to close his eyes, and the gun clicked hollowly.

Hey, Wyatt Earp, point that thing some place else ... Leigh had smiled and brushed the gun aside. He seemed easy to like.

'I just got a call from Hasky,' Leigh informed him. 'Said the search didn't turn up anything, but he's keeping his people on the streets all night. Also said he's set a curfew.'

'Good.' Jay nodded. 'You know how to use that thing?' He indicated the gun on Leigh's hip, police issue .38.

Better than nothing ...

'I point it and pull the trigger – yeah?' Leigh grinned. He had spent more than a few mornings at the range learning firearms control when it became evident that Hasky might need him one day, as he himself sometimes depended on the Sheriff at fire scenes. He was no marksman, but could just about hit a barn door at ten feet.

'I don't like us being separated,' Jay had told Leigh.

'Ellen's watching a movie. Once it's over I'll bring her back and you guys can get some sleep while I stay on the door.'

... fourteen ... fifteen ...

And that was all.

He began reloading the bullets into the magazine, when he noticed Kirby spying on him from under the covers. He winked at the boy, and grinned. A false façade, a lie – and Kirby was not convinced. He came from under the sheets, but with no answering smile.

'Why do you do that?' Kirby asked softly.

The voice was barely a whisper, but Jay heard and when he answered it was in similar fashion. He realised that Kirby had never been asleep, but watching and listening ... frightened.

All four of them were frightened ... and Jay knew that the kid knew that.

'Just checking,' Jay assured him.

Exaggerated images of what had happened filled Kirby's mind, and although he tried to block it all out, the gun – what it stood for, what it meant, and all that it could do – brought back the traumatic events in chilling colour, as if they were happening all over again.

But at the same time the gun symbolised protection. And the man, Jay, he also offered protection and a warm, fatherly comfort that had always been missing from Kirby's life. The man and the gun ... with them here, he knew he would be safe.

Jay was the person his father should have been; and Ellen, the woman he had saved – they all agreed on that; it was Kirby's foolish bravery that had saved her from the killer – reminded him of a person he had never known ... the person his mother should have been.

They were his surrogate parents, and he liked being with them.

In the afternoon, regardless of all he had been through, Kirby's father had slapped him across the face, just for being at the Centre, just for getting involved – something a McCaul had successfully evaded for generation after generation. Kirby was the good seed in a rotten pod. After his father had left the room, Kirby had wept; not because of the slap, which so often in the past had been a fist – but because he was afraid.

Afraid of the pain, the knife, the glass raking across his back ... the man's cold, yet burning eyes....

Kirby was terrified, and nothing either of his parents did could change that. Despite their presence, he ignored them.

Jay came in half an hour later, wearing the blue gown which looked silly on him and made Kirby laugh, and he had rubbed frantically at his eyes, trying to wipe the tears away. While Jay changed into his jeans and sweater, he asked the kid why he'd been crying.

Kirby's response was slow in coming. 'I was alone,' he said eventually. 'I'm afraid.'

'Me too,' Jay told him, not lying because he knew the boy would see through it to the hard truth. 'It's nothing to be ashamed of.'

'It's not?' Kirby asked.

'No.'

Five minutes later, while Jay lay above the covers, a cool breeze drifting through the open window, the boy came and crouched at his side ... crying onto his shoulder.

Let it turn, Jay had whispered into his ear. *Let it all turn to something else.*

'Feel better?' he'd asked, when the well dried up and Kirby could cry no more even if he wanted to. 'You want to know what I turn to when I'm afraid?'

Kirby had nodded – and that was when Jay pulled out the Beretta, and the demonstration had begun. A new education, something no school would ever teach, not in this world anyway ... survival.

Kirby liked Jay. He did not patronise him, or speak to him in a condescending manner. Jay could appreciate all he had been through. He did not laugh if Kirby asked a question that sounded stupid. He spoke to him as if he were a man, not a schoolkid; as if they were on the same level.

And it was then, looking into the boy's fearful red eyes, that Jay realised he was responsible to more people than himself now. There were two others. He cared for the whole town, but these were special people. For the first time, he had come out of the deep abyss into which he had slipped when he'd first heard of Susan's death.

He was no longer cold inside. He could feel again.

'Will he come?' Kirby asked now.

'Yes,' Jay told him.

'Will you protect me?' Kirby asked.

...the woman, his mother, rushed at him, pounding his chest with hard, tight fists. My son is dead, she cried. My Billy – you let him die...

Jesus, Jay thought, feeling tears in his eyes. Tears that hurt...

The stubborn passion that burned bright within, to kill the man who had taken his beloved sister's life, was slowly fading; it was being replaced by a stronger, more vibrant passion for life. He would never see the boy die, or Ellen ... not before their natural demise. He would protect them. He would do his best.

They were more important now.

'*Will you protect me?*' Jay whispered back, and the boy came running across the room, jumping on the bed, hanging his arms around his neck.

Jay felt his tears fall, like rain trickling down a window. Silent, so that Kirby would not know of them. He did not really want any of this. He did not want to get close to Kirby or Ellen. He did not want to feel anything. No love, no compassion, nothing ... in case they should die.

But it was too late now.

'Let it turn,' Kirby whispered softly.

Chapter Seventeen
Rampage

Hasky could feel the pressure coming down on him as he sat in his office, doing his best to keep a grip on things. He ran his hands through his hair, a couple of strands coming away, and he stretched them between his fingers.

What the hell was happening to Haddonfield?

His manpower was a joke, completely inadequate. It was wrong that he'd had to force Leigh's men to help out, but it was the only way he could see it working. If it came down to it – and he would see that it did not – there might even be a vigilante force down at the bar, ignoring the curfew...

He hoped that people were sleeping peacefully, but he knew how gossip usually spread through the town, no matter how hard you tried to keep a lid on it. Then there was fucking El Paco...

While Leigh's men were working as volunteers, carrying their own weapons, Constantine was demanding double time to work the night through. Hasky had seriously considered canning his ass right there and then, but as he didn't have a clue what might go down tonight – if anything – Paco was on the streets – on double time ... but on his very last shift.

Hasky had heard through the grapevine that Paco was balling some chick from the rich north end of town. If that was true, then come morning he could afford to lose his job.

He listened to the radio chatter and wished they would keep it to a minimum.

Lulu had been in the office all day, co-ordinating the search. She knew the town better than anybody, and had the cars and foot units well spread out. They were covering a lot of ground. But finding nothing...

Hasky rubbed sleep from his eyes.

Perhaps the killer *had* left, after all ...

Paco sat in his patrol car, looking through his binoculars at the young couple making out down the hill, supposedly hidden in some trees. He thought about driving down, giving them a scare, and smiled.

He opened his lunch-box, and found a note in with the snack his girlfriend Debra had prepared for him. He managed to take his attention off the couple for a second and unfolded the paper. It read:

I love you

There was a little heart at the end of the words, and Paco smiled. He chewed the sandwich and read the note again, feeling good inside.

He looked down the hill. The young couple were getting dressed. He wondered where their car was parked, couldn't see it. He thought about Debra...

Something slammed on his side of the car, and he spun quickly, the lunch-box flying off his lap, tuna mayo hitting the ceiling.

It was just some drunk making his way home, coughing phlegm all over the car door. Paco wound the window down.

'Go home before I book you, asshole,' he told the drunk, and looked down at the couple. They were walking up the hill. When they got close he would remind them of the curfew, tell them to get inside. 'I said—'

He turned back ... and Daniel was smiling, the knife in his hand.

'Shit!'

El Paco went for his gun, but Daniel pulled the door open and dragged him from the car. Across the road and out of sight...

Hasky picked up the phone and punched in his own number. Alice answered on the first ring.

'Yes?'

'It's me,' Tom told her. 'I was just making sure you're all right.'

'When will you be home?' she asked.

'Not for a few hours. Maybe not until sunrise,' he sighed. 'But if it comes to that, I'll let you know.'

Lightning struck outside, and thunder boomed. Rain suddenly slashed on the window, the storm unprecedented. Hasky wished he did not have to go out in it, wanted to be by his wife's side, holding her in his arms ... protecting her against the night.

'Good,' she told him. 'Baby Hasky misses you.'

'He does?'

'Yeah, and so do I.'

'Are all the doors and windows locked?' he asked.

'Yes. Tom ... come home soon. Please.'

'I will. Alice, I love—' Suddenly the line went dead.

Hasky looked out the window, trying to get a dial tone. The winds were blowing hard – a line must have gone down somewhere close by. He put the phone down, thinking about what he had been saying to his wife.

Alice, I love you.

It was a bad omen that he had failed to complete that sentence. A bad sign. He felt butterflies dance in his stomach.

Were the winds strong enough to take a line down?

Or had he returned?

Hasky stood and grabbed the holster, quickly fastening it around his waist. He pulled the gun out and checked the load.

Lightning flashed again, and Hasky reached for his hat and jacket. He stepped into the next room, where Lulu was trying to get through on the phone.

'Line's down,' he told her.

He looked at her face, saw his own fear reflected. She was old, and had lived a long and pleasant life. She did not want a violent death.

'Come on,' Hasky said, and held out his hand.

'Wait. I just got an incoming call from a couple of kids. Said some jerk stopped by a patrol car out near the cemetery. They think they saw him drag El Paco out of the car and into the trees.'

'The bastard must know they are at the hospital,' Hasky whispered. 'Get the nearest units up into the cemetery. I want a search of that whole area. Tell the others to stay sharp. You'll be safe enough here.'

Tom was out of the door, but stopped when Lulu called his name.

'You be careful, Tom Hasky. That baby will need a father.'

The Medical Centre was a round building on one level. At its centre was the only operating theatre. Off this were situated various offices, a medical records library, consulting rooms and a lecture hall. Forming a third and final ring were the patients' rooms ... more than enough for a town twice the size of Haddonfield – but one day, the town meant to be that big. From the centre led off four spoke-like corridors, each leading to the outer ring. If you were to look down from high above, the Medical Centre would look like a giant wheel.

Jay stared out of the window, watching the rain, wondering how much longer it would be before the man came. He resisted the temptation to go out looking for him. His hand rested on the handle of the Beretta, sticking out from the top of his jeans.

He spotted a pair of headlights through the trees, and then, as they came closer, the light cutting a soft path through the rain and dark, he recognised the vehicle as a patrol car. It was only when the car stopped, just out of view, that he realised Kirby was standing next to him.

'Is he here?' Kirby asked.

'No,' Jay assured him, and ran a hand through the boy's fine hair. 'It's just a cop. Wait here.' He was protecting Kirby even then, not wanting him to hear anything bad. Protecting him ... *will you protect me?*

Jay was at the door when he heard the first shot. He had to go out and see what was happening. Nichols ... *he's dead* ... would need his help.

There was a second shot, and Kirby ran to him. He held the boy behind him as he slowly opened the door. He pulled the Beretta free from his jeans.

'Stay back,' he whispered.

He peered out and saw the killer looking down the corridor in the other direction. Jay was about to duck back inside, when Daniel turned suddenly and spotted him. Daniel quickly lifted the auto-shotgun and fired, the expended case popping out, before hiding in the doorway through which he had just come, listening to the rain on the glass.

They were alone.

Hasky drove urgently through the night streets. He had

to get to the Medical Centre, warn Leigh and the others. He pushed down on the accelerator and the car splashed through puddles, its headlights fighting to cut a course through the night.

'You out there, Hasky?' It was Lulu.

He grabbed the radio. 'Got you. Any word on Paco?'

'They found him, Tom. His face is cut up bad.'

Jesus . . . 'Is he—'

'He's dead, Tom. I can't get through to the Centre.'

'Keep trying,' he told her.

'Tom . . . I'm scared.' Her voice sounded lonely and distant.

'Don't worry, Lulu. I'm on my way there.'

He hit the siren and drove faster, the bad feeling in his gut taking over his whole body. He shivered in the cold night.

'Lulu, you still there?'

'I'm here.'

'If anything happens to me, will you go see Alice, sit with her? Tell her I said I love her?'

'Jesus, Tom, you're talking like you're not coming back from that place alive.'

Hasky paused thoughtfully, the gun pressing on his hip, and clicked the radio off.

Jay stepped out of the doorway and fired four shots in quick succession, waving Kirby out as he did so, giving the boy a chance to get across the corridor and into the spoke opposite.

Jay hid in the doorway again.

If Kirby followed that corridor, and then went around the operating theatre, he would be able to get out on the other side of the building. Either that, or find help on his way.

Daniel fired as Kirby dashed across the passageway. The boy dived into the spoke, unhurt.

They had the killer's full attention.

Nichols had to be dead. And Ellen, she – but he could not think about that. He had to get the boy out. At least while the killer was chasing them, he could not be hurting her ... if she was still alive.

Kirby turned once he was certain he was hidden by the wall of the corridor, in relative safety. Daniel fired the auto-shotgun, and Kirby saw Jay huddle in the doorway as large splinters of wood and burned chips of paint came down on him.

Jay looked up and saw the boy watching, transfixed. He waved him away. 'Go!'

But Kirby did not move, knowing he could do nothing, but afraid to leave Jay to die.

'Jesus fucking Christ!' Jay whispered harshly, as the killer fired again and more splinters cut into his arms. 'Go ... go!'

Jay returned fire, a couple of shots, just his arm poking out of the door, and then quickly stepped into the corridor.

He had intended to fire a couple of times, giving himself cover as he jogged across the open space into the spoke where Kirby still stood, but the last thing he expected to see was the killer, less than fifteen feet away, walking towards him, the shotgun already aimed, ready to fire.

Ready to kill.

Jay fired, but the bullet went inches wide of his adversary's face. He continued to side-step across the corridor. He was squeezing the trigger again, less than half second after his first shot, when the killer fired ... and everything happened in a horrible slow motion, as suddenly Jay was hit.

The shell took him high in his right arm, shattering the bone as it passed through and out. Shot from such close range, Jay felt himself lift up as he was thrown back, a splash of blood leading his flight, out of sight of the boy as he twisted in mid-air ... and the gun, with its valuable death-bringing, life-saving bullets, fell from his hand and landed at Kirby's feet.

Kirby looked down at the gun, larger than it had ever seemed before. It filled his vision, and his mind. Eyes wide with morbid fascination, he bent down and picked the gun up, holding it in both hands.

Kirby moved forward, taking slow lethargic steps, figuring there was no way the killer would suspect him of still being there. He saw Jay's blood on the floor, and splattered on the wall opposite ... blood, not unlike the blood the gun would soon yield.

... and Jay, his arm clinging to the rest of his body by gory threads, the pain intense enough to make him want to pass out and accept the darkness that beckoned him, so that he did not have to watch the figure of Death that approached, walking towards him, grieved over all the pain and the agony he had seen and been through, all of the innocence he had seen lost, just to become a victim himself, to become one of the many ... *oh, there must be so many* ... to join his sister in her territory of lost souls dancing in the fire.

He felt dizzy ... His eyes closed and he collapsed, tumbling into unending Infinity. He propped himself up on his surviving arm and blinked his eyes open. As he fainted, in his peripheral vision he saw Kirby pick up the gun ... the killer was still approaching, laughing and swaying in his blood-filled vision ... and Kirby walked forward, closer to the killer, instead of running, running scared ... and how scared he must be.

No, Jay struggled, but no words were forthcoming, so he tried to raise his other arm, the one that was bleeding, to warn Kirby away, but the pain was incredible. Nerves were out of control, dancing and twitching to their own music, refusing to obey ... and the confusion ... *Susan, he could see Susan* ... coming slowly with the darkness, but he had to stay and fight, as much as he wanted to be with her, had to—

Ellen ran down the Medical Centre's long white corridor, not daring to cut through one of the spokes for fear of getting lost. She cursed the corridor for being so long, and Leigh for leaving her alone and going to check on the others.

More loud shots fuelled her burning energy and fear drove her on.

Then she saw Leigh, slumped on the floor, his back

against one wall, and she slowed to a stop. There were two giant cavities in his chest, and blood trickled from his mouth.

'No . . .' she cried, and fell to her knees.

His hand reached out, and she almost staggered back.

He was alive.

'Gun . . .' he whispered, but she could not make out the word.

And then she saw it, hanging loose in his grasp.

'Gun,' he whispered, stronger.

She took it from his hand, and held him for a second.

'I'll get help,' she promised.

But Leigh Nichols died in her arms.

And she stood there, strong – but needing comfort, needing to be with Jay and Kirby.

Daniel walked fast, eagerly anticipating the death to come.

This was it! Let the woman and child run and hide. He'd waited far too long for this moment. He could taste the sweet excitement in his mouth, could feel it whip through his whole body, driving a fast course through his veins . . . the death he carried inside, a natural part of him.

Kirby was walking slower, so as they came to the corridor's intersection, it was the killer who stood in the opening, unaware of the watching boy behind him.

The gun still in both hands, Kirby aimed patiently,

not wanting to miss, afraid to pull the trigger but knowing that he must.

Suddenly aware of a presence, Daniel turned and saw the kid, a gun in his hands. He grinned – and then chuckled as he decided to kill the kid first, just to make the man from his past suffer that little extra. Let him see the blood paint the walls red as the small body was ripped apart by the shells. Laughing wildly now, he pointed the weapon away from Jay . . .

. . . who crawled uselessly forward, reaching out with his good arm. He could not let the killer harm the boy. He inched his way forwards, leaving a trail of blood on the floor, like a snail leaves slime. And then Jay saw something that neither Kirby nor the killer had noticed . . . the safety had got jammed on the Beretta. 'Safety,' he tried to say, blood trickling from his mouth. *Fucking safety* . . .

Kirby pulled the trigger, knowing that there was no more time to aim and delay, knowing what had to be done. He shut his eyes in preparation for the loud explosion of sound and blood. He squeezed hard, but still the trigger pull would not complete, just a soft metal clicking sound rising above the killer's shrill mirth.

Click . . . click!

Louder than any explosion.

'Safety . . .' Jay finally managed.

Daniel sniggered. 'Nice try,' he whispered, congratulating the boy on his foolish effort, and then placed the barrel of the auto-shotgun to his head.

Jay, only inches away now, reached up, knowing how

futile his actions were, coughing more blood because of the strain. But he reached further, hearing only the killer's laughter in his ears, trying to knock the gun away, trying to gain just a few seconds more so that Kirby would snap out of his shocked daze, flick the safety off and blow this fucker into next week. But Jay was out of reach – only centimetres, millimetres away, yet it might as well have been a mile, because it was too far. The killer's finger was closing on the trigger—

—Then Daniel whirled round, pain erupting in his side – as a bullet hit him – the shotgun lifting up as the trigger pull was completed. The shell hit the ceiling behind Kirby.

And Daniel saw the woman walking towards him, her gun aimed right at him. He brought the shotgun down ... *and another bullet hit him, knocking him further back* ... and he fired off-balance, expending another useless round. The woman walked closer, firing again ... *the third bullet, the first two having hit him in his barrel torso, hit his hand and the shotgun came free* ... and the corridor ran with his blood.

She was a fierce representation of all the women he had ever killed ... *a fourth bullet hit his knee and he felt it explode, felt it fold underneath him, causing him to fall to the floor* ... Daniel did his best to crawl for the shotgun, leaving trails of blood everywhere, but could not reach it ... *all the times they had begged and cried for mercy* ... he could not reach the shotgun ... all those times now one as he looked up to her – their expressions etched deep into his own face for eternity.

363

But mostly his eyes, pride not allowing him to speak, pleading and begging.

Jay smiled grimly as he watched the ice within them melt.

Daniel nodded slightly, commanding her to pull the trigger a final time ... *and the fifth bullet hit his face ... the only shot she aimed with any real accuracy ... above his nose, between his eyes; driving a hard course through the bone of his skull and his brains, and then out the back, ripping short hair away and into the floor ...*

Kirby hurried to Jay's side and Ellen, the gun falling from her hand, ran over to join them. Quickly she began to bind a tourniquet around the wound, ripping the sleeve of her gown, although everything she did seemed to be useless. The amount of blood he had lost was already great, and his arm, a sickening sight, seemed to be hanging by a thread.

They hugged and cried, and Jay did his best to join in all of that, and then, while Kirby ran for help, and Sheriff Hasky arrived, finding his best friend dead, Ellen whispered her love for him in his ear, and for just a second, Jay looked at the bleeding body next to his.

As the killer's muscles and nerves finally relaxed and died, a small sweet and innocent smile – *the smile of a lost child* – appeared on his lips. And a single tear rolled down from one eye ...

Susan was finally at rest. Her killer, the killer of so many, was slain.

But with this death, revenge fulfilled, came none of

the elation Jay had expected to feel. No joy, or sense of great salvation.

Only cold satisfaction . . .

And then nothing.

Chapter Eighteen
The Edge

Daniel came close to the edge – and then fell ... deeper and deeper, the blackness encompassing him, slowly becoming tainted by orange, before he was surrounded by fiery red. And still falling ... Melissa came forward, a floating apparition, her face was red as the fire behind her, and she still looked as beautiful as ever. *I've brought some of my friends to see you*, she said, and Daniel was confused because her voice was more like a thought his whole body heard ... *felt*. And then there were more faces and bodies. The first one was the girl from Manhattan – Susan Austin – and as he looked at her face, rushing towards his, long blonde hair flowing far behind, he realised who the man from Detroit was, the man who had brought him to this place. It was her brother ... *the daunting horror as this realisation dawns* ... her angry face coming so close to his ... *his terrified expression because he knows* ... cold metal, claws and hooks and chains, ripping and shredding his flesh as she floats before him ... *his mouth forms a neat little 'o' of silent surprise* ... which he sees on Susan's face as she mimics him, and he remembers the photograph. The physical pain is intense as he tries desperately to suck in his final breath, knowing that here, his final breath will never be. His body, useless and tortured, falls away and all that is left, unguarded and unprotected, is his empty soul ... and his victims' exacting, ETERNAL VENGEANCE ...

Epilogue
Resolutions

Two days later, a report on the television news brought Ellen out of her drug-induced slumber. She sat up and managed to hear the newsman for a brief minute, before falling back into the light clouds. It was a safe sleep – one without dreams. For her, the fires were over.

'...believed that the real-estate baron is the only person trapped within the building. Fire-fighters are—'

The reporter was wrong.

...and Angie laughed and cried as the flames lit up Griffen like a firework. He ran and screamed and grabbed her, the hot flames taking a hold, engulfing her. They danced a painful, macabre dance and Angie screamed ... and screamed ...

On the day of Bobby Roberts's funeral – police officers saluting, watching him put in the ground, children playing touch football alone, Dawn Taylor weeping,

369

each saying their own silent goodbye as the priest intoned the final prayer – Alice Hasky decided upon the name of their child, to be born a healthy baby boy six months later.

Leigh Thomas Hasky.

Their close friend had to be remembered for his sacrifice.

He was a good man, sorely missed by the whole of Haddonfield.

Tom Hasky hung up his spurs and spent those six months trying to convince himself that Leigh's death had not been his fault, that he had done all he could during the *bad time* . . .

It was a psychological scar he would carry for ever.

Ellen woke, looking around, confused, afraid. And then she remembered . . .

There was a moment, the single most frightening moment in all of her life, when she believed Jay was dead. And then, his eyes blinking open as he coughed more blood, he had managed a grin. Ellen was laughing with relief when Dr Mayberry and Sheriff Hasky arrived soon afterwards.

She smiled now. Jay was alive.

Sleeping by her side, holding her through the nights.

The nightmares were back.

'It's not over,' Jay whispered.

Ellen held him close. He'd been suffering badly. He would wake in the dead of night, screaming out loud and sweating, and only her soft touch would calm him.

'We saw him put in the ground,' Ellen told him. 'It's over. He's gone.'

'No,' he warned her.

The court order came through a week later.

After an extensive investigation into the McCauls' abusive parental behaviour, Kirby was to be put in a foster home. His new guardians permitted Jay and Ellen to visit when they liked.

Kirby looked a lot better, and a lot happier. The psychological scars the doctors worried about never appeared. He was resilient and intelligent, and had already suffered much – he would come to terms with what had happened on his own ground when he was older.

He was visiting Jay and Ellen when Caldwell phoned.

'What do you want?' Jay asked bluntly, motioning for Ellen to stay as she was about to leave.

'Jesus . . . it's good to hear from you too, Jay. It took me a while to track you down, so the least you can do is give me a few minutes. I need you to come back and—'

'No.'

'But Jay, it's—'

'I don't give a fuck. I made it clear in my letter. I'm through.'

Ellen was at his side, stroking his arm. 'Listen to him,' she whispered. 'For me. It's time you let the nightmares end.'

'I know you're through, Jay. You disappeared off the face of the planet. I only found you because of the foster-care papers. You need to clear your name – people are asking serious questions. And there's something else, too. Can you come home for a short while?' Caldwell asked. There was a secret in his voice.

Jay thought for a minute and looked to Ellen, who nodded.

'Give me a couple of days.'

It's not over . . .

Those words haunted him now as Caldwell placed the book in front of him.

'Some jerk mailed it to us a couple of months ago,' Alan explained. 'The guy must have stolen the four by four – missing from the scene, remember? – and found it later.'

But Jay did not want to remember. He had been unconscious for three days, and had spent the past six months putting all this shit behind him and starting over with Ellen. Now Caldwell was dragging him back in.

'It's the real deal, Jay.'

Jay opened the book and read the first couple of pages – a child's handwriting, littered with spelling errors. He flicked through the pages, looked at grainy black and white pictures, and then colour. Jay saw how full the book was.

'Why are you doing this?' Jay asked Caldwell, feeling the unwanted tears as he found *the* date, and read of

Susan's murder, recoiled at the photograph. '*Why did you do all this?*'

'I've read it cover to cover,' Caldwell said, reaching out and closing the book. 'Over and over. This man thought he was some kind of child. He felt alone and afraid, fighting the urge to kill. He wanted it to end: you saved him. Nobody ever knew how big this thing was, Jay. The FBI think you're a hero. You've probably halved their unsolved case load.'

'I ... I did the best I could and ... and ...'

'Hey! You can lose those tears right now. If Teressa comes down and sees you crying she'll kick my butt. Just listen. People in Detroit started asking questions – mainly politicians looking for a big score, wanting to know why charges had not been brought against you – people who did not understand what had happened. You made the front page – "missing cop wanted for questioning", all that kind of stuff. Of course, they would never recognise you with that beard, and hair down to your shoulders.'

'I kind of ... I just ...' Jay began, and was suddenly hugging Caldwell, who held him tight. 'It's good to see you.'

'I know, man. I know,' Caldwell said, letting go. 'It was all fucking bullshit, but they were looking to hang you.' He gestured at the book. 'It was these people who pulled your ass out of the fire. The friends, the families ... it took me a while, but I got in touch with them all. They wanted to give you a fucking medal.'

Caldwell grinned. 'There are a few people waiting upstairs whom I want you to meet, Jay.'

And then they came down – the old, the young, the male, the female, people of every creed and colour. Mothers and fathers, sons and daughters, brothers and sisters ... *friends*.

They were led by the mother of Billy Rogers, who kissed him on the cheek and whispered words of sorrow and thanks to him. Kirby and Ellen came down last.

Ellen held Jay and whispered sweet words of love.

Later, from a window, they watched Kirby running and playing with Caldwell's children. The sun was bright, and the sky golden.

They were the future.

A selection of bestsellers from Headline